Wrath

Laurann Dohner

An Ellora's Cave Publication

www.ellorascave.com

Wrath

ISBN 9781419968082

Edited by Pamela Campbell.
Design by Syneca.
Photography by Fotolia.com.

Electronic book publication March 2012
Trade paperback publication 2013

Dedication

ꝏ

To the love of my life, Mr. Laurann. Here's to a new chapter in our lives and to a love that grows deeper every year we spend together. You are truly awesome!

Prologue

ꕥ

919 tensed, watching the other males in the room with a mixture of awe and trepidation. His future rested in two of those males' hands. Justice North sat calmly behind his desk while Brass paced in front of it. Brass paused.

"They are new to freedom and I don't trust them yet. It is too dangerous to have them leave the NSO."

Justice's mouth flattened into a grim line and his gaze fixed on the only human in the room. Tim Oberto sat in a chair near the corner. He seemed angry, the way his features were slightly reddened and his fists were clenched along the arms of the chair.

"I want to pick men for this joint venture, Justice." He glanced at 919, the male next to him, and finally the third male standing before him. "My men haven't trained with these men and they don't even have names. Let me meet with some of your officers and choose from them."

Anger stirred in 919 at the insult but he fought back a snarl. Who did the human think he was to doubt his word or his commitment? He stepped forward to stare at Justice and waited for the male to address him.

"What is it, 919?"

"This is important to us. There is no denying we are newly released. We haven't made strong bonds yet that would prevent us from putting our lives at risk." He glanced at the male at his side. "358 and I are close. We come from the same place and have the same experiences." *Nightmares.* He didn't say that word aloud, fearful it would make the other males worry about his motivation. He stared deeply into Justice's eyes. "You already have the name that I would have chosen. I want justice for our people and I am willing to risk my life to track down the humans who have harmed our people. We realize that some humans are good while the ones who worked for Mercile are not. We've seen their faces and can identify them. I am calm. I can handle this assignment."

358 stepped closer to him. "We will watch out for each other. We'll do the NSO proud. We wish to work closely with the task force."

Justice leaned forward in his chair, studied both of them intently, and focused on 919. "Why?"

919 hesitated. "I don't understand your question."

"Why is this so important to you? You should be enjoying your freedom. You could make friends, flirt with our females, yet you want to put your lives in danger. Why?"

He said nothing, unsure the truth would get him what he wanted, which was to be assigned to the task force.

"I asked you a question. Answer it."

919 glanced at the human, Tim Oberto, and then back to Justice.

"He's a trusted friend. Speak freely," Justice urged. "There is nothing you could say that would shock him. He knows what has been done to us."

"I spent too much time alone and I'm uncomfortable around large groups of people. I also have no desire to flirt with females." Anger burned but he managed to suppress it. "After what was done to me, I worry about being intimate with one. The task force is all male. The three of us will live together and I want to track down the ones who hurt us. I don't sleep well knowing they are out there and that more of our kind may be suffering what we endured."

The New Species leader didn't look horrified at his answer when he relaxed in his chair. "How are you doing on managing your anger? Would you tear apart the enemy if you came into contact with someone who hurt you?"

"No. I admit I would be happy to capture them but I want them alive and well to spend many years suffering behind locked doors. That is the best punishment." He believed that. He hoped it showed in his eyes and the truth sounded in his voice.

Justice glanced at 358. "What about you? Speak the truth."

"I'm damaged as well, my social skills aren't great, but I manage my anger by taking it out on punching bags. I also want any humans we capture to suffer confinement but not death." He paused. "I go where he goes. We've been together for a long time and he's the one thing I care about. We are brothers."

The human's eyes widened. "They are biological brothers? They don't look anything alike besides being mixed with canine. Is that the blood connection because it sure doesn't appear to be from the human traits?"

"It's emotional," Brass stated. "They have bonded as brothers due to their long-term association. They have kept each other strong and they should remain together to help stabilize them."

"What about you?" Justice addressed 922. "You are from a different facility than they came from."

Tim frowned. "919 and 922 are from different testing facilities? Are you sure? They are just a few numbers apart."

Fury leaned against a wall across the room. "That doesn't matter. There was one genetic scientist who created us, according to what we've learned from the Mercile employees we interviewed. We were all born in the same location but sent to other testing facilities after birth. Our numbers have no relation to where we were sent."

Justice addressed 922. "Why do you wish to be part of the team?"

The male hesitated too, probably trying to form his words carefully before he spoke. "Mercile gave me a mate but murdered her. I don't sleep well nights. I'm not social either and I want to track down the humans who hurt our kind to make them pay. I feel useless here but this will give me a purpose." He growled the last words. "I have no reason to exist any longer and I need one."

Justice frowned but stared at Tim. "I understand why you are concerned but most of my people don't want to go into your world to live there. We've all agreed though that it's an advantage to have some of our males join your team. They can identify some of the Mercile employees, they have enhanced senses, and it would benefit us all to have this joint venture succeed. It's also highly dangerous to send them into the out world despite the precautions we've agreed upon, like having them live inside the basement of the task force headquarters. I toured the place and it is too similar to the cells we were kept in. Many Species would have an issue with that after living away from that environment for this long but these three are volunteering, knowing the living conditions." He paused. "No others have."

"We could order them to," Fury admitted. "We just don't wish to do that."

Justice nodded in agreement. "We don't want to do that. They were given their freedom and we refuse to ask them to sacrifice it. These three are new enough to avoid being traumatized by the tight living spaces. We understand your concern and I agree." His gaze slid to Brass.

Brass took a deep breath. "I will come with them. I'm not mated." He glanced at Fury and Justice before staring at Tim. "I have been free for quite a while. I've trained with some of your team and they trust me. I'll take charge of these three and they will be my responsibility. I will have them picked up if I see any signs of them becoming unstable."

Tim nodded. "Agreed. Okay." He glanced at 919, 922, and 358. "They need to fit in with my teams though. The long hair has to go, they'll need to wear sunglasses to hide their eyes and it might distract people from noticing their features as much. I insist on assigning at least one member of the team to be on duty upstairs every evening. Your men can't drive and they don't do anything without my permission."

"That's fine about assigning someone to be on duty to drive for them." Justice picked up a pen on the desk.

"Wait," Brass growled. "I'm willing to do a lot to help his mission succeed but I'm not cutting my hair."

Justice glanced up at him and grinned. "I forgot. Sorry." He stared at Tim and shrugged. "He's got a thing about keeping his hair long. They used to shave all of it off while in captivity and he's got scarring he wishes to never see again. He will braid it back."

"He needs to fit in." Tim shook his head. "That won't work."

"He can wear a cap. I've seen some of the males on your team do that." Anger narrowed Justice's eyes and his features hardened. "You take orders from me and that is how it will be."

919 noticed the human backed down immediately but he didn't appear happy about it.

"Fine. He can wear a cap but the other ones get haircuts."

"I saw one of your males outside and he is shaved bald. I will agree to that," 358 said as he reached up and fingered his hair. "I won't miss it."

"Short is good enough but whatever you decide is fine." Tim Oberto frowned at Justice. "They need names."

Justice glanced at 922. "Pick one."

"Vengeance. I want it for my female."

"Fuck," Tim grumbled.

Justice glanced at Brass, then Fury, and back at 922. "Vengeance it is. Just keep a tight leash on your temper or you'll be sent back here."

"Understood."

Justice glanced at 358. "Do you have a name in mind?"

He shrugged. "I like Elvis movies."

Justice grinned. "I like them too but it's too obvious. I doubt the humans will let that one pass without teasing you. Any second choice?"

"I like the name Shadow. I like to stand still and watch others."

Brass nodded. "Good name."

Justice turned his attention on the third male.

919 tensed, put on the spot, and had no idea what to name himself. "May I think about it?"

"I've got paperwork to do." Tim stood from his chair. "I need a name."

919 stared at 358, his friend who'd just chosen a name. Shadow met and held his gaze. They knew each other well after having spent years in cells close together and both had suffered the same damage.

Shadow finally spoke, never looking away from him. "He should take the name Wrath. He allowed his anger to simmer, relied on his intelligence, but he made them pay when the opportunity presented. The humans always knew he'd eventually get even after they abused us or at least the smart ones did."

919 felt pride surge and he nodded. "It is a good name." He glanced at Justice and Brass to see their reactions.

"Just make sure you keep hold of your temper." Justice scribbled on a folder lying on his desk and passed it to Tim. "Here you go. Here's information on all four of your new team members. Make sure they are protected but don't baby them. You wanted them for their skills and strengths. Allow them to use them." He stared at Brass for long seconds. "You're in charge of our males. Tim takes orders from you. You can take control of any situation if you deem it necessary."

"Damn it," Tim spat. "Now wait a damn min—"

Justice snarled, flashed sharp teeth and shocked everyone in the room except Brass and Fury with his show of temper. Tim backed up enough to almost trip on the chair he'd just vacated and sealed his lips together.

"You work for us. Brass is a seasoned officer of the NSO, I know him well and he has my complete trust. He's not newly free or unstable. He's highly intelligent and it's a joint operation." He relaxed slightly. "That means your team and ours will work together but Brass is in total charge of my males. Understood?"

"Yeah." Tim still looked angry. "I got it."

"Good." Justice met and held the gazes of the four men who were leaving the NSO. "Be safe and you take your orders from Brass as if I were speaking. Understood?"

"Yes," they agreed in unison.

Wrath turned and left the office. His friend followed closely behind until they were outside. They both paused, waiting for further orders.

"Shadow is a good name."

"So is Wrath." His friend grinned. "I knew you'd pick something kinder but you have strength and a strong sense of justice. It is too bad that name was already taken."

"Wrath suits my purpose. We'll find the humans who hurt our people and bring them in to pay for their crimes."

A scent drew their attention as a female Species neared the office. She smiled and her gaze wandered over Wrath from head to foot. She paused next to him, peered into his eyes and softly purred.

"Hello."

He didn't know what to say but Shadow came to his rescue. "We're leaving with the human task force. We don't have time to socialize."

The female's smile faded. "Good luck. You both are very brave." She walked inside the building.

Wrath relaxed and met Shadow's eyes. "I'm glad there won't be females where we're going."

Shadow nodded. "They are drawn to your looks and strength."

"I need more time to heal before I even consider sharing sex with one of them. I'll be happy to be away from here for a while."

His friend reached out and gripped his shoulder. "We share that in common."

Both of them remembered being drugged while hooked to machines and the horror of their seed being forced from their bodies. Wrath shivered from the vile memories and the uncertainty of what had been done to the sperm taken from them. Some of it had been sold and shipped to other countries, where scientists planned to use human female surrogates to birth human/Species hybrids to be sold to the rich as exotic pets. The thought of them succeeding made rage burn inside his soul.

Shadow's eyes narrowed as they stared at each other. "We'll capture the ones who hurt our kind and bring them to justice. You are thinking about what I do so often but you heard what the NSO doctors said. They are doubtful any children were produced from our stolen seed. The drugs used on us damage the sperm and nature has a way of only making it viable when we are highly aroused. They are pretty certain it only seems to survive inside a living female when *we* put it there. They said they would have heard about any babies put up for sale on the black market, even if it is in Europe."

Wrath relaxed, comforted by the words. "We'll make all of them pay for what they've done to our kind."

"Yes, we will." Shadow released him.

Chapter One

ꟃ

"You aren't really going to eat that, are you?" Lauren curled her lip, staring with horrified fascination at what sat on her friend's plate. "It looks like someone slaughtered a salad with all that green and red."

Her best friend, Amanda, laughed. "It's the latest diet trend. It looks like hell but I'm supposed to lose twenty pounds a month if I eat this every day."

Lauren pushed a stray lock of blonde hair behind one ear. "I'd lose that much too if I had to try to choke that crap down. I wouldn't eat." She sighed. "I know all about diets and I think I've tried them all. Trust me, that isn't going to work. The only way I can lose a few pounds is by downing water and exercising until I can't breathe."

"You only need to drop thirty pounds." Amanda pouted. "I need to lose twice that much. This spinach salad and hot sauce thing is supposed to work. I want to have a shape again."

"You and I both have that already." Lauren winked. "Round is a shape. Look, I am tired of being unhappy because my butt doesn't fit into the same jeans I wore when I was fourteen and I've got love handles. I enjoy eating and detest starving. It sucks being hungry all the time. Those diets just made me miserable, hungry, and depressed." She pointed at the burger on her plate and used her other hand to push it closer to her friend. "Take a bite. You know you really want to. Eat a fry. Live a little and save yourself from misery. You'll enjoy my food way more than yours."

"I haven't had anyone ask me out in two months, Lauren. Two whole months. You've got big boobs, the long hair, and pretty blue eyes going for you. And you're short. You are cute to men even with the excess weight."

"Yeah. Men are just breaking down my door." She snorted. "I just must not be home when they do it. No one is still there when I get off work. They have to be skilled carpenters too because they are amazing at fixing any damage they did to get in."

"That one man asked you out last week and he was cute."

"Cute? He reminded me of a puppet with his frizzy red hair and the unibrow."

"At least you got asked out by someone." Amanda sighed. "I'd love a puppet type myself. You could have so taken him home to keep. I bet he's into cuddling."

Lauren shook her head in disgust. "Imagine doing someone who reminded you of a childhood cartoon. Give me a break. I didn't want to keep him or take him home. He was kind of weird besides. He has a real freaky thing going on with his mother. She called me five times to tell me her son was a nice man I should date. I was afraid they'd invite me to dinner and it would be located next to some remote house on a hill that stood beside a creepy motel."

"Funny." Amanda hesitated before she popped a French fry into her mouth. "He was cute though, in that movie. Too bad he was a knife-wielding murderer. I mean, come on. Stab the naked girl in the shower or try to do her?" She rolled her eyes. "What a waste."

"I worry about you," Lauren commented, smiling to soften her words.

Brown eyes twinkled with amusement. "I wouldn't mind a psycho if he was into stabbing me in a sexy way with a big body part."

"You're sick." Lauren laughed. "You—"

Her phone rang. She groaned and reached for her purse under her chair. One glance at her caller ID made her wince. "Lauren here. What's up, Mel?"

Lauren listened to her boss and closed her eyes. "Tonight? Why can't someone else—" She paused. "But I'm in the middle of dinner with my friend. I can't possibly—" She shut up and gritted her teeth. "But can't you go instead because—" She was getting angry. "Fine. Right. I'll go. Fine. Bye." She hung up. Lauren shoved her phone back inside her purse and stood, giving her friend a regretful look. "I have to go."

"Seriously?" Amanda's smile faded. "Now? What did your bitch boss want?"

Lauren slapped a ten-dollar bill on the table and grabbed her coat off the back of the chair. "It seems one of the agents had an emergency. I have to show a building in the Industrial Park area right away. Some big fish is out there wanting to see it tonight. She told me it's so important that I'm fired if I don't go. She can't meet him because of her plans. I guess mine don't mean squat. God, I hate that witch."

"Damn. Well, go. Maybe you'll sell it and we can take a trip somewhere nice, on you. I've always wanted to go to Jamaica."

"Yeah. With my luck he's just some guy who was bored, with nothing to do on a Friday night, and decided to spin my wheels. I'll call you tomorrow. Are we still on for seeing a movie?"

"Yeah. Good luck. Break a real estate sign." Amanda ate another fry.

"Cute." Lauren waved and headed toward her car.

* * * * *

Lauren glanced at her GPS navigator for the fifth time ten minutes later and cursed as she looked around at the empty streets. She had a bad feeling about showing a property after hours. The Industrial Park was virtually abandoned since most businesses had closed for the night or were just warehouses. She was a single woman going to meet a strange man in an unfamiliar area at night. She took a turn when the computerized voice ordered her to.

An expensive red sports car was parked in the otherwise empty parking lot when Lauren stopped her car next to it. She hesitated before climbing out. Every bit of common sense told her to flee. It screamed "bad idea" but she'd lose her job if she didn't get her ass inside there and show the thing. Her fingers gripped her keys and her thumb hit the door-lock button.

The building was a huge one-story, similar to dozens of others on the block and the old business sign declared it had been some shipping company she wasn't familiar with. Her high heels clicked loudly on the pavement as she approached the double doors. The key box sat on the ground, open. She bit her lip.

Only realtors had the combination to open them to get the keys but someone had obviously given it to Mr. Herbert. It made her dislike her coworker even more. The jerk who was supposed to show the property had obviously betrayed the seller's trust. It was a huge no-no. They used the same combination on all the properties they represented, including homes that people still lived in. If Mr. Herbert was a pervert or a thief, he now had access to a lot of properties. She silently swore to have a talk with their boss about it.

The doors were unlocked when she tested them and one side easily opened. It wasn't a mystery anymore where the prospective client had gone. He hadn't waited until she arrived to go on a tour but had already entered the warehouse. She stepped inside, glanced around the barren reception area, and cleared her throat.

"Hello?" she called loudly. She peered at a dim corridor. "Mr. Herbert?"

She stepped into the darkness and turned her head to search for the light switch. The outside lights in the parking area didn't extend far into this section of the building. Relief was instant when she found it and she could see the room. Mr.

Herbert wasn't there but the double doors to the hallway leading to what appeared to be offices were wide open.

"Mr. Herbert?" She yelled the man's name louder.

No response.

"Damn. I don't like this," she whispered.

It went against the grain to meet a stranger in an empty building. She wasn't stupid. Mr. Herbert could be a rapist or a killer. It was her job to meet clients and lead them through empty properties. *The commission on this baby though…*

That prospect propelled her closer to the dark hallway to hunt for another panel of switches. The lights in the hallway flickered and stayed on when she found it. Her gaze traveled the long length of open office doors on both sides and it seemed to end at the warehouse part of the building, judging by the massive double doors. *Where the hell is this guy?*

"Mr. Herbert?"

She stepped into the hallway with dread pitting her stomach. One by one she paused in open doorways and searched the empty dark offices with a sweeping glance. The feeling of something being wrong only intensified. She'd have turned tail and fled if she wasn't desperate to make the sale.

Lauren reached the end of the hallway without finding the guy. She wanted to go home, didn't want to be there, and that inner voice urged her to return to her car. The lights hadn't been on which made her wonder why the buyer would willingly wander around in the dark. *Who would do that? Isn't it basic instinct to turn on lights?* There was no way she wanted to walk around the eerie building blind.

She stared at the massive metal double doors and her heart raced. Her rent was due, she had a car payment, and less than two grand to her name. She'd be in deep shit if she didn't make money in the next few weeks. Homeless hadn't been her goal when she'd put herself through school. The buyer was somewhere—he'd unlocked the door and the sports car had to be his.

What if he had tripped? He could be hurt and the lights might have a timer on them. She glanced up at the lighted beams and knew she'd freak out big-time if she were suddenly left in the dark if they turned off.

"Too many horror movies. This is what you get for watching them." She reached for one of the door handles, paused, and noticed her hand trembled. "You'll totally feel like shit if this man had a heart attack and he's lying in there dying while you're being a chickenshit."

The pep talk helped.

Lauren straightened her shoulders and gripped the cold metal handle. It twisted easily and she shoved hard. The door opened to reveal pitch blackness and cooler air. A shiver ran down her spine as she paused there.

"Mr. Herbert?" She lowered her voice to mutter, "Answer me. You better have had a heart attack or something to explain why you're scaring the shit out of me by not answering. God knows I'm about to have one."

Her gaze paused on the light switch inside the warehouse section and she moved fast for it. She'd do a quick walk-through to see if the client was there but afterward she'd split.

She had almost reached it when total darkness closed in around her and the door slammed loudly at her back. She gasped and froze. Her eyes widened but she couldn't see a thing. Goose bumps pricked her skin and she hoped she wouldn't seriously have a heart attack.

Calm down! She forced herself to take a breath. *The doors are probably weighted to close. Turn on the lights! Damn Amanda and her talk of serial killers.*

She found the wall with her franticly seeking hands, brushed her fingertips along the smooth surface, and finally touched the switches. She flipped them on and prayed they'd work. A slight hum startled her but the room brightened as the lights flickered a few times rapidly but stayed on. *Oh, thank God!*

She turned her head to stare at the vast warehouse. It had to be fifty feet in height from the concrete floor to the metal ceiling beams. The previous owner had left big metal containers inside that blocked her view of large sections but she could see parts of the back wall to judge that it had to be a good six hundred feet long and probably five hundred feet wide. Lauren frowned as she looked at the four rusted hunks of junk—shipping containers similar to the ones she'd seen leaving the harbor on cargo ships.

Why didn't the owner remove them? It looks bad for a sale. She really wasn't familiar with the property. It was Brent Thort's listing. She briefly wondered what Brent's big emergency had been that made him duck out on Mr. Herbert. If the potential buyer asked about those containers she wouldn't have an answer.

Is the owner going to have them removed under the contract or is the building selling as is with those massive babies? Damn. Lauren gripped her purse, ready to call her boss to ask, if she ever found the elusive buyer.

"Mr. Herbert!" She yelled for all she was worth.

Movement made her gasp. The man who stepped out from behind the container wore all black. Lauren's heart hammered and she stiffened. Fear didn't inch up her spine. It jolted lightning-quick from her heels to her brain.

He was dressed wrong to drive the fancy sports car outside. He definitely didn't look like a Mr. Herbert. He was a big man and reminded her of a mix between a ninja, with the all-black clothing, and a soldier, with the bulky bulletproof vest. Black material encased everything on the man except his tan throat and head. Spiked black hair also gave her the impression that he was military but the dark sunglasses didn't fit with the look. She couldn't see his eyes at all.

He slowly stalked toward her, closing the distance while she stood there frozen. It gave her time to take in more details of the stranger. He had wide shoulders and his shirt stretched tightly over thick, bulky biceps. Her fear notched higher. That screamed "ex-convict" to her. She had a neighbor with arms nearly that size and he'd told her lifting weights had been the only thing to alleviate boredom while he'd served nine years for armed robbery.

Lauren swallowed hard. Her neighbor scared the crap out of her but this guy was ten times worse. Her gaze lowered to his black boots and she openly stared at them since her legs still refused to work. Definitely military. Her cousin was in the Marines and she'd seen him polish his boots a few months before while visiting an aunt. The kickass chunky boots were almost exactly the same as the ones she'd seen.

Whoever he was, she bet he wasn't Mr. Herbert. She knew that but was hopeful to be wrong. She finally backed up and nearly tripped. She fought down a scream of terror. Her gaze had located the two guns holstered to his thighs, a sight she had missed until her brain began to function better.

A soft whimper escaped her parted lips. The man wore black cargo pants that had pockets running up both legs. He not only had guns but a long knife was strapped over one thigh as well. Her terrified gaze landed on his gloved hands. They were open at his sides and it reminded her of something out of an old western as they twitched, almost as if they were about to draw down on someone, gunslinger fashion.

"Are you Mr. Herbert?" She hated the crack she heard in her voice.

The man paused and cocked his head slightly. His mouth twisted into a tight line, giving the appearance of either anger or confusion. She wished he wasn't wearing the glasses so she could see his eyes. His bone structure was pronounced—strong cheekbones, full lips and a masculine, square chin. She retreated another step while the silence stretched between them.

Something moved at the corner of her vision and she jerked her head in that direction. Another man stepped out from behind a second container. He was blond, tall, huge, and dressed just like the first guy. The rest of his looks didn't register to Lauren. All she saw beyond the basics was the big weapon he gripped with both hands. It looked like a wicked mean shotgun.

Oh dear God. Lauren freaked out, totally lost her cool, and spun. She ran right into the doors and bounced back enough to nearly fall on her butt. Her fingers frantically grabbed at the bar that would open the door and gave it a mighty shove. The thing still didn't open. She threw her shoulder against the door while pushing frantically on the bar again but it wouldn't budge.

"No!" She kicked at the locked door and hurt her toes in the process but wasn't willing to give up. Two terrifying men were behind her. "Open up. Damn you, open up!" she yelled but it wouldn't let her through.

Her heart raced and she panted after she gave up. The doors weren't going to let her pass and she was trapped. Her fingers released the bar and she slowly turned to face the two men who were probably sickos targeting real estate agents.

The men remained in the same positions and she glanced between the black-clad figures. The blond wore dark glasses too. He lowered the big gun to aim it more at the floor than at her. It was the only upside she could find.

Lauren remembered her purse dangling from her arm. Her gaze darted between the two men in absolute terror before she frantically searched for another door. She didn't see one. Her hand slid down to her purse, brushed her car keys clipped there, and her brain began to work.

Panic button. I have one! Her thumb brushed the square pad and she pushed the button. In the distance, although muffled, her car alarm began to scream in rapid bursts. She swallowed hard. *Maybe it will draw the attention of…no one. The area around the building is deserted. Damn it.* Her hand inched toward the flap of her purse and her cell phone.

"Turn it off," one of the men ordered in an unnaturally deep voice. "Now."

Lauren gawked at the blond who'd spoken. He was holding the weapon near his hips but he could easily aim it at her again. She didn't look at his face since the gun held her full attention. *Is he going to shoot me? Are they rapists? Worse? Oh God!* her mind screamed. *Worse would be so bad.*

Her car alarm suddenly silenced and shock tore through Lauren. She hadn't moved her thumb to turn it off. Someone else had to have done it, which meant there were more of them. She pressed her back against the door, pushed with her weight and prayed that it would move. She wanted to flee in the worst way.

"Where is he?" the blond asked.

"Who?" She barely got the word out. Her throat felt closed off with her heart seeming to sit inside it.

The blond man shifted the gun, gripped it with one hand and slowly stepped forward. Her gaze lifted to his face, couldn't miss his frown, or that he was coming right at her.

"Stay away from me." Lauren's voice grew stronger, louder. "Stop right there. I don't know who you are but I want to leave."

The blond kept coming. Lauren's heart speeded up painfully. The urge to scream rose in her throat, her lips parted, but nothing came out.

"Where is he?" The blond stopped just feet away.

Lauren noticed he had a good foot of height over her and it made her feel small. That would put him in the six foot five range. His shoulders were wide and muscular arms bulged beneath his black clothing. Her gaze couldn't penetrate those black glasses to see his eyes. It was unsettling and made him an even scarier figure to confront.

She focused on his face, taking in the high cheekbones, square jawline. She guessed he had an abundance of testosterone from how masculine his features were. His voice reminded her of gravel—deep, rough, and gritty. Her gaze lowered to the gun gripped within his right hand and couldn't look away from the scary thing. She would do anything they said just to survive the nightmare she'd fallen into.

"Who? Mr. Herbert? I don't know. I was looking for him," she managed to whisper. She hoped he'd heard her. "Please. I want to go now."

Silence stretched and she finally tore her focus off the gun to look up at his face. His full lips were twisted downward and lines had appeared at the edges of them. She noticed his odd-looking nose for the first time. It wasn't exactly flat but it had a smashed look as if he'd taken a few too many hits to the face.

"He goes by the name of Brent Thort. Where the hell is he? I won't ask nicely again."

Surprised, Lauren knew her mouth dropped open. "You're looking for Brent?"

She glanced at the blond and the other scary guy. She didn't like Brent but these men were seriously armed and dangerous. Her coworker was a loudmouthed, sexist jerk. He made a point of being offensive to all women with his crude remarks but she suddenly had a hunch that he had a gambling problem. Were these two men bill collectors from some illegal bookie? The color drained from her face. Or maybe Brent was into drugs. He did drive a really nice car and bragged about all the women he nailed. Any woman who purposely slept with him had to be paid to do so. He was good-looking but it was only skin deep in his case.

It explained why Lauren was trapped inside a warehouse with thugs. They'd been expecting Brent. She studied the terrifying man in front of her and could totally see him being the hired muscle of the worst type of criminal. *Oh crap! I showed up instead of Brent.* Some of the terror eased but not much. *They'll have to let me go,* she hoped, now that they realized their trap had caught someone innocent instead.

"Some emergency came up. My boss called me to show the property instead of Brent." She was proud her voice sounded more normal. "Can I go now? Obviously you aren't interested in buying the building, right?"

The blond's mouth tightened into a firm line. His hand slowly lifted to his ear to touch his earlobe. "Say again. I didn't get that. There's interference from the steel in here in some parts."

The dark-haired man moved forward and Lauren squeezed tighter against the door. All of her terror returned when she focused on him. The men could almost be twins in sheer size. They were both towering above her, wide shouldered, and muscular. She couldn't see his eyes either through the dark glasses but she sensed that he stared at her too. She didn't try to make eye contact since it was pointless. Her gaze dropped to the concrete floor while she started to pray. *Please have them let me go. Please God.*

"Lauren Henderson."

Lauren's gaze snapped up to the dark-haired one who'd said her name. He turned his head to glance at the other man. He shrugged.

"My com was fine. Lauren Henderson is her name. She works at the same company as our target."

The blond turned his head and Lauren stared up at the black sunglasses. She swallowed again and nodded. "I do work with Brent but I don't know him well."

The fact that they were calling Brent a target didn't bode well for her or her coworker. Her knees shook almost as much as her hands. *Target means they are probably hired hit men. Jesus! What in the hell is Brent into?*

"She is his girlfriend." The dark-haired one had a deep voice too but his didn't sound like gravel.

"I'm not dating that creep. I swear. I'm not dating anyone." She had to convince them or they might decide to hurt her instead of Brent. "I don't even like him. He's a dick."

Two pairs of sunglasses were aimed in her direction and she felt them watching her. She quickly got the impression they weren't buying it when both of them frowned. Seconds ticked by with excruciating slowness.

"Let's be rational, okay?" She forced air into her lungs. "Look at me. Do you know Brent? He's into skinny, tall women. That's not me. He goes to bars all the time but I don't even drink."

She knew she was babbling but didn't care. She didn't want them to break her legs as a warning to a boyfriend she didn't even have. "I don't even like the guy. He's rude and we don't get along. He came into work last week showing pictures on his cell phone of women's bare asses and he said some mean things when I told him I didn't appreciate it. I don't like the guy and he doesn't like me. I am not," she almost yelled the words now, "his girlfriend or his friend! I'm just the idiot who answered her phone when her boss called and actually got my ass down here to show this property." She closed her mouth.

"They are sleeping together." It was the dark-haired one. "We do know Bill." His mouth twisted into a grin and white teeth flashed.

The blond nodded. "Yes. We do."

"I'm not sleeping with him." Lauren was shocked. "Hello? Didn't you hear me? I'm not his type and he's sure as hell not mine!" It took her seconds to realize they'd called Brent by another name but they probably went after a lot of targets. It had been a slip. She wasn't about to point out the error to them either. "I have standards."

"Bill's type has breasts and you have those." The blond sounded amused.

"I haven't slept with anyone in a long time. Trust me," Lauren stammered in a rush. "I wouldn't sleep with that jerk. He is a man slut and a total pig. I am not dating anyone and haven't in almost a year. I really am serious. I don't like Brent, Bill, or whatever his name is."

The dark-haired one's smile died. "Almost a year, huh? Now I know you're lying."

She shook her head. "That's the truth. I wouldn't touch him with a ten-foot pole and we don't like each other. We don't even talk unless it's to argue. I don't know what you want with him and I don't care. Can I please go now? Please? If you think I'd warn him or something, I wouldn't. I swear. You can have him. Take him please. He's a jerk who I'm sure deserves to have his legs broken or whatever you need to do to get your money. Sometimes I wish I could hurt him so have at it. Please can I go now?"

The blond bit his lip. "Who do you think we are?"

Her heart pounded as she stared up into the dark sunglasses. "Bill collectors?"

The other one laughed. "You think we're…" He laughed harder. He turned his head toward the blond man. "She thinks we're hired muscle, as in those films we've watched."

The blond grinned. "I wouldn't mind breaking Bill's bones. He does owe a lot to us."

The dark-haired man nodded. "I'd do it for free."

Lauren pushed harder on the door at her back but it didn't budge. "Can I please, please go now? We all agree that Brent is a piece of shit. Think of me as a cheerleader. Go team, and beat him up! Give him an F, I, S, T."

Two pairs of sunglasses swung her way and their grins faded. The dark-haired man moved. "No." He reached for Lauren. "You're coming with us."

She saw a gloved hand reach for her arm and lunged forward. She shoved at the blond, surprised him by the attack, and pushed with all her might. The man stumbled back and Lauren dashed away to run toward the containers. Once she made it behind one, she kicked off her heels and reached down to grab them. She straightened just as the blond nearly slammed into her when he rounded the corner.

Fear made her spin away and flee again until she nearly collided with the dark-haired one who came from the other side of the container. Their bodies missed touching each other by mere inches. A shriek of terror came out of her mouth.

On instinct, Lauren threw one of her high heels at the man's face. It afforded her the benefit of dodging his hands, which he had to use to shield his face. She ran for the back of the warehouse, fisted her keys in one hand and her remaining shoe in the other.

"Leave me alone!" she yelled.

The sight of a back door urged her to sprint faster. Hope flared that she might make it out of the warehouse alive but heavy breathing sounded right on her ass. One of them was gaining on her fast. She screamed, terrified, and ignored the cold concrete floor that hurt her bare feet.

She didn't slow, knew it was a luxury she couldn't afford, and dropped the items in her hands. She really hoped the thug tripped on them. Her open palms slammed hard into the door, hoping that hitting the bar latch would force it open when her body barreled against it too. Pain exploded through her chest and the side of her face when the thing didn't budge. She could suddenly sympathize with a bug hitting a windshield since she felt she'd just survived the rough impact of being in flight and hitting a solid object.

Two large hands gripped her upper arms and she managed to suck in enough air to let loose a shriek. She still gripped the bar handle and shook it with all her terrified strength. The door didn't budge and she found herself still trapped. She twisted, tried to get away from the hands. He refused to let her go and she glanced up to see it was the dark-haired one who had her. Her foot kicked out frantically, trying to nail him in the shin.

"Stop it." He snarled the words, a scary sound that just made her freak out more.

Lauren kicked again but missed. The man could move quickly and dodged her foot with ease. She did brush the material of his pants though with her toes. He hissed out a curse before he spun Lauren back around to face the door and pushed her against the wall next to it hard enough to knock the breath from her lungs.

One of his hands left her arm and fisted into the bun at the back of her head. He released her arm and that hand pushed hard against her back, pinning her tightly against the wall. She struggled but he was too strong.

"Freeze," he demanded. "Before you are injured. I don't want to hurt you."

Lauren stopped struggling when it became apparent that each movement brought her pain. Her breasts felt smashed and it was really uncomfortable. Tears blinded her from the pain of her hair being pulled. She closed her eyes, trying to calm her ragged breathing. The firm hold on her hair eased until it wasn't painful any longer but she still couldn't turn her head.

"Where is Brent?"

"I don't know. I keep telling you that. I just work with the guy."

The dark-haired man sighed. "You lie."

"I'm not lying."

"You just said you haven't dated in a year. That was a lie."

She wanted to glare at him but she couldn't turn her head without him ripping out hair in the process. "That wasn't a lie. I haven't been in a relationship in that long."

"You just share sex with men? How many times have you allowed Bill to touch you?"

"You mean Brent? I have never slept with him! I don't do that stuff. I'm telling the truth. You can call my boss. She might know where Brent is. I'll give you her number. Her name is—"

"Stop," he ordered, cutting her off. "Obviously you aren't going to give him up easily. We'll have to change your mind."

The door next to them opened. Hope leapt inside Lauren that help had arrived but one glance at who entered just made her fear notch higher. The bald man was dressed exactly like the other men who'd confronted her. He kept the door open as he frowned, met her stare, and his icy-cold blue eyes narrowed.

He didn't wear sunglasses but she suddenly wished he did. She'd never seen eyes like his before. The shape of them was strange and they were chilling, with no emotion. A shudder ran down her spine. His stare seemed to grow even colder, leaving her shaken, until he shifted his gaze to the big thug behind her. It broke the spell and she glanced at his face. It was strange too but she didn't have time to really study him to discover what was wrong with it.

"We need to leave now. Our escorts are nervous about this and have threatened to place calls. Wrap her up and let's move."

She closed her eyes again. *Wrap me up? As in kill me and leave my body rolled inside a carpet?* She wanted to scream, maybe cry, but she sure didn't want to die. The hand fisted at her back, grabbing the material of her shirt. He used it to haul her away from the door and force her to move. He kept hold of her hair too, a double insult, and she knew she couldn't get away from her captor.

"Walk through the doorway and don't fight me. I would hate to harm you but I will if you don't follow orders. You'll walk or I'll have to hit you, knock you out, and carry you."

They were taking her somewhere and she couldn't escape. The thug holding her was huge, a real freak of muscle. She would have fought to be free of his hold on her shirt but grabbing her bun had been sheer genius.

"Please?" Lauren wasn't above begging.

"Silence." He lowered his voice as he leaned in to put his lips closer to her ear. "No harm will befall you if you just cooperate. You have my word."

The word of a hired killer. Yeah. That's comforting. She managed to refrain from snorting, afraid he'd pull her hair just for the hell of it. He wasn't going to let her go regardless of what she said.

The back parking lot was dimmer than the front. There were fewer lights set farther away but it was easy to make out the large, black, unmarked commercial van parked ten feet from the door. The side door was open, she was led to it and her hair was finally released.

"Get in."

She climbed into the back of the van, not seeing another choice, and he kept hold of her until he'd angled her toward the back. She couldn't see much without interior lights but didn't try to escape. He stayed too close, his fist kept a firm grip on her shirt, and she collapsed to her butt when he seemed happy with where she'd stopped.

The front passenger door opened. She glanced that way and spotted the dark head of a driver wearing a black cap. The bald man climbed into the passenger seat. He turned to stare at the two guys wearing sunglasses.

"Close the door and let's go. He sent someone in his place but we'll get answers from her."

I don't know anything! Lauren kept her lips sealed though. They obviously weren't going to believe her. She really hated Brent now.

"We'll send a team to his condo." The blond sighed. "It's all we can do. Someone had to have tipped him off. He wasn't sure though since he sent her."

The dark-haired man still gripping her said, "That or he wanted us to get rid of her for him." He paused. "Female, you wouldn't happen to be recently pregnant, would you?"

Shocked, Lauren turned her head. She couldn't see him now that the doors had closed but she knew where he was. "No. I keep telling you, I've never slept with Brent, I mean Bill, or whatever you want to call him. Never."

"Let's return," the dark-haired man rumbled. "We'll get her to talk once we're back at headquarters." He paused. "Tell Brass that she's our only lead."

Dread and terror filled Lauren.

Chapter Two

ꟗ

Lauren figured they were going to kill her. It would explain the room she sat in, chained by her wrists to a big table that looked more like something found in a morgue. The entire thing could tilt, it had a rim along three sides and a big drain, which was centered over another drain in the concrete floor. The walls were equally grim with the dungeon décor of dull gray bricks. The only splash of color came from the yellowed light that ran the length of the room about eight feet above her head. They were underground, backing her theory that it very well could be a morgue.

The blond shifted where he stood against the wall. Sunglasses still hid his eyes but she knew he wasn't happy since he hadn't stopped frowning after she'd been led into the room.

"How long have you been sleeping with Bill?"

She'd left fear behind and moved right into feeling pure frustration. "I keep telling you that I've never slept with my coworker. You can call him any name you want but if you're talking about Brent Thort, the real estate agent, I've never touched him."

"Where is he?"

She took a deep breath, really wishing the blond would stop asking the same questions over and over. He was the only one who'd spoken to her since they'd brought her into the room. Hours must have passed and she yawned.

"I don't know." Her voice rose. "I really don't. The answer isn't going to change, no matter how many times you ask me the same questions. I have told you at least a hundred times that I am not sleeping with him. I have never even gone on a date with him and I only see his face at work. Call my boss, I say again, and ask her. She has to know where he lives. It would be in his employee files." Anger stirred, at Mel, who'd sent her into this nightmare. "Go kidnap her!"

He sighed. "What has he told you?"

"Nothing. I don't talk to the jerk! I'm tired, hungry, and I want to go home. I don't know where he is but I'd tell you if I did. Trust me. We aren't friends. We've hardly said two civil words to each other since I started working there three months ago. I avoid him, okay? He's loud and rude. Crude. He tells offensive jokes at the office, which is very unprofessional."

She took a deep breath, trying to calm down. Her temper was borderline explosive. Why wouldn't they listen to her? "He goes to a lot of bars and brags about all the women he picks up. He's also recently made a habit of taking inappropriate cell phone photos of the women he dates and shows them around the office. That's all I know about the guy. I swear I'm telling you the truth."

The dark-haired man pushed away from the corner where he'd been standing quietly since she'd been handcuffed to the table. He frowned as he moved closer. His weapons and belt were gone but it didn't make him appear any less dangerous. He paused near her.

"It could get really ugly if you don't stop protecting your boyfriend. He obviously doesn't care about what happens to you or he wouldn't have sent you in his place. He must have suspected it was a trap since he didn't go there." He paused. "He sent you alone without his protection, knowing something was wrong. Do you understand that, female?"

"Stop calling me that," Lauren snapped. "My name is Lauren and my boss, Mel Hadner, sent me to that warehouse. That's all I know. She called me on my cell while I was at the restaurant to tell me Brent had some kind of emergency. She was busy and ordered me to show the property instead. I didn't want to but it's my job. I was the last hired and you know that saying. Last hired, first fired. I need to keep my job so I left the restaurant and here we are."

His lips twisted into a mean grimace. "You just showed your ability to lie. You said you didn't date. Were you eating alone?"

"I was having dinner with a friend."

"I see. Do you call men you share sex with your friends? How long have you and Bill been friendly?" A strange, animalistic noise came from him. "Stop lying. You are Bill's type of female. We interviewed many of the ones he used to share sex with." He bent a little, drew closer, and those dark glasses just made him look evil. "We're not easily fooled. He is not a male you wish to protect since he is not one who would protect you. He's free and you are not. You seem intelligent. This is only hurting you."

"I was having dinner with my friend Amanda. Don't twist my words and stop accusing me of screwing that loser. He isn't my type. I'll say it again. I wouldn't touch him with a ten-foot pole!" She pushed back in her chair and glared at his sunglasses, resisting the urge to scream from the frustration.

"We won't release you until we have Bill. That is a promise."

She believed him and anger turned to fear all over again. They were going to hold her hostage until they had her coworker. It was beyond shocking. "You can't do that. Please? I just want to go home. If this is about money, how much does he owe? I'll try to pay it. Whatever it takes but please, let me go!"

The man drew closer. Lauren felt fear but he suddenly spun away.

"I can't," he snarled.

She swallowed but the blond took his place. The guy crouched near her chair. "You are now willing to pay his debts but you aren't sleeping with him? You are bad at lying."

"That's not what I mean. I'm scared, you won't believe the truth, and I'll do anything you want if you just let me go."

"He doesn't owe us money."

Lauren lost the last bit of hope. These guys were criminals and would probably kill her. She stared at the guy, trying to convey her sincerity. "You have it wrong. The only thing I did was answer my phone when my boss called me to show a property. That's it. I don't care if you want to beat on Brent. I'm sure he deserves it, he's a jerk, but I'm innocent in this."

"You were having dinner with Brent? Just tell us the truth if you want out of here."

"Do you want me to lie? I will. I was having dinner with my friend Amanda but I'll say anything you want if it makes you happy enough to release me."

The man took a deep breath. "I see."

"You believe me now, right? I am not sleeping with Brent."

The man moved quicker than she thought a person could. Lauren didn't even have time to gasp before his hands gripped her waist, he flipped her and her back slammed on top of the table. The handcuffs pulled painfully on her wrists, which were hooked above her head now.

Her heart hammered and pure terror tore through her as he leaned over her. His weight caused the table to tip until her head was higher than her feet as his fingers gripped her jaw. He kept her pinned with one hand on her waist and a snarl came from deep within his throat. It mimicked the sound from a vicious dog.

"I'm done playing nice. Hurting a female isn't something I wish to do but I will. Did you see the drain in the floor? It is there to clean up blood easier."

"Shadow." The dark-haired one gripped his shoulder. "I can smell her fear over that horrible perfume even. Back off. You made your point and are going too far with your attempt to make her comply. Let's give her time to let the situation sink in. We could all use a break."

The blond released her. "I made certain I didn't cause her any harm."

The hands tore away from her body and both men left the room. The door slammed loudly, the twist of a bolt being thrown unmistakable, and she stared at the yellow light hanging above her head as the metal table chilled her body through her clothes.

"Oh my God," she whispered. They were going to kill her and they wouldn't believe anything she said. Brent must owe money to the mob or something. Those guys had a room for torturing people and it was designed to make their kills easier to clean up.

She tried to twist to get off the table but it was useless. The edges of the table had those horrible ridges, probably to keep blood from spilling off the sides of it, and gravity held her in place from her body being hung by her wrists. Lauren stared down at her feet and saw that drain from her position with the table tilted upright.

The door suddenly opened. She gasped, turned her head and stared at the bald man who entered. With the bright lights, she got a very good look at his features and they still looked strange. Something wasn't quite right with his prominent, wide cheekbones and those blue eyes of his were just as icy cold as she remembered. He still wore the uniform but his weapons were gone as well. He crossed his arms over a broad chest, displayed some seriously thick biceps stretching the shirt he wore, and gave a smile that could have frozen hell.

"I was told you refuse to talk, that you are protecting Bill. They don't believe you will break from the fear they caused when they tried to intimidate you."

He had a gruff voice, raspy, and it just amplified his scary appearance. Her mouth opened but nothing came out.

"I don't play games and I don't care what the booklet says on interrogation and scare tactics. I will be honest." He licked his lips. "We know you are Bill's female. Your scent gives it away. He has a favorite one that you wear." His gaze lowered to her chest. "All his females have large chests, just the way you do." He dropped his hands to his sides and marched forward until he glared down at her from the side of the table. "You stink of belonging to him."

Her mind blanked, too afraid to make it work properly. "What smell?"

"The perfume you wear. It is rare and the same one he gives to all the females he takes to his bed. It is offensive, messes with our noses, but it's probably why he chose it. It's to hide things from us."

Terror struck Lauren as the guy leaned closer and his hands came down on the table inches from her waist, pushing it back to nearly horizontal. She saw her own death in his cold eyes as his face came closer to hers too. He was really angry, talked crazy words she didn't understand, but she was innocent, damn it. She'd never slept with Brent. He was a jackass, a conceited jerk, and as for her perfume...

"I got it at the Christmas gift exchange at work last month," she told him quickly. "Maybe he's the one who bought it. I don't know! I swear I don't. This perfume was the gift I was given. We were all told to bring something to the Christmas party and names were drawn. If this is Brent's favorite one, if it's hard to come by, then he must have brought it. I have never slept with that man."

He shook his bald head slowly, snarled low, and leaned in so close his breath fanned her face. He'd drunk coffee recently. "Wrong answer. You will tell me where he is and help me find him. You don't know what kind of monster you've been trying to protect, little female." He snarled the words. "He killed a female who was loved and I know the same loss. I haven't found the animal who murdered mine yet but I will have vengeance for others."

Wide eyed, Lauren stared up at the very angry man. He was livid beyond reason and it frightened her even more.

"I am not sleeping with Bill!" she yelled in his face. "No matter how much you try to scare me, I still haven't slept with Bill. I am not protecting anyone. I don't know where he is or I'd tell you!"

The man's mouth tightened into a firm line. "Don't say I didn't warn you."

A whimper escaped that she didn't even try to stifle. Was he going to torture her? Strike her? If she knew where Brent was she'd tell him in a heartbeat. Why wouldn't they believe her?

The man's hands suddenly fisted in the material of her skirt and yanked hard. Alarm tore through Lauren as it was ripped from her lower half and the destroyed thing was thrown to the floor. Cold air from the room hit her thighs, hips, and bared lower stomach. Her mouth opened to scream.

His icy gaze locked with hers. He shook his head, warning her not to scream. She was so petrified that nothing came out and she couldn't even draw breath. He gripped her shirt next, tore it wide open and spread it apart. The man had bared her to her panties and bra. He backed up enough to run his gaze down her body to take in every exposed inch of her.

He was just trying to scare her, Lauren hoped. She stared in horror as the man reached up, ripped the vest off his chest and dropped it. The sweater-type shirt was torn over his head next to reveal bare skin, lots of it, and enough muscles to assure her the guy probably had spent years in a prison yard pumping iron while he'd served his time.

"Oh God," she finally got out, able to breathe again, since fear made her pant. "Don't do this."

His head lifted, enraged blue eyes glared at her, and his fingers began to unbuckle his belt. "Where is Bill?"

"I don't know!"

He growled. "Your loyalty to him is over. You will tell me what I want to know. He is no longer your male. I am. My name is Vengeance and you are mine."

He tore the belt off. She wondered if he'd hit her with the black leather but he dropped it on the floor. She screamed when he unfastened the front of his pants, no doubt left that he'd rape her. She tried to roll away. Sheer panic helped her find the strength to ignore the pain in her wrists caused by the frantic motion that made the handcuffs dig into her skin.

A hand gripped her hip, shoved her down flat, and her head turned. His pants were undone, they'd lowered when he'd lunged forward and he wasn't wearing underwear. She saw his cock, something she couldn't miss since it was hard and large. Another scream tore from her throat and she lifted her knees, tried to kick at him.

His free arm forced her thighs flat as he used his weight to pin her down. Those icy-blue eyes drew closer as he bent over her until only inches separated their faces.

"Don't fight me. You no longer belong to Bill. I won't cause you pain but you will learn to enjoy my touch."

She closed her eyes and screamed.

The door was thrown open hard enough to hit the wall. "What is going on?" The words came from a harsh, deep voice, and Lauren's eyes flew open as she twisted her head. The dark-haired guy had barged into her worst nightmare.

He moved fast, grabbed Vengeance, and tore her attacker away. Lauren lay there unable to do anything but watch as the two faced off. The taller one, still wearing the sunglasses, put his big body between her and the other man.

"Get out, Wrath. She is no longer a concern to you." The bald man tried to step around him to return to her.

"You aren't going to do this." The dark-haired man had a name—Wrath. His fingers curled into fists at his sides as he moved to stay between them. The gloves were gone and she could see tan skin. "I won't allow you to harm her. We aren't like them. We were only willing to frighten her into talking but you have gone too far."

"She isn't going to protect him any longer," the bald one snarled. "She won't talk but she will change her mind about helping us find that monster. Leave. She's his female and he owes us a life. Vengeance is mine, Wrath. I claim her. She will take the place of my murdered female."

Wrath didn't budge. "She isn't our enemy. You can't take her to replace the female you lost. You aren't thinking right in your head. I hate them as well. I can't look at her without reliving what was done to me. She has pale skin, a soft body, and I remember the hours of being drugged while they forced me to give them samples. The images of ones who look similar to her were used to obtain them. I know she isn't responsible and I won't harm her for what others have done to me. Calm down, Vengeance."

He snarled in response.

"I know the rage inside. I suffer it too. She knows nothing of who Bill really is or she wouldn't be protecting him. He is pretending to sell property and she believes we are hired males who beat on people who owe money. He sent her in his place, believing we'd kill her. That is not something he would do if he cared for her in any way."

"I want her. She is mine," Vengeance demanded harshly.

Wrath inched closer. "You do this and she will hate you. I won't allow it. I already suffer guilt from watching her be fearful when Shadow tried to scare her into submission. Remember the female who held your heart?"

The bald man lowered his head and pain flashed across his face. "Yes."

"This one will never be her. She will never look at you the way yours did or welcome your touch. You can't force her to feel what you once had with another and she can't replace what you lost."

Tears streamed down Vengeance's face when he lifted his head. "I miss her."

"I know." Wrath reached out and gripped his shoulders. "We will find all of them but this is wrong. We don't hurt females. It's one thing to use their own fear to make them talk but force breeding them is something our enemy would do. Take a walk, let your rage cool, and tend to your needs. It will help."

The bald man bent, grabbed his discarded clothing, and rushed out the door. Lauren was confused, terrified, and in pain. It was apparent that the thugs were insane. Wrath slowly turned and she was not sure what he'd do.

"Are you all right?"

"No." Hot tears poured down her cheeks now that the danger had passed. She'd come close to being raped. Nobody would be okay after that.

"Easy." His voice lowered to a husky tone. "I will take care of you."

She didn't know if that was a good thing or not. Was that mobster talk for he'd kill her? She wouldn't put anything past them now. He strode closer and a soft noise came from his parted lips.

"Your wrists are bleeding."

He gripped the slanted table and leveled the thing until her weight no longer pulled against the cuffs. Gentle, warm fingers carefully touched her skin near where they ached. He unlocked the cuffs and freed her.

Lauren jerked her arms down, covered her bra with her hands and stared at the face hovering above hers. She flinched when he touched her again but his hand only cradled the back of her neck while he helped her sit.

"I'm going to take my shirt off to give to you. Stay calm. Your clothes are destroyed and you must be cold." He hesitated. "I have a first-aid kit inside my room. No harm will come to you there."

Lauren sniffed, trying to fight back tears.

The guy hesitated. "I am so sorry." His voice came out raspy, almost sounded sincerely apologetic, though she knew better. "This went too far. We were just trying to frighten you. You believed the worst of us and we needed to locate Bill. No one was supposed to harm you in any real way. Even Shadow was careful not to bruise you when he flipped you over on the table. His hands braced you to keep you from hitting your head or landing too hard. It still worried me enough to call a halt to your interrogation when I saw your reaction. I nearly hit him because I couldn't stand to see you that terrified. You're little and I am just very sorry. That is why we left. We were discussing how to get you to work with us without using fear."

He backed away and she noticed for the first time that the vest he'd worn earlier had been removed. He worked the shirt over his head, managed to keep the glasses on, and she wondered why he wore them inside. Maybe it was so she couldn't identify him later and that gave her hope once again that at some point she might survive her ordeal. Of course she'd seen the bald man's face so that probably was a bad thing.

Wrath had saved her from a horrible fate. That had to mean something and he had apologized a few times. Maybe he was a thug with a conscience, despite having such a horrible nickname. She could work with that. Her mind began to plot and she wanted him to see her as a real person. She'd read once that if a kidnapper grew to care about the victim that the chance of survival was better.

"Thank you." It was tough to force out those words.

She couldn't help but notice how buff he was. Maybe he and Vengeance had shared a prison cell since they both seemed to have spent a lot of time working out. They'd have to, to gain that kind of mass. He worked to right the inside-out shirt while she stared at his flat, six-pack abs. Her gaze lifted to his arms, watched his muscles flex and she shivered. She wasn't going to be the one to suggest he give up a life of crime to perhaps start competing in bodybuilding competitions. He probably could win them.

He held out the shirt to her. "Here, female. Please allow me to help you. I wish to soothe some of your fears."

"My name is Lauren." Her hands trembled as she accepted it. The material was still warm from his body and held his masculine scent as she pulled it over her head. It was large on her—something that made her shiver since she wasn't a small woman—which only emphasizing how much bigger he was. She tugged it down her body to hide her underwear from him.

"Let me help you."

She froze up as he gently rolled the too-long sleeves until her hands and injured wrists were revealed. He stopped when they were almost at her elbow. They were a bit bulky but they wouldn't get blood on them from the scratches the cuffs had caused.

"Your feet are bare and the floor will be cold. Don't be alarmed. You are safe with me."

That was the only warning she got before he scooped her up into his arms, pressed her against his hot skin, and turned with her. He strode to the door and carried her into the hallway. Lauren closed her mouth firmly, didn't protest, and fought down her fear.

Be nice to the kidnapper and maybe the kidnapper will be nice to me.

Wrath was furious as he carried the female down the hallway to his room. He was glad he'd decided to check on her and heard her screams. He'd felt very guilty while watching Shadow use her assumptions about them against her. Fear made humans talk more easily but it had been hard to see her tremble at times.

His blood boiled over Vengeance's behavior. The male couldn't just force a female to be his. Why didn't he know that? Perhaps he shouldn't have been assigned to the team. The fact that Vengeance had caused her to bleed, had stripped her of her clothes, made him want to beat the male. No one should harm a female physically.

He inhaled and bit back a growl. She was so soft, smelled so good, and the feel of her in his arms turned him on. She rested her cheek against his chest, her silky hair tickled slightly, and his fangs dug into the inside of his lower lip. The last thing she needed was to fear him more and she would if she realized how she affected him. It confused him that he felt attracted to her.

The door was difficult to get open with her in his arms but he managed, kicked it open, and turned to get them inside. He pushed it closed with his foot and glanced around his barren room. It was a square room with dull bricks for walls and concrete floors. He only had a bed with one nightstand and the bathroom to call his own. He gently placed her on the mattress, wished the blanket was softer, and released her.

"Stay."

Big blue eyes stared at him with trepidation. Guilt ate at him. She was a little thing compared to the females he was used to, softer, and obviously not accustomed to stress. Her hands trembled when she tugged at his shirt, trying to hide her blue panties and the tops of her creamy thighs. She looked as if she worried he'd attack. It wasn't a stretch of her imagination after what Vengeance had pulled.

"Easy," he crooned and tried to express that he wasn't threatening as he backed away. "Do not run. There is nowhere to go and Vengeance is out there." He hated to use that threat but figured it would be effective. The terror that widened her eyes assured him he'd been correct. "I'm getting the first-aid kit to take care of your injuries."

He spun quickly to stalk into the bathroom and flipped on the light. The kit was a white box with a red cross on it and was hooked on a peg inside the door. The female didn't attempt to flee in his absence. She sat huddled on his bed with her arms wrapped tightly around her waist.

She started when he crouched before her. His heart hammered as strongly at them being so close but she needed medical attention. Tim's team wouldn't return until morning and that left just him to tend her. Brass was above, using the telephone to speak to Justice while Shadow had gone to eat. He sure wouldn't allow Vengeance near her again.

He placed the kit down, opened it, and tried to ignore his body's response to the female. Memories surfaced of what humans looked like naked. A stream of images from the movies he'd been forced to watch played through his mind—images of them touching their own bodies. Another growl rose inside his throat that he barely swallowed down. Fear quickly followed. He'd been conditioned to react to human females and he wasn't sure if he could trust himself, alone in a room with one.

"Let me see your wrists." He winced when his voice came out deeper than he'd intended.

She cautiously stopped hugging her middle to show him her arm. The cuts weren't deep, just scratches, and relief swept through him. She wouldn't need more medical attention than he could give. Wrath took his time to unpack the kit and get what he needed, while he battled with the desire that rose within him.

"You live here?" She glanced around.

"Yes."

Her teeth bit down on her lower lip and drew his attention. Memories hit him of other females doing that while they moaned. Their hands had traveled over their breasts and stroked their spread pussies. Blood rushed to his cock, made his heart pound, and the air froze inside his lungs. Her voice forced him to concentrate on something besides his body's responses to the flashbacks he suffered.

"Why? I mean, we're underground, right?"

He refused to answer, opened the alcohol, and dampened one of the cotton balls. "This may sting."

A small sound came from her. She gasped when he applied the wet cotton to one of the deeper scratches. He remembered something he'd seen on television when he'd tried to get used to the outside world. A mother had blown on her child's injury to alleviate the burning sensation. He leaned in and fanned his breath over it.

"Does that help?"

"Thank you. Yes."

Wrath quickly cleaned and bandaged both her wrists. He packed away the medical supplies, closed the lid, and rose to his feet. He just wanted to put some space between him and her scent, which drove him a little insane.

The female stared at him as he paused by the bathroom door when he turned to peer at her. Her heart-shaped face was attractive, her nose strange but not unappealing, and she seemed to have a tendency to chew on her full bottom lip.

"I won't identify you to the police. I want to put that right out there. I don't care what you do with what's-his-name, that's none of my business, but I do want to survive this. Tell me what that's going to take. Do you want me to sign a sworn statement or something that I won't go to the cops? I'll do that."

"I'm not concerned with you going to the police."

It shocked him when tears welled inside her eyes and slid down her cheeks. She didn't bother to wipe them away. He took a hesitant step forward, alarmed that cleaning her wounds might be causing her pain. Her next words halted him quickly.

"I'll do whatever you want but please don't kill me. I have a whole list of stuff I want to do before I die and I haven't done any of it yet."

"I'm not going to hurt you."

"Right. That's why you're hiding your face." She pointed up at him. "You're making sure I can't see your eyes. Is that supposed to terrorize me more, because it's working? This might be some kind of sick sort of amusement for you but not for me. I'm hungry, tired, and scared. Don't you have a heart at all?" Her hand lifted to wipe at her tears.

"I am not wearing them to frighten you. My intention is the exact opposite. I wear the glasses to keep you at ease with me."

"Big fail."

He hesitated. "Do not be alarmed. I swear I won't hurt you. Humans are afraid of us."

Her eyes widened. "Humans? What are you? An alien?" She frowned. "Crap. You're nuts too? Really? Shit."

Wrath reached up and slowly removed his glasses. He stared at her calmly while she paled. Her mouth opened, closed, but nothing came out. He figured it was a good sign when she didn't scream.

Chapter Three

ꟹ

Lauren knew she was gawking at Wrath. His eyes were strange. She was adding up facts and it all slammed together in her brain on why his features looked so masculine.

"Oh God."

"Do not be frightened."

Is he kidding? Relief swept through her and her fear eased. "You're not some ex-con who works for the mob. You're a New Species, aren't you?"

He gave a sharp nod of his head.

"You don't just have weird nicknames. They are actually your names!"

"Yes." His lips twitched. "And I don't think our names are weird."

"Most men have names like Joe or Ralph but I shouldn't have used the term weird. I know that New Species have names like Justice and Fury. I have seen both of them on television and I heard or read somewhere that you all pick names that have meaning for you. So you really are New Species. I've never met one of you in person."

"I am New Species."

"I didn't know any of you kept your hair short. I should have realized when I saw your cheekbones and that nose…damn. I feel stupid for not putting it together. It's just that the bald man's eyes are really weird and he doesn't exactly look like you."

His eyes widened and he appeared confused.

"I can't believe I'm in a room with a New Species." She blushed a little and knew she probably sounded a bit nuts but she was a huge supporter of them. "My best friend and I, well, we've followed the news closely since that first facility was raided."

She rose to her feet and took a few hesitant steps toward him. It dawned on her that it might not be a good idea and she paused. That's when she remembered they could be dangerous to their enemies. Her eyes widened.

"Brent worked for Mercile? Is that why you're after him?"

His lips pressed firmly together then he said, "Yes."

"Son of a bitch!"

Eyebrows arched.

"Sorry." She tried to tone it down a little. "I really didn't like him. He's a dick, treats women like crap, and is a ten on the *eeew* scale." She was nervous suddenly. She was alone in a room with a real New Species.

They'd suffered so much. New Species had been created by a pharmaceutical company, using various combinations of human and animal DNA. The company, Mercile Industries, had used them as test subjects, imprisoned them, tortured them, and treated them like animals.

She tried to get a handle on her emotions as everything snapped into place. They were hunting Brent because he was a douche bag who helped suppress them. Vengeance's words finally made some sense and she paled. "Brent helped kill that bald man's girlfriend? One of your women?"

He hesitated. "Bill worked for Mercile Industries and isn't worthy of you protecting him. You are aware that Mercile Industries used our kind to experiment upon. You know they created us to do illegal testing on our bodies. Bill worked for them and he tortured many of my people. He enjoyed causing us pain. Vengeance is so enraged because he was joined to one of our females for a long-term breeding test. He mated her and when they ended the test, they tried to take her away. A fight broke out and she was murdered by the technicians as punishment to him for attacking them. Vengeance was only trying to protect her. Bill didn't kill the female but he killed another male's female out of revenge. Bill reminds him of all he lost."

Horror and shock tore through Lauren. She had heard Mercile Industries had done some horrible things to New Species but she hadn't heard that they had murdered their victims.

"Brent killed someone?" She shook her head, taken aback. "Are you sure you have the right guy? I mean..." She kept shaking her head. "He's an asshole and creep but I never would have thought he was pure evil."

"We have the right male, Lauren. I am telling you the truth. He tortured my kind in the facility where he worked. He brutally raped a female and slit her throat in front of a male as punishment for his refusal to do as he was ordered in a breeding test. The male whose female was murdered, along with other victims from that facility, have all identified Bill by photographs we were able to obtain. She wasn't the only female he raped and he enjoyed hitting males while they were helplessly chained." His voice deepened into a snarl. "He deserves to be punished for his crimes and he is one of the humans we want most."

It was beyond appalling to hear that the guy she worked with was capable of such monstrous atrocities but she believed Wrath. A shiver ran down her spine. She backed up to the bed and sat hard. Her legs shook a little at the thought of all the times she'd spoken to Brent, totally unaware of what a vile person she dealt with. She'd even filed complaints with their boss over his rude behavior. He could have killed her in retaliation.

"I am sorry for Vengeance's behavior toward you. He thinks you are Bill's female. The pain of what he witnessed with his own female and the rage at her loss has driven him a bit crazy. We haven't found or identified the male who killed his female but Bill is so similar to that human that he's taken this mission to his heart. I apologize. It will never happen again. You weren't supposed to really be harmed. You assumed we were similar to those males we watch in criminal movies and we allowed you to believe it. We don't hit or torture females but we thought your fear of us would make you talk. We played the part you expected."

Lauren still reeled from finding out she'd worked with a rapist and murderer. "I understand. I feel so bad for Vengeance now that I know why he was so awful to me. I don't condone it but I get it." Her arms hugged her waist and she peered up at the New Species. "I had no idea who Brent really was but I'll do anything you need to help you track down that piece of shit. I mean that. I know you guys think I'm dating him or sleeping with him but I have better taste than that. He's a creep."

"How well do you know Bill?"

"I know him as Brent. Everything I've said is true about just knowing him from work. I started there three months ago and I didn't like him from the get-go. Vengeance said I smell like perfume that Brent likes, that it's rare, but I got this at a Christmas gift exchange at work. It must have been the gift he brought. I took men's cologne in for the exchange. It's a common thing to buy for those things."

"We've talked to many females who Bill has dated and shared sex with. You carry the scent he buys them and prefers they wear. Perfume confuses our sense of smell. We aren't picking up any trace of sex from you or even the scent of a male but we can't read you accurately. I can faintly scent another female. Did you hug or brush up against one?"

"Wow. You really do have an enhanced sense of smell, don't you? I read about that. I hugged my friend, Amanda, when I met her for dinner. You won't smell sex on me." She blushed at the thought that he could smell her that well and hoped her deodorant was really as good as it boasted.

Wrath's intense gaze studied her body. "You are his type. Has he ever approached you with an interest in sharing sex?"

She hesitated. "The first week I worked there we had an incident."

"Explain what an incident is to you."

She sighed. "I was bent over a desk reaching for the phone. He walked by and smacked my ass. He made a sexual comment, he hit me hard enough that it hurt, and I was mad. I threatened to bring him up on sexual harassment charges and raised hell. We deal with each other in the office but it's tense at best. Now he's taken to bringing his cell phone to work and showing off pictures of naked women's body parts. It's disgusting."

"He wanted you but you weren't interested." Wrath nodded. "Does he go out of his way to annoy you?"

"Sometimes I swear he does but I can't prove it. Otherwise I'd have gotten him fired. Mel, our boss, says we're just different people and I need to try to get along with him. I just can't."

Wrath stepped closer. "Vengeance didn't believe you because of how you look and smell. You lied to him about not having sex in a long time so he refused to believe you about anything."

"I didn't lie about that."

Wrath frowned and his gaze narrowed. His eyes were rounded but slanted slightly at the corners, giving them an exotic appearance. The irises were a dark brown, almost black. His slightly flattened nose twitched.

"Even I don't believe that. You are attractive with a body that draws attention. Males would want to touch you and they would approach you often for shared sex."

"Well, I don't want to be touched." She frowned at him. "I was in a really bad relationship. Do you know what a stalker is?"

He hesitated. "No."

"I dated a guy for about six months and I thought he was someone nice. We moved in together but he got weird. He wasn't abusive. He didn't hit me but he got really creepy and it turned so bad that I moved out. He started stalking me. That's following me around and leaving threatening notes on my door. I finally had to get a restraining order. I had to have the police make him leave me alone. It was a bad experience and I haven't dated since. I thought he was normal but I obviously have bad taste in men. I haven't met anyone since then that I'm interested in enough to take another chance."

"How was he creepy and weird?"

She hesitated. "As an example, I came home and he was wearing my panties." She made a face. "Just my panties. He picked up his belt and told me he wanted to spank me. I moved out after that. Creepy, weird, and kind of scary. I'm not into guys who wear women's panties and I'm sure not into being spanked."

Wrath nodded. "Human males are freaks."

Lauren smiled. "Some of them are and I found one who turned me off men. Then I found out he'd been sleeping with another woman while we lived together. He told me, trying to hurt my feelings, but I think he really thought I'd be jealous enough to want him back. I just felt sorry for her and glad I wasn't with him anymore."

Wrath appeared a little surprised. "What do you know of Bill?"

"Just what I said. I know he goes to a lot of bars and brags at work about how he can pick up women easily. He's good-looking until he opens his mouth."

Wrath grinned. "Do you know what bars?"

She shrugged but a memory surfaced. "I don't know where he lives but he did mention that there was one around the corner from his place and he goes there often. He was telling someone he never had to worry about getting popped for a DUI because he just walks there and back."

"What is a DUI?"

"Driving while under the influence of alcohol. I guess he gets pretty drunk. It's illegal to drive after drinking."

"I have his address and I'll have it checked out. Thank you."

"May I ask you something?"

He didn't say anything. She figured that wasn't a "no".

"Everything I've ever heard or read about New Species says all of you live at the NSO Homeland or the NSO Reservation but you are here. Why?"

He took a breath. "Some of us want to find the humans who harmed us, though it is risky for us to leave the safety of the NSO. Bill is at the top of our list of people to find. We're going to bring them in to be punished for their crimes or…kill them. Whether they live or die depends on their willingness to be taken in. We have formed a small team to hunt and locate them. We also work with a team of humans who work for the NSO but they aren't here right now. This is their task force headquarters. They have homes elsewhere. It is not safe for us to live with them so we stay here in the basement where it's secure. It's a joint venture between the New Species Organization and the government."

"I hadn't heard about a task force but it's good that you have one and they are helping you find the people who hurt you." She hesitated. "I'm on your side and I want you to arrest Brent, I mean Bill. Now that we're clear on that, can I go home?"

He slowly shook his head. "You know who we are and that we are on the hunt for Bill. You could warn him. Even if you would not, you could give us away by accident by looking at him differently since you know his true identity. You will have to stay here until he is captured or killed."

"But what if that takes days? Or weeks? What if you never find him? I have a life, a job, and bills to pay. I have plans to go to the movies with Amanda tomorrow. I can't stay here."

He frowned. "I'm sorry. Finding Bill is more important."

"You have to let me go. What if that…Vengeance comes after me again?" She felt pure terror remembering what he'd nearly done to her in that interrogation room. It was understandable, but the guy had some screws loose and unfortunately he'd picked her to take it out on. "He scares me."

Wrath stepped a little closer. "I apologize for what he tried to do to you. It is the pain he suffered at the loss of his loved female. He won't do that again now that he's realized how wrong it was to allow his rage and grief to get the better of him. I swear that no one will force mate you here."

"Force mate?"

"You would consider it being held hostage by one male for the rest of your life…and rape."

Shock tore through Lauren. Wrath had saved her. She wasn't afraid of him and she did understand why they wanted to keep her there. It just wasn't something she agreed with. No way would she warn Brent that his days of being on the outside of a prison were limited. It would be doing all women a great service if he was locked up forever. The guy was dangerous.

Wrath strode to a dresser and opened one of the drawers. He withdrew a folded pair of sweatpants and cautiously approached her. Lauren didn't tense up or feel fear. He offered them to her.

"Why don't you put those on? Your legs must be cold. There isn't much heat down here and your skirt was destroyed. I'll take you to get something to eat. Your stomach keeps growling from hunger."

He can hear that? Wow. Not only did he have a super sense of smell but his hearing had to be pretty keen too. She accepted the folded pants and stood as he backed away.

"You may use my bathroom."

The human female intrigued Wrath. He really wanted to believe she was innocent of being involved with Bill. The idea of someone as sweet as her allowing that monster to touch her made him furious.

The violence Vengeance had subjected her to had shaken her badly. That was nothing compared to the kind of evil Bill had done. He hadn't threatened to force mate females in the testing facilities, he actually had assaulted some of them to achieve his own sexual pleasure. It hadn't been for any other reason except the ability to inflict suffering on others.

Lauren stirred emotions inside Wrath that left him feeling unsettled. She hadn't screamed when he'd revealed his true identity but instead seemed relieved. Him being Species was preferable to her than him being hired muscle for a criminal. She'd been very accepting of his origins.

She'd felt soft, slight and fragile in the cradle of his arms when he'd carried her into his room. It made his protective instincts flare to life. Lauren Henderson was trouble in a small package. A supple, seductive one that encouraged him to learn more about her but she was a curiosity he couldn't afford to explore.

He was severely damaged inside, a victim of abuse, and human females were his trigger. Coldness settled inside him over the desire she stirred. The parts of him he tried to control, those animal instincts, fought to be free. He wanted her but he needed to resist. The sounds she made in the bathroom drew his attention as he waited for her to return to the bedroom. He'd get her food, keep her safe from Vengeance, and he'd focus on the simplicity of those things instead of the way his blood warmed with the temptation to hold her again.

The room was tiny—just a toilet, sink, and shower stall. It was bare basics, something found in a business rather than a home, and Lauran felt a little sad for Wrath for having to live in such a stark environment.

The sweats were huge and the legs way too long. She had to roll them to avoid stepping on the excess material. She used the toilet, washed her face and hands, and opened the bathroom door.

Wrath had taken a seat on the bed. His tall, large frame dwarfed the twin-sized, long mattress. He rose to his feet quickly and his gaze traveled down her body. He frowned and returned to the dresser then offered her a pair of thick white socks.

"Your feet must be cold."

His concern warmed her heart and made her like him even more. For a guy she'd thought was a murdering ex-convict, she was really glad to be far off base. He wasn't scary at all and was actually sweet to be worried about her catching a chill from the concrete floors. She put the socks on and had to roll those as well. One glance at his boots assured her the guy had huge feet and that's why the socks would have probably reached her knees if she'd tried to straighten them out.

He hesitated by the door. "Come with me. They keep a small kitchen on this level for us and it is stocked with sodas and sandwiches. We have chips too. I apologize but it is all I have to offer until our main meals come. I will call and ask them to bring you cooked meat."

"Cooked meat?" She walked toward him.

"We don't enjoy our meat cooked much. We just sear the outside but enjoy it very rare inside." He paused, his gaze studying her. "You may not wish to watch us eat in the morning. That is our next main meal delivery. I won't forget to ask them to bring a human breakfast for you."

"I can't stay here until morning. I get why you want to keep me but I really have to go to work. I need my job. Maybe you don't understand what rent or bills are. I don't know how that works with the NSO but our world we have to make money to keep a roof over our heads. I'm almost flat broke and can't afford to take any time off. I need to be out there showing properties, making sales. I earn a percentage of that."

"I apologize for keeping you in captivity but there is no choice. Bill is too dangerous to risk allowing him to get away from us. They are not easy to track. They take false names and sometimes they try to harm our kind in retaliation for tracking them down. They are stupid and don't feel they should be punished for what they have done to my kind." His gaze softened. "I know how it feels to be held against your will but I promise, catching him is worth the time you'll spend here."

She could see from the determination in his steady gaze that he wasn't going to budge. "I guess I should be grateful to come out of this alive. I really thought I wouldn't."

"No harm will come to you." He opened the door to the hallway. "Please follow me and stay close. There is nowhere to escape to. The elevator needs a code to work and I doubt you would enjoy running into Vengeance after the scare he gave you."

A shiver ran down her spine over that prospect. The bald man terrified her. Nothing was going to change that after what he'd nearly done to her. She quickly reached Wrath's side. Once again she felt dainty compared to his tall, muscular form. New Species were much larger in person than in pictures and on television.

Amanda was going to flip when Lauren told her what had happened and how she'd been kidnapped by a few of them. New Species were their favorite topic of discussion and sometimes they watched television specials on them together. Two weeks prior they'd watched a documentary on how the New Species had been transferred to remote locations after their initial freedom to get used to life on the outside. The reporter had said they had to learn simple things such as how to use the phones and microwaves. None of those things had occurred to her until then.

Wrath stepped out of the room and she moved with him. She wasn't about to lose him and risk running into Vengeance. He glanced at her.

"You are safe."

She nodded, pretty sure he wouldn't hurt her. "I know."

His hand lifted and he motioned her to precede him. "Walk straight ahead and I'll tell you when to turn to reach the kitchen."

"I'll just stick to your side, if you don't mind."

"Vengeance won't hurt you. He's calmed down and will be over his behavior."

Lauren licked her lips. "I'm not." She wasn't embarrassed to admit how much she'd been frightened. "He's scary."

Chapter Four

ജ

Lauren felt trepidation as Wrath led her down a long hallway that opened up into a large room. There was a pool table in the corner. Couches, tables and a large television sat in the center, and along one corner was a kitchenette with a large refrigerator, cabinets, counters, and a sink. There was also a table and chairs. That's where her attention fixed and she halted in fear.

A hand gripped her elbow gently and Lauren's gaze darted up to Wrath's face. He gave her a small smile. "It's all right, Lauren. These are the males I work with. You've met one of them."

She had no choice but get closer to the table since Wrath held her arm and tugged her along. Two men sat at the table opposite each other. One was the large blond from the warehouse, minus his sunglasses, and his eyes were clearly displayed. He was obviously New Species. He had blue eyes, unlike Wrath, but their features were similar. The blond man frowned as he watched their approach.

"This is Shadow," Wrath introduced.

Shadow glanced at Wrath. "Why is she out of the holding cell?" He studied her with a quick sweep of his gaze. "Was her perfume bothering you so much while you interrogated her that you made her wear your clothing?" He sniffed. "I do admit I prefer being in her presence now more than before."

Wrath ignored Shadow. He nodded toward the second man. "This is Brass."

Lauren studied the man with brown hair and almost-black eyes. He was big too, had wide shoulders, and was as muscular as Wrath and Shadow. Brass frowned too.

"Why is she out here? We were trying to intimidate her."

Wrath hesitated. "We'll discuss that later. Right now she needs food. I believe she is not Bill's girlfriend but only works with him. She told me that he said he likes to hang out at a bar within walking distance of his home. We should have Tim send a team there and put it under surveillance. Perhaps he will show if it is a regular place he visits."

Footsteps sounded behind Lauren and she turned her head. Vengeance stepped into the room. He had changed into a tank top and cotton shorts. The skimpy outfit showed off his big muscles. It only took one look at him before terror hit her faster than a bolt of lightning. She whimpered and jerked out of Wrath's hold. She stumbled backward, looking for a place to run.

Wrath moved fast and grabbed Lauren around her waist. Strong arms hauled her against his chest. He turned in a way that blocked her from the source of her fear and glanced down. "It's fine, Lauren. He won't touch you again."

Her fingers clawed at Wrath's shirt. She didn't fight to get away but instead clung to him. He had saved her once and she felt safe huddled against his big frame.

"What is going on?" Brass stood. "I can smell pure terror coming from her."

"That's an interesting reaction to Vengeance. Is it his shaved head? It does look strange. Was she too distracted to notice him when we took her from that building?" Shadow chuckled. "Are you all right, Wrath? Do you need help before she climbs up you?"

Wrath snarled and his body tensed against hers. The sound was vicious and threatening. Lauren would have pushed him away and tried to flee but his arms were locked tightly around her waist. One of his hands rubbed her back even as he made another scary sound.

"See, Vengeance? See what you've done? If you can't contain your temper then you should be back at Reservation until you can."

Another growl sounded inside the room. "I said I was sorry."

"Sorry for what?" Brass snarled now. "What did you do, Ven?"

"I scared her," Vengeance admitted.

"How? I think if she could climb up Wrath to escape you, she would." Shadow even sounded angry. "Did you cross a line?"

"She shared sex with that monster." Vengeance's voice deepened. "I lost my temper. She's protecting him when she shouldn't. I'm going for a walk."

Long seconds ticked by but Lauren wasn't willing to release Wrath until she was sure Vengeance had left. Brass finally spoke.

"What happened?"

Wrath continued to rub Lauren's back. "I heard her screams and ran in there. He had torn her clothing off and was about to force breed her to get her to talk. He thought mating her would make her switch loyalties to him."

"Son of a bitch," Brass ground out. "No wonder she reacts to him that strongly. Is she all right?"

Wrath's arms still gripped Lauren, but he said, "He's gone. You can let go now."

Lauren released him and stepped back. She leaned sideways to peer around Wrath to make sure Vengeance had really left. The fear faded and she peered up at her hero. Wrath watched her calmly.

"Thank you." She swallowed.

Wrath touched Lauren and turned her to face the two New Species. They were now standing only feet away. Lauren gasped and quickly put more space between them. Her back slammed into Wrath's chest. His arms wrapped loosely around her waist to anchor her there.

"Easy," he urged. "You're safe."

Shadow smiled but it looked forced. "We aren't going to hurt you. We only tried to frighten you into giving up information but you were never in any real danger. We don't harm females."

Brass' expression was grim. "Ven never should have touched you that way. We don't condone forced mating or rough physical treatment of females."

"I was careful not to harm you when I put you on the table." Shadow frowned. "It was just to shake you up a bit but Wrath said I took it too far. That is why he had us leave you alone. I apologize."

"I explained. Her wrists were a little torn from the handcuffs when she fought to get away from Vengeance but I bandaged them." Wrath gently eased Lauren a few inches from his body. "I brought her in here to get something to eat and drink. Her stomach rumbles from hunger."

Brass sighed. "You must think the worst of us. I apologize for Ven's rage."

Wrath released her. "She isn't happy about having to stay here until we capture Bill."

"Who would be happy to be kept prisoner?" Shadow turned and sat down but his gaze remained on Wrath. "I'm shocked you didn't tear his head off when you walked in on that."

"I would have if he hadn't calmed." Wrath was grim. "Brass, you might want to talk to him. He has no business being part of his mission if he can't control his anger. He should return to Reservation. They handle irate males there much better than at Homeland."

Brass nodded. "I will go have words with him." He paused. "She's your responsibility, Wrath. She seems more at ease with you than the rest of us."

Wrath paled. "I thought we could turn her over to the task force to hold."

Shadow shook his head. "No." His blue gaze traveled over the length of Lauren's body. "I would feel better if she were with us. I am sure they are fine but we don't know these humans well enough to be certain they can be trusted with a female. We brought her here. She should be our responsibility to protect until she's released."

"She's our responsibility to protect," Brass agreed. "I know it doesn't need to be said but don't leave her with Ven. I'm sure he's fine now but his behavior is alarming. Perhaps he's not as stable as he seemed. We're all under a great deal of stress on this mission. I'm sure the female won't want to be left anywhere near him."

Wrath frowned. "Where do I put her?"

Brass shrugged. "Close to you."

Shadow nodded. "Better you than me."

Lauren darted a glance at the three men. Brass looked indifferent, Shadow seemed uncomfortable, and Wrath flat out frowned. It was clear he didn't want to be stuck with her, nor did the other two. It might be time to try to gain her freedom again.

"Can't I just go home? Please? I won't tell Bill anything. I want you to catch him."

Three pairs of eyes turned on her with grim expressions and she swallowed. No one said a word. She sighed and knew she wasn't going anywhere.

"Fine. I am hungry. I was just sitting down to dinner with my friend when I got the call to show the warehouse. I didn't get to actually eat."

Wrath moved away from her. "Have a seat. Do you like roast beef or ham sandwiches? I'll make you one."

"Roast beef, please. No mustard. I'm allergic."

"I understand." Wrath kept his back to her as he started pulling things from the fridge to make her a sandwich. "Feeding you should be easy."

She sat and eyed Shadow as Brass left the room. He held her gaze and frowned. He kept glancing at her hair though.

"What?" She reached up to touch her head, felt the bun still in place, and no parts of it sticking up. "Is something in my hair? Tell me it's not a cobweb. I hate spiders."

"No spiders are there. Why do you do that to your hair? It looks uncomfortable."

She let her hand drop. "I look more professional with my hair up. I should cut it but I always had short hair as a kid. I always wanted long hair so I let it grow out when I got my own place after high school."

"Why didn't you just stop cutting it when you were young?"

She hesitated. "My grandparents raised me. My Grandma said it was easier to care for if it was short and my grandfather was afraid boys would take notice of me so he agreed with her. They made me cut it every few months until I moved out. It was their house, their rules." She smiled.

"Can you take it down please? I am curious."

Lauren shrugged. She reached up and started pulling pins. She knew it would look messy but wanted to appease his curiosity. She understood it since she had a ton of questions about New Species. She realized that she might seem as strange to him as they did to her.

She placed the pins on the table and unwound her hair and then pulled the ponytail holder out. She ran her fingers through her unbound hair, happy to have it down since she usually brushed it before bed, and met Shadow's gaze to see his reaction.

His lips were parted and his blue eyes were wide as he gaped at her hair. He blinked a few times but finally smiled.

"It's beautiful and longer than I thought it would be. I miss my long hair."

She glanced at his short-cropped hair. "Why did you cut it if you like it long?"

"The mission was more important and it will grow back." His smile faded. "I had to cut it to look more human and fit in with the task force. It wasn't as long as yours but it hung past my shoulders."

She could understand that. "I keep mine up for my job. Maybe instead of cutting it you should have put it up."

Glass broke in the kitchen area. Lauren started and her head jerked in the direction of the loud sound. Wrath stared at Lauren, openmouthed, and the plate that held her sandwich was broken on the floor at his feet, where he'd dropped it.

Shadow chuckled. "It's beautiful, isn't it? Much longer than I thought."

Wrath's face tightened and his gaze lowered to the floor. A growl tore from his throat as he crouched and started picking up the mess. Lauren was confused and she glanced at Shadow.

"Did he just growl? I thought I imagined it before."

"We all growl. It's the change in us. We snarl too. Howl." He chuckled. "We show teeth. Have you seen them yet?"

She shook her head. "They look like regular teeth."

"That's because we've learned to only open our mouths so far around humans. We practice speaking and smiling in front of a mirror so we don't frighten humans when we deal with them. Would you like to see my canines?"

She hesitated. "Sure, if you don't move closer."

He laughed and opened his mouth all the way. Lauren couldn't help but gawk. She swallowed hard. Shadow's teeth were beautifully white and looked human until his fangs were revealed. They extended longer than a normal person's canines and they turned into sharper points at the end. He slowly hid them.

"We're all canine on our team. That's what we were mixed with. The feline mixes have the same anomaly, only they roar when they get emotional. We howl and snarl." He shrugged. "We all growl. Don't be alarmed when you hear it. We do it often. It doesn't mean we're angry."

"Feline?"

"Some of our people were mixed with large-breed felines, what we believe were lions, tigers, and the black big cats—your people call them panthers. It's just a guess but they have the catlike eyes and they roar. Canines are better trackers and deal with each other better. Our sense of smell is stronger and we enjoy company. Felines are faster and they can leap a floor or two in height. Most of them aren't real social though, long term. They prefer solitary situations."

"Justice North is feline then, isn't he?"

"He's the exception. He is feline but he's very social."

"I have seen him on the news plenty of times. He seems really nice."

"He is."

"Here." Wrath placed food and a can of soda in front of her.

She carefully studied the sandwich.

Shadow laughed. "It's not the one that hit the floor. He made you another."

Lauren blushed, embarrassed that he'd guessed what she was thinking. She turned her head and stared up at Wrath. "Thank you."

He took a seat next to her but his attention remained focused on her hair. For whatever reason, he seemed fascinated by the sight of her blonde hair flowing down her back almost to her waist. She mentally shrugged it off. Shadow had said they liked long hair.

The roast beef sandwich was good, he'd put mayo on it, cheese and fresh lettuce. She smiled at him.

"Thank you. This is great. I appreciate it." Lauren opened her soda.

Wrath turned his head to glare at Shadow. "You should protect her and keep her close to you."

Shadow's eyes narrowed. "No."

Wrath growled. "Please."

Shadow stared at each other for a long time. Lauren ate and watched the two men, wondering if they were silently communicating. It seemed as if they were having some kind of silent discussion as their eyes narrowed at each other and they made some strange facial movements around their mouths.

"Are you two reading each other's thoughts?"

Both turned to gape at her.

"No." Shadow flashed a grin. "But it would be cool if we could. We were just studying each other. There are some things between us that go unspoken. We're from the same testing facility and we have spent all our time together since being freed. We know each other well enough to understand how the other thinks." His gaze turned to Wrath. "No."

Wrath looked angry. "She would be safer with you."

Shadow's features softened. "That wasn't your fault that you tried to attack a female while drugged in captivity, Wrath. You must get past it. You're stronger than the conditioning and this will be a perfect way to do it."

Wrath suddenly stood. "How?"

"You won't harm her and you're much stronger than you believe. We both know she's not one of the humans who harmed us. She had no part in the things done and the drugs are long gone from our bodies. You will be fine."

"You are better natured than I."

Shadow frowned. "I have the same memories as you. We shared that hell together and you were stronger then. I was overdosed because I couldn't manage my rage. She trusts you and you won't betray that."

Lauren figured the "she" they spoke of was her. "What are you guys talking about?"

Shadow slowly rose to his feet. "Our life in captivity. It is a private matter."

That made her realize she'd overstepped a boundary. She finished her food while they continued their staring contest. Wrath finally broke the silence.

"You're afraid too."

"Always," Shadow admitted. "You were always stronger than me."

Wrath broke eye contact with his friend to peer at her grimly. "Lauren? Let's go. You'll be staying with me in my room. You can have the bed and I'll sleep on the floor. I won't harm you."

She was shocked. "I have to sleep in your room with you?"

He hesitated. "Would you prefer to sleep in Vengeance's room?"

She stood on shaky legs. "I'm ready to go with you."

Shadow chuckled. "That was smooth."

Wrath snarled at him and gripped Lauren's arm gently. "You can clean up the dishes. I will see you bright and early in the morning."

"Trust yourself," Shadow called out as they left.

Lauren was uncomfortable as Wrath led her back to his bedroom. He closed the door behind them, a grim look on his masculine features. He released her instantly, moved a few feet away, and appeared as ill at ease as she felt being closed inside a room together. It made her feel a little better knowing he wasn't thrilled with having to spend a night together.

He finally looked at her. "There's no television but I have a radio and a few books on the dresser. I am going to take a shower." He shifted his stance. "Don't leave my room. Vengeance is out there and I don't want there to be a reason for him to confront you. He will believe you are escaping and he's already emotionally stressed. The bed is yours. I'm sure you're very tired after all you've been through. Rest."

He walked to the dresser to grab a change of clothing before closing himself inside the bathroom. Lauren glanced around the room, hoped it would only be for a night, and missed her own bedroom. She took a seat on the bed. The mattress was firmer than she liked but Wrath wasn't the pillow-top bedding type.

Her arms hugged her waist as she listened to water turn on in the other room, still couldn't believe she was with New Species and that they'd kidnapped her. Wrath was hot, she had to admit that, and he'd saved her from Vengeance.

She bit her lower lip, her gaze fixed on the closed bathroom door, and realized the Wrath was less than ten feet away, naked in a shower. *Amanda is not going to believe me when I tell her this.* She smiled.

Wrath clenched his teeth and allowed water to strike his face. A female was going to be sleeping in his bed just feet from him and she was human. Images flashed through his mind, the human women he'd been forced to watch to help them steal his seed from his body. His cock stiffened and he barely managed to hold back a howl of rage.

Lauren wasn't responsible for the cruel testing he'd survived. The Mercile employees who had kidnapped him from the testing facility before the police had raided it and freed others of his kind were to blame. They'd kept him caged and chained, hooked him to machines, put a helmet over his head that showed naked human women touching themselves and pumped his body full of breeding drugs to drive him insane with lust.

He turned his head out of the spray of water, gasped in air, and glanced down. His hand gripped his cock. The feel of his rough palm was much different than the machine that had milked his seed for the humans to sell for experiments. He stroked the shaft to help ground him to reality. He wasn't a prisoner anymore. No machine would be strapped to his body and Lauren was a real person instead of some nameless human in a video used to help arouse him.

Pleasure helped soothe some of his anger. He was in control now and he leaned back against the cold shower stall. His eyes remained closed and images of Lauren filtered in. Her smile, the way her blonde hair fell down her back and how soft her skin was. Her body was so different from Species women. Pale. Generous with curves.

He groaned as he stroked his cock faster and sealed his lips tightly to avoid making any sound when he came. The tension in his body eased as he recovered from the fast climax and reached for the shampoo. He missed his long hair but it was easier to care for as he quickly washed it and his body. He hurried in case his guest was afraid. She was in a strange place with males unfamiliar to her.

Chapter Five

ꟾ

Lauren decided she really hated Brent. He was far worse than just a crude jerk. He'd committed serious and horrible crimes against New Species, but she was the one paying for them currently. She turned on her side on the mattress and used her arm to pillow her face.

She inhaled Wrath's masculine scent, decided it was pleasant and allowed the sound of the shower to soothe her. A yawn broke. Wrath was being kind now but a few hours before had been a different story. She'd never been more afraid than when she'd been kidnapped and Vengeance had threatened to rape her.

She fought sleep and wondered if her captor had dozed off in the shower. He'd been in there for a long time. The water suddenly cut off as if he'd read her thoughts and she waited for him to come out. It would be rude to go to sleep without telling him good night.

The door opened within minutes and her sleepy mind jerked wide awake at the sight of him stepping into the room wearing nothing but a pair of boxers. His naked chest was all tan skin, muscles and pure perfection. His biceps were well defined, thick, and he had the broadest shoulders. Her mouth turned dry.

He paused to stare at her with a curious look and tilted his head as he faced her. "Are you well?"

Her gaze lowered down his body to the low-riding boxers and over them to his bulky thighs—more muscles. He was the epitome of masculinity and looked better than any of the models on her wall calendar at home.

"Lauren?" Wrath frowned. "You look paler."

"Where are the rest of your clothes?"

"I usually sleep without any clothing but I am properly covered." He glanced down before meeting her gaze again. "My dick is hidden."

She had nothing to say to that. Her mind blanked for seconds as her gaze traveled over every inch of him.

"I wear clothing during work hours and enjoy relaxing when I sleep. It's been a long day and we both need sleep. I will be right back. I forgot to grab spare bedding for the floor. They keep sleeping bags and extra pillows in a storage closet down the hall." He paused. "Do you need a drink before bed? I could get you a glass for water or a soda."

"I'm good." She swallowed.

He turned around. The boxers outlined his beefy, perfect ass nicely and his back was broad. He opened the door to step into the hallway and turned left. Lauren rolled onto her back to stare up at the ceiling and suddenly laughed. It was a good thing she'd been the one kidnapped instead of Amanda. Her best friend would have seen Wrath's body and attacked him. Wrath could tempt a saint to sin. He had a bod that didn't quit that any woman would appreciate.

Movement drew her attention and she was glad he'd been quick about running his errand. It wasn't Wrath who stepped into the room though. The door closed quietly while Vengeance glared at her. Terror made her jerk upright to gape at him.

"You have fooled Wrath with your pretty eyes and soft voice." He growled a threatening sound. "But not me." His hands fisted at his sides as he took a step closer. "I have scented you today and you stink of the enemy. You will be my mate and do as I ask by taking me to Bill. You no longer belong to him and will carry my scent."

Lauren knew she was in danger as the bald man growled again while blocking the door he'd come through. Her gaze darted to the bathroom. It was only a few feet from the end of the bed but it didn't have a lock on the inside. She lunged toward it anyway. It would at least put a door between them. She almost made it when hands suddenly grabbed her.

The scream she tried to get out was cut off when he spun her and her side slammed into the wall inches from her goal. The rough impact knocked the air from her lungs and a hand tangled in her hair at the base of her neck. She battled for breath as he shifted his hold to wrap his arm around her waist and yanked her off her feet to lift her against his body. He spun and stormed for the door.

She finally sucked in a lungful of air and screamed. She kicked frantically in an attempt to trip him but he succeeded in staying upright no matter how hard she nailed his lower legs. The hand let go of her hair when he yanked open the door and carried her into the hallway. Two doors down, he entered a room and slammed the door. She guessed they were now inside his room.

Another scream tore from her throat as he threw her on a firm mattress. She landed facedown on his bed and it took her stunned seconds to realize what had happened. She spit hair out of her still-open mouth as she lifted her head and stared at him in horror. He was mere inches away.

"I claim you," he snarled. "You are my mate now."

He reached for the front of his shorts and the reality of what he planned sank in. Lauren reacted. "Fuck you," she yelled and rolled away.

His bed wasn't against a wall, the way Wrath's had been. It was in the center of the room and she hit the floor hard on her side. The mattress creaked as Vengeance stepped onto it. He glared down at her until she rolled under the bed, trying to get away. She had nowhere else to go as she frantically scanned the room, looking for an escape. The doors to the hallway and bathroom were too far away for her to make it.

Feet hit the floor less than a foot away from her face when he jumped off the mattress and she gasped when the bed was suddenly gone from above her. Vengeance had thrown it out of the way. The sound of the frame hitting the wall was loud and she stared up at him with dread.

"You want to be taken on the floor? Fine." He lunged.

She wanted to roll away again but he moved too fast. He just dropped his big body down. The pain of being crushed never happened. Instead his arms caught most of his weight and he settled down over her slowly, pinned her to the concrete, and braced his weight on one arm. His free hand clutched at her sweatpants while he rolled enough to put space between their hips and yanked hard. Fabric ripped.

Lauren screamed again and tried to claw his face but he jerked away. She found his neck instead and dug her nails into the hot skin. He howled in pain. His hands became brutal. He rolled her onto her stomach, pinned her painfully against the floor and snarled.

"Don't fight or I will hurt you."

"Go to hell," she cried out, struggling to knock him off her back. "Let me go!"

"I claim you for my mate. You will learn to enjoy my touch."

"You sic—"

The door burst open and hit the wall hard. Lauren twisted her head enough to see the source of the vicious snarl that sent chills down her spine. Shadow and Wrath entered the room and both of them looked furious.

"Help me," she panted, her gaze locking with Wrath's.

"I claim her as mine," Vengeance bellowed. "Get out and leave us to form a bond."

Brass rushed inside the room, shouldered Shadow aside, and revealed sharp teeth as he snarled. "No. You can't force mate her. What is wrong with you, Vengeance? Release her now."

"I claim her as my mate and she will do as I tell her," Vengeance snarled viciously. "I will show her my dominance until she obeys me."

Wrath's nose flared as his fingers curved into claws and he lunged at Vengeance. All Lauren could do was tense from the knowledge that another body was about to slam her into the floor. Instead Vengeance's body rolled from hers and crashed into the wall.

Hands grabbed her upper arms and dragged her toward the door. She looked up to see it was Shadow who did it. Brass moved, grabbed Lauren's other arm, and both men lifted her upright to her feet. They shoved her backward, closer to the door and put their bodies in front of her.

"Should we break it up?" Shadow rumbled, anger in his tone.

"No," Brass growled back. "Ven has gone too far. So be it if Wrath kills him. He went after a female. He's unstable."

Lauren was shaking badly as she leaned against the doorframe. Their words sank in and so did their meaning. She inched over enough to peer around them and the sight shocked her. Vengeance and Wrath were attacking each other but it wasn't like any fight she'd ever seen. They were kickboxing, exchanging punches and wrestling at times as she watched. The men collided at one point and rolled on the floor. Sharp teeth slashed and they clawed each other until they broke apart. Both men sprang to their feet.

Vengeance kicked out suddenly, trying to nail his opponent in the stomach. Wrath dodged the heel and threw a roundhouse kick that hit Vengeance in the face. The man was thrown backward into a wall. He hit it hard, grunted, and spun. He snarled as he flashed deadly looking teeth and tried to tackle Wrath around the waist to take him down. Wrath snarled back, showing his own scary teeth, and twisted out of the way to avoid Vengeance's outstretched arms. His clawed hands slashed at Vengeance and both men slammed into the floor again. They rolled, exchanging slashes and fists. Blood smeared their bodies.

Lauren pleaded, horrified at the show of pure violence. "Stop them."

Shadow reached back to grip her arm gently. "They fight over you. Wrath has to do this and Vengeance needs to learn he can't harm females."

The two men sprang apart again, snarling at each other. Vengeance suddenly howled and lunged. It was apparent that he was going for Wrath's throat but Wrath threw his arm up, shoving Vengeance's clawed hands to the side. His elbow slammed hard into Vengeance's neck. The man made a choking sound and hit the floor. Wrath dropped down on top of his back and his arm hooked around Vengeance's throat, squeezing tightly.

"You touched her again," Wrath snarled. "You took her from my bed. You are out of control."

Vengeance tried to lift his body enough to roll but he couldn't do it. He collapsed back to the floor.

"I should kill you. I should snap your neck. If you ever even look at her, go within scenting distance of her again, you will die," Wrath snarled, enraged.

Wrath's arm muscles bulged while Vengeance choked and gasped. His body jerked and his fingers clawed the concrete as his face turned a sickly color from lack of oxygen. Vengeance's eyes rolled up into his head and he went limp. Long seconds ticked by before Wrath softly cursed. He released the man's neck and climbed to his feet.

Blood was smeared around Wrath's mouth and down his chest. More of it was on both arms and ran down his torso to the waist of his boxers. Even one thigh and one knee were bloodied. He glared at Brass.

"He is not fit for this mission or to be around others. I will kill him the next time I see him if you don't send him to the

Wild Zone of Reservation. He should be with the other untamed males. He is lucky to live."

Brass nodded. "I will guard him and call for them to pick him up. He will not leave the Wild Zone."

Wrath growled. "He's dead if he's here in the morning. He's dead if he steps foot from the Wild Zone." His furious gaze turned to Lauren. His voice came out unusually deep but he stopped growling. "Let's go to my room."

Lauren's legs wouldn't move, shock holding her still. She wanted to do whatever he said but her body didn't respond. Wrath slowly stalked toward her but paused a few feet away. He took a deep breath.

"Until he is gone you are going to my room. Turn around, Lauren. I don't want to touch you with blood on me. Please go now."

She managed to get her body under control and turned around. Wrath stayed close behind her until they entered his bedroom. The door slammed behind them. Lauren jumped, spun, and stared wide-eyed at Wrath. He still appeared furious, his eyes black from his rage. She tried to remember it wasn't directed at her.

"I'm going to shower to wash off the blood. Sit on the bed and don't move." He drew in a deep breath. "I won't let you out of my sight until Vengeance is gone." He took another deep breath. "Go to sleep and know this won't happen again. He's dead if he comes after you again."

She nodded mutely, not sure what to say. She was badly shaken. Her legs were so wobbly she barely made it to the bed where she collapsed. She lay on her side, facing away from Wrath, and stared at the wall. Tears filled her eyes and she trembled.

Wrath's heart raced and he needed to put space between himself and Lauren. Adrenaline from the battle surged through his body until his skin itched. The urge to run, to howl, or to keep fighting had him on edge. He could have killed Vengeance, nearly had, but he'd regained control in time to prevent it. That should have counted, calmed him some, but he didn't trust himself to be near her.

His rage over Lauren being attacked in his room by a male who was intent on taking her body and claiming her had boiled over into violence. The scent of her fear had flipped a switch inside him, one that had sent him into pure bloodlust.

Vengeance's blood and his own coated his skin as he entered the bathroom but the violence and rage of battle quickly turned to desire and the need to claim Lauren before another male could attempt to take her away from him again. His dick swelled with blood at just the thought of returning to his bedroom and stripping her bare. His hands clenched as he breathed through his mouth to lessen the stench of blood. The primal side of him wanted her so bad it hurt. His body trembled from the need to go after her.

Brutal images filtered through his thoughts and it cooled his heated blood enough to keep control. He would hurt her in the state he was in. He'd take her roughly, without consideration, just to satisfy the need to make her his. He'd be worse than Vengeance if he did it. Wrath knew it was wrong to force a female to become his mate.

His cock throbbed painfully and he knew he had to attend to his own needs before his instincts overrode his control. She was human and not his. He guarded her and she trusted him. For one instant he remembered all the human women who had been used in videos to torment him and the craving to seek revenge struck.

It scared him, knowing what he was capable of doing in that moment. Lauren wasn't his enemy and didn't deserve to become the vessel of his revenge. She was soft, nice, and hadn't done him any personal harm. He wouldn't mean to hurt her but at that moment he had no gentleness to give. His hands unclenched and he frantically stepped inside the shower stall. He needed cold water and a way to unleash his building aggression. He had to remember that he was strong enough to keep his baser side leashed. Hurting Lauren wasn't acceptable and it was the last thing he wanted to do. Unfortunately, the urge to claim her lingered.

Lauren tried to keep it together. Falling apart in front of Wrath after he'd just brutally fought to rescue her wouldn't be something he needed to see. He'd done more than enough already without having to hold her hand through a sobbing scene. Men hated tears, she knew that, and didn't want to inconvenience him further.

The sound of water didn't surprise her. Wrath had said he planned to shower but the door hadn't closed between them. She turned her head to peer in the direction of the bathroom and was shocked when Wrath's blood-streaked back was in clear view. He bent, jerking down his bloody boxers. His ass was as tan as the rest of him, no tan lines there, and his butt was a thing of beauty.

Her lips parted in silent surprise. He'd said he wouldn't let her out of his sight but showering with the door open was taking it a bit far. He stepped inside the shower stall and the glass door was clear enough to see every exposed inch of him. Wrath didn't glance her way as he lifted his chin and shoved his face under the spray. He reached up to rub at the blood on his arms.

Water ran red as it sluiced down his back and she knew she should face the wall again. It was rude and totally wrong to spy on him but she just couldn't make herself stop. Wrath had the best body she'd ever seen in her life. He was so fit, muscular and attractive that she couldn't resist. His back stayed to her and he seemed oblivious to her watchful gaze.

He turned sideways and tipped his head back under the water. His eyes were closed as he scrubbed his face. Her breath caught as his palms slid down the column of his throat to his chest. It was a great one—broad, smooth. He didn't have any hair on his chest. Those hands blindly reached out, captured a bottle of body wash, poured some into one palm, and returned to soap his skin.

Lauren couldn't stop watching his hands as they lathered dark, taut nipples and dipped lower to his belly. She didn't even want to blink. His stomach was hard and flat, the ridged muscles well displayed. She bit into her lower lip as her fingers twitched. She envied his hands, touching all that beautiful skin. She'd bet he felt as good as he looked. Her physical reaction was surprising as her nipples tingled and her stomach clenched. Wrath was incredibly hot.

He leaned back more and turned her way as he washed off the soap. Her mouth dropped open as her gaze lowered to his waist. His cock was displayed clearly through the glass. It was hard, thick, and the guy had balls. Big ones and no hair covered him there at all that she could see. He either shaved or naturally didn't grow it in his groin area.

Lauren turned her head and stared with wide eyes at the wall. She didn't want him to catch her gawking at him if he opened his eyes. She swallowed hard but the image of a naked, wet Wrath was burned into her brain.

New Species were circumcised, or at least Wrath had been. He was also larger than any guy she'd seen in person. Magazines and porno videos didn't count but he could hold his own in a size comparison to them. She'd heard adrenaline could be an aphrodisiac but hadn't believed it until that moment. The attack she'd suffered should have turned her off men, sex especially, but instead it only seemed to heighten her emotions. Watching Wrath lather up his muscular body was making her feel plenty.

She glanced back at him, unable to resist the temptation. He was proportioned big all over. His hands had moved lower, the movement more of a caress now, at least in her mind. Her breath halted when his fingers curled around his cock, slid lower down the shaft and opened to cup his heavy balls. The hand lifted, fisted his cock again and slowly stroked from tip to base. She jerked her head around until she couldn't see him anymore. *Is he masturbating?* Shock tore through her. *He can't be. No way. I'm right here and the door is open!*

Long seconds ticked by but she had to look. Her head turned in his direction and she glanced at his face first to make sure his eyes were still closed. They were. She braved trailing her gaze down his sleek, sexy body, and that hand still worked his rigid cock. Heat warmed her face as she watched. He was soapy there, his fingers gripped the shaft tightly and his other hand lifted to brace against the shower wall. His hips slowly rocked back and forth in a sensual way that made it possible for her to imagine him fucking someone in that slow, provocative method.

Her breasts ached and she could feel how damp she'd grown between her legs, turned-on by the sight of what he was doing to his body. It made her hotter, knowing he was unaware that she watched him. It made her feel naughty and downright wicked. A decent person would keep her back turned but she couldn't move, her focus locked on his every movement. His dick seemed to grow even larger and his body tensed, muscles strained, were more defined as he came. His head tipped all the way back, his lips parted and his canine fangs flashed. She heard him groan.

"Oh fuck," she whispered, turned her head before he caught her watching him like the voyeur she was, and stared at the wall. Her heart pounded, her body tingled, and her clit throbbed. Wrath was so sexy that she felt warm all over.

She figured he had been affected by the violence too since he obviously had gotten turned-on. Of course with men it was probably caused by the aggression of fighting but her arousal was totally his fault with the peep show he'd given her.

Her feelings were slightly wounded. Why hadn't he hit on her if he wanted sex? She glanced down and stared at her body. Wrath was perfect and she wasn't. Tears burned behind her eyes and she fought them back. She knew it was stupid to feel the way she did but it hurt. She knew her emotions were running rampant after all the stress she'd gone through. *Don't go there and feel rejected, damn it.* She forced her thoughts away from her weight. *Men like that don't go for women like you. They date those skinny chicks with big boobs that a plastic surgeon perfectly aligned.*

She heard the water turn off, the shower door opened, and she sat there staring at the wall while she imagined Wrath using a towel to pat all over that sexy body of his to get dry. Seconds ticked by into a good minute.

"I'm done with my shower." His husky voice startled her, sounding close.

She twisted her head to stare at him over her shoulder. He had a towel wrapped around his waist but wore nothing else. He stood by the dresser, bent and pulled out a fresh pair of boxers. Their gazes met when he straightened and faced her.

"I'm going to drop this and put on my boxers. You might want to close your eyes."

She gave him her back instead, stared at the wall once more and heard him rustling around. She counted for thirty seconds and shifted her body as she changed positions to sit facing him again. Wrath had put on loose black boxers and picked up the towel he'd dropped. He gave her a half smile, returned to the bathroom and threw the wet towel over the top of the shower. He stepped back into the room.

"I'm going to grab that sleeping bag and pillow from the hallway where I dropped them when I heard you scream."

He opened the door and stepped into the room. She saw his back there were multiple scratches with fresh blood running from them. The blood he'd washed away hadn't just been Vengeance's. She gasped. He turned and frowned as he stared at her.

"Your back is bleeding."

He shrugged. "I was lucky." He walked out of sight.

Lucky? Did he really just say that? What is so lucky about having deep scratch marks on his back? He returned carrying the bedding, used his foot to close the door, and tossed everything on the floor. He crouched and unrolled the sleeping bag.

"Aren't you afraid someone will open the door and hit you with it? You're kind of close."

He shook his head. "Vengeance will leave first thing in the morning but we have a few hours before they'll be able to transport him. He won't get past me if he manages to escape from Brass and wants to try to claim you again."

"Oh. Do you want me to bandage your back for you?"

He tossed down the pillow and straightened to his full height. His dark gaze swept the room before he walked to retrieve the small first-aid kit he'd used earlier to clean and bandage her wrists. He moved closer to her with the box in hand.

"That would be nice if you tend my wounds. Thank you."

She accepted it when he held it out. He sat on the floor in front of the bed. She scooted closer and put her feet on each side of his hips. Her hands trembled slightly when she opened the kit, placed it on the bed next to her, and removed what she needed to clean and bandage the injuries. One look at them made her wince. They looked painful but weren't bleeding too much.

"He scratched you badly."

"It is our way when we fight."

"What did it mean exactly when he wanted to claim me? I get that he wanted sex but it was more than that, wasn't it?" Lauren wanted to be distracted from the fact that she was about to touch him and he was so close.

Wrath tensed. "It is always something that should be agreed to by both parties. What he did was try to force it upon you and it's wrong. He wanted to claim you as his mate."

"What does that mean?"

"It's similar to your human marriage but in Species' terms it means for life. You only mate with the one you have strong feelings for. Species commit until one of them dies. After a time we scent imprint our mates. With some it happens very fast while in others it may take a few weeks."

"What does scent imprint mean? I've never heard of that before." She blew on the cuts she cleaned in case they burned. He didn't flinch and his voice remained calm when he spoke.

"It is to help form a bond between mates. A male who scent imprints a female will only want her scent around him and she will only want his scent around her. It comforts each of them, smelling like their mate. Once it happens they can't stand the way others smell."

"They stink?"

He chuckled. "Not exactly, but others smell wrong or bad to a mated couple. I don't know how else to explain it. They just need each other and no one else."

"I read that a few women married a few of your guys. Did it happen to those women? You know, like me? Did they get all weird about the men's scents?"

He glanced back and flashed her a grin. Amusement twinkled in his dark eyes. "No. They don't have our sense of smell or memory of scents. We are strongly dependent on our sense of smell. The couple you would have heard about the most is Ellie and Fury. She loves him and he loves her. When we mate we are very caring of our females. He will make sure she never has a want or need he will not fill."

Lauren was impressed. "That sounds kind of cool."

"Do you want Vengeance to claim you?" Wrath turned his head toward her, the look in his dark eyes almost scary, his expression downright pissed.

"Hell no. I can tell you right now that if he'd claimed me it sure wouldn't have been for the rest of my life. Well, maybe the death do us part would have worked because I would have killed him the first chance I got."

Wrath relaxed. "I would have killed him if he'd forced you to mate with him. You could not kill one of us unless you got your hands on a gun. We are too big, fast, and strong for someone your size to do any damage otherwise."

Lauren couldn't disagree. "Yeah. I saw that. Thank you for fighting him and saving me. I was terrified."

"I know. I smelled it on you strongly."

Lauren finished putting on the last bandage. "Well, I shouldn't smell like fear anymore. I feel safe with you."

Wrath inhaled deeply and his body tensed. His gaze dropped to her lap to stare between her thighs. He inhaled again slowly and a soft growl burst from his parted lips. His eyes widened when he met her gaze.

"You're aroused."

She felt the color drain from her face. "What?"

He rolled to his knees, gripped the edges of the cot, and sniffed again. The color of his eyes seemed to darken as she watched. His lips parted, a deeper growl came from him, and she saw those sharp fangs of his when he bit his lower lip.

"You're scaring me," she admitted.

"You're aroused. I can smell you, Lauren. Why?"

Shit. He can smell I'm turned-on? She wasn't about to tell him she'd been watching him while he touched himself in the shower or admit what a turn-on it had been to see him masturbate.

He tilted his head and closed his eyes, inhaling deeply. Another growl eased from his throat. He moved closer to lean down and Lauren gasped when Wrath dropped his face onto her sweatpants-covered thighs. He inhaled again as his face pressed tightly against her lap and a low rumble came from him.

Wrath wanted to howl. The scent of Lauren's need drove him nearly insane. He knew she was alarmed at having his face buried in the seam of her thighs while he breathed in her feminine scent but he couldn't draw back for anything. She smelled so good he couldn't force his body to move.

Blood rushed to his dick, filled it, and he had to spread his legs to make room for the massive hard-on he suffered. The desire to shove her down, tear her clothes from her body and fuck her was so strong he had to grip the bed until his arms shook from the strain. She'd be terrified if he didn't regain some control. She was human, not a Species female, and he didn't dare try to tempt her into sharing sex with him the regular way. He'd terrify her by snarling and showing pure dominance. It wouldn't impress her to show off his strength.

He took another deep breath, groaned, and battled for logic to take over. He hadn't been with a female in a very long time and they'd always been Species. He no longer trusted himself after the years of being drugged. Sex had turned into a brutal battle of wills and that was why he hadn't tried to initiate sex with anyone since he'd been freed. He doubted even a Species female would want to take him on. He couldn't be sure it would be safe.

Memories flashed of those human women, lying on beds with their legs spread wide while they'd used their fingers and sex toys on their own bodies. The images had aroused him as the machine forced his seed from his body. He opened his mouth to breathe through it but Lauren's scent was strong enough to taste. It just made it worse. His dick throbbed painfully, the desire to fuck her intensified, and he whimpered.

Don't, he ordered his body. *Take control.* Another memory flashed, a foggy one of trying to attack a human female, a real one, and it cooled his desire. The day he'd been freed from captivity he'd been high on the Mercile drugs he'd been forced to take, enraged by what they'd done to him, and he'd gone after an innocent because he'd hated all humans.

Brawn had fought him to protect Becca, his mate. Wrath had been too confused to understand their bond in his altered state. He'd just seen her human body and wanted to kill her in a fit of revenge. It haunted him, always would, and his body relaxed. His dick stayed hard but he managed to leash his desires.

"Wrath?" Lauren's voice shook with fear. "What are you doing?"

He didn't want to scare her, refused to hurt her in any way, and that helped calm him. She had a need and he wanted to meet it. He could do it without losing control. It would be a test and he wanted to tackle his fear head-on for her.

He made a decision. He was Species. Strong. A male in control of his own body, free, and no one could make him hurt anyone else. Lauren was so sweet, she scented so good, and he was curious.

Chapter Six

ꟙ

Wrath lifted his face and Lauren was shocked at the pain she saw in his dark gaze.

"You smell so good."

His voice was super deep, gruff, and should have frightened her. She admitted experiencing some fear but he wasn't hurting her. His behavior was more shocking than terrifying. Her body heated up more as they stared deeply into each other's eyes. He was so close she could have just lifted a hand to touch him, and time seemed to stand still.

His breathing increased and he seemed to be searching her gaze for something. She just wasn't sure for what. He growled and his hands released the edge of the bed to lightly settle over the top of her thighs. Fingers rubbed and slid upward to the waist of the sweatpants, where they hesitated. He suddenly pushed. She landed flat on the mattress. His fingers hooked the waistband and he tugged. She stared down at him, his gaze held hers, but she didn't protest.

"I won't hurt you, Lauren. You smell so good."

"Wrath?"

She didn't know what to do but she didn't want to tell him no. A little voice reminded her that she shouldn't be considering having sex with a stranger, something she'd never done, but Wrath was different. That whole rule about not even kissing a guy until the third date suddenly seemed pretty outdated and stupid when someone as sexy as Wrath was so close and she wanted him so much.

"Close your thighs for me."

She hesitated for a second but did it. Her body felt alive, ached, and the desire that darkened his intense gaze was reason enough to do as he demanded. She pushed her legs together and lifted as he pulled the material over her hips. It slid down her thighs until he removed them.

Lauren knew she should twist away and tell him to stop. He was New Species, a stranger, and she didn't know much about him but desire overtook common sense. She couldn't ever remember being more drawn to a man. She was sick of regrets—she had a lot of them but this wouldn't be added to her list.

He dropped the sweatpants on the floor, removed her socks too, crouched over her, and gripped her knees. "Open up for me. I won't hurt you."

"I..." She was self-conscious about her naked body and especially of showing him her sex—spread open for him to examine. No guy had ever really looked at her there. She'd always been too embarrassed and they hadn't exactly pressed the issue. Curiosity was strong though over finding out what he'd do.

"Are you afraid of me?" He sniffed. "I don't smell fear."

Her cheeks grew warm. "I, um, the lights are on and they are pretty bright."

He frowned. "I don't understand."

"You want to have sex, right? Can we turn down the lights first? I don't want you to see me." She pushed the shirt over her lap to hide her bare lower half.

"Why?" Confusion was an easy emotion to read on his face.

"Nobody has ever really looked at me down there and if I spread my legs...you're on your knees. You're going to get a really good view."

"Your face is a bit red."

"I'm embarrassed. My sexual experience isn't, well, I haven't slept with many guys and the ones I did, they didn't want to see me with bright lights on. I can't say I wasn't upset by that. I'm a little overweight and aware of how I look naked."

"Open up for me. I want to see you and I think you are very attractive."

"You are curious?" She could understand that. "Have you ever seen, hell, are you..." She couldn't say it. Wrath was way too attractive to be a virgin.

He sat back on his heels, frowning. "Am I what?"

"Have you seen a girl naked before? I never really thought about it before but you were locked up for a lot of years. All of your life, from the stuff I read. I guess it was like prison."

"I've shared sex but it has been a long time." His features softened. "Are you shy?"

"Yes." She blew out a relieved breath, grateful he wasn't a virgin. The thought of having to teach him about sex stressed her out. *Talk about pressure.* "I'm not comfortable being naked in bright light."

"You will learn not to be shy with me. There is no reason to be." His thumbs rubbed her inner knees. "Open up for me."

"You want to take a look at my, um, down there?"

"I want a taste." He licked his lips and dropped his gaze to her lap.

Her mouth opened but no words came out. The thought excited her yet left her unnerved. "I've never, I mean, no one has ever..." Embarrassment hit and she realized she probably shouldn't have admitted that aloud. "You don't have to do that."

"Don't be afraid by my dominance. I won't hurt you, Lauren." He suddenly slid his fingers between her knees, dragged her down the bed and forced her legs apart.

It shocked her and his strength made it impossible for her to slam her knees together. Wrath suddenly bent. Hot air blew over her exposed pussy and a hot tongue traced her clit.

Shock made her gasp and her fingers clawed at the bed. She didn't fight but her body tensed. Wrath snarled, a loud, animalistic sound, and he licked her again. He pressed tighter against her pussy, moved his tongue and she moaned as the sensations of pleasure reached her brain. It felt really good. Her back arched off the mattress.

He was merciless with his tongue, licking and sucking on the bundle of nerves. He growled, it sent vibrations against her clit, and she panted. He wasn't gentle as he shoved her legs wider and nuzzled his mouth tighter against her sex.

It felt so intense it nearly hurt. It half mortified her when her hips bucked against his mouth but she couldn't stop, gripped in the throes of passion. His mouth grew more aggressive and a moan tore from her throat. Wrath was doing amazing things to her with his lips and tongue. The sensation was overriding everything inside her until all that was left was pleasure.

She climaxed hard, her body jerked from the force of it, and Wrath tore his mouth away from her clit. Her vaginal walls twitched in the aftermath but his tongue suddenly pushed inside her pussy. She cried out his name, half from the shock and half from how good it felt.

He fucked her with his tongue, burrowed in deeper, and snarled. She didn't care how scary he sounded. Fear was the last thing she felt as he withdrew and speared her again. She stopped worrying about anything but the way it made her shiver with ecstasy.

He slowly withdrew his tongue and she opened her eyes to stare at the ceiling, tried to catch her breath, but gasped loudly when his finger pushed inside her pussy. He slid the thick digit in deep, withdrew it, and a second finger stretched her slowly.

She clawed the bed and arched her hips against his hand. He paused.

"You're so tight. Am I hurting you?"

She shook her head, unable to answer him.

He pressed in more, made her take both of his fingers, and her muscles squeezed around them. He snarled, suddenly jerked his hand away, and released her thigh so he wasn't touching her anymore at all.

Lauren lifted her head to stare down at him, still crouched over her. Their gazes locked and he looked at her with such longing in his eyes that she reached for him. Her hands opened, urging him to come closer. He moved higher but didn't allow her seeking fingers to brush against his skin.

"I want to bury myself inside you," he rasped. "But I can't."

She frowned. "I'm protected against pregnancy. I take a birth-control shot every three months. If you don't have condoms it's okay. I don't have any STDs. Do you?"

"We carry no diseases. That is not why I can't bury myself in you. I want to so much it hurts me. I am so hard it is painful. I want to taste you and touch you all over but I will take care of my pain. I just don't want to alarm you."

"I don't understand that part about you taking care of your pain."

He lowered his head and brushed his chin across her stomach. His hands moved up her body, pushing her borrowed shirt higher until it was bunched over her breasts. His eyes fixed on her breasts and he growled again. He moved over her and she felt his heavy, stiff cock brush against her thigh. His head lowered, his mouth opened and he licked the underside of her breast. His tongue ran upward until it reached her nipple. Wrath's mouth closed over the pebbled bud.

Lauren gasped when he sucked her taut peak inside his really hot mouth. She felt his sharp canines but they didn't hurt. She raised her thighs, gripping his hips with her lower legs to urge him to fuck her. She arched her hips until the head of his cock pressed against the slit of her pussy. She moaned and tightened her legs around his hips, pulling him closer until he began to enter her. His cock was thick and her body protested, not easily taking him, but she wiggled her ass, spread her thighs wider and dug her heels into his skin.

"Take me," she moaned.

Wrath's body tensed over hers and a low sound came from him, almost a whimper, and he tore his mouth away from her breast. His hands flattened on the bed next to her shoulders, shoved up, and he twisted his hips. She had no choice but to release him since he was strong enough to force her to. He threw his body back away from her and landed on his ass off the bed on the floor.

Lauren jerked upright to a sitting position to gawk at him, wondering what had happened, and the enraged expression on his face made her freeze. He clawed his way to his feet and stumbled toward the bathroom. He didn't close the door and just yanked the shower door open. He bent, the water came on and he stepped into the stall. The shower door slammed closed.

Lauren was shocked. She watched him through the glass but he didn't look at her. He grabbed the body wash, dumped a generous heap on his palm and lowered his hand to fist his stiff cock. His hand moved furiously, pumping the hard flesh.

Her gaze jerked up to his face. His eyes were squeezed tightly closed and his head lowered. He kept his eyes closed. She heard a vicious growl tear from his throat and his hand moved faster, almost violently. His body tensed, his muscles bunched and then he growled loudly. She lowered her attention to his hips and watched as he came. His semen hit the tile in front of him as his body shook from every pump of his fist, which made him keep coming.

What the hell? Lauren felt hurt as well as shocked. She'd offered him her body but he'd preferred to masturbate. Was he too good to enter her? Was she not attractive enough? She fought tears. She knew the guy was hot but she still thought he wanted her since he'd nearly attacked her with his mouth.

She rolled over and yanked her shirt down to cover her body, which he must find unappealing to reject it. She heard the shower turn off but kept her back to the bathroom while fighting tears. The guy would rather touch himself than make love to her. It was devastating to her feelings and her pride.

A minute later he walked into the bedroom. "I'm sorry."

Lauren wiped at her tears and turned her head. He had a towel wrapped around his waist again. The look on his face was grim as their gazes met.

"Why are you crying?"

She hated the sound of pain in her voice. "You would rather jack off than enter me?"

He blinked. "I would never enter you. I would hurt you and I'd never risk causing you pain."

Confusion hit her hard. "How would you hurt me?"

He moved closer, cautiously, and crouched next to the bed. The look in his eyes softened. "I am larger than your males and rougher. I would hurt you, Lauren. I would be too violent and take you too hard. I will never enter you or make you suffer my body inside yours."

Lauren didn't even know what to say to that. She was speechless. She finally found her voice. "Then be gentle."

He swallowed and his Adam's apple bobbed. "I don't have that kind of control or trust myself that much."

"I don't understand."

"I know but I do this to protect you. I will never hurt you, Lauren. Never." He blinked. "I would like to hold you and sleep with you in my arms. May I?"

She grappled to understand his logic but the main point was that he wanted to sleep with her. She nodded. The guy wouldn't fuck her but he'd engage in oral sex. He was really good at it too. He was afraid he'd cause her pain and she could understand why it might be a concern. His cock was large. Maybe he'd hurt a woman before because he was so well endowed. She'd always heard bigger was better but she figured it just might hurt.

He smiled. "Thank you. I would enjoy holding you in my arms. Let me put on boxers."

He stood, spun, and opened a drawer to grab a fresh pair of boxers. He just dropped his towel this time, kept his back to her and she got to view his great ass again. She watched him bend as he slipped on the boxers. His dark gaze locked with hers when he turned and slowly stalked closer to the bed. It was majorly sexy to see him move that way, something almost primal, and she remembered he wasn't completely human.

Wrath reached out to her when he paused at the edge of the bed and she put her hands in his. He gently pulled her to her feet. He smiled and released her to ready the bed for them by pulling down the blankets. Lauren didn't mention that they were going to have a problem fitting on that bed together unless they were really tangled together in the limited space. Wrath turned her.

"Take off the shirt. I want to see you and touch you again."

She hesitated but Wrath didn't. He reached for the shirt and slowly pulled it over her head. Lauren felt self-conscious instantly as she stood naked in front of him. His heated gaze lowered and slowly slid down her body. A soft growl rumbled from his parted lips. His eyes met hers.

"Lie down for me and open your thighs. I want to taste you again."

Her heart missed a beat, stunned that he wanted to go down on her again. Oral sex meant tasting to him? She made a mental note of that but moved to lie on the bed flat on her back. Nervousness struck at being completely exposed to his view but he didn't seem to notice her excess weight, judging by the way he quickly took a seat on the edge of the mattress. One hand curved around her inner thigh, pushed them apart, and he twisted his body to face her as he lowered to get closer. Another one of his sexy growls filled the room and she was learning fast that it meant he was turned-on.

Lauren closed her eyes. It helped her be less self-conscious about her body as his hands spread her open. He licked her and his tongue felt heavenly as he teased her clit. She moaned when he growled, creating soft vibrations over the bundle of nerves. She turned her head when her passion ignited, quickly getting over her hesitation to have him do anything he wanted to her body and she stared at his lap. He sat on the edge of the bed, facing her, as his upper body twisted enough to reach her pussy. His boxers were raised in the front from the thick erection that couldn't be hidden.

It was easy to twist her upper body on the mattress and reach out to cup him through the thin, black material. His cock was really hard as she stroked it. His reaction was instantaneous. His mouth tore away from her pussy and he snarled when he jerked his head up to meet her startled gaze.

"Don't."

"I want to touch you too."

"That's not a good idea."

"Please?"

He growled again as he released her thighs and sat up. "My dick is larger than your males and at the end I swell up. It only happens right before I experience strong pleasure. I will stay swollen for a few minutes afterward. I don't want to make you frightened of me."

That news was a bit stunning. "You swell how?"

"I swell up right before I come. I'm different…changed, Lauren. This is one of the ways. It is another reason I will never enter you. I grow thicker around the base of my dick and it would cause you pain and discomfort. If I were inside you when I did that, I could not leave your body until the swelling passed. Our females find this pleasurable but not all of your females do from what I was told."

"You've slept with someone like me before?"

He looked grim. "No. I haven't shared sex in a very long time with a female. It's why I will never enter you."

She stared into his eyes. He had a look in them that she'd almost call haunted. "I thought maybe you just didn't want to be inside me."

He growled. "I want that so much it hurts."

Lauren licked her lips. "Take the boxers off. I want to touch you. You won't scare me if you swell."

He studied her eyes for long moments before he nodded. "I will not harm you, Lauren."

She watched him stand up and he hesitated almost as if he expected her to be afraid of him. He only shoved his boxers down when he seemed certain she was fine. His cock was large, thick and impressive. Wrath held perfectly still for her inspection.

"Sit down." She scooted her hips over a little closer to the wall to give him more room. "I'm not afraid, Wrath."

He hesitated before he slowly lowered his ass to the edge of the bed. He paused again before turning enough for her to be able to reach out to him. Her hand lifted and she gently gripped his steel-hard shaft. Hot, firm skin felt nice to touch and she slowly lifted her gaze to watch his face as she stroked his cock up and down.

He tipped his head back, his mouth parted and he softly growled. His fingers gripped the edge of the bed and he white-knuckled the metal almost as if he were afraid to touch her. It made her more brazen as she wiggled to get upright, released him, and their gazes met as she climbed off the bed.

"Thank you for touching me." His voice came out really gruff, passion flared in his eyes and he gave her a curious look. "What are you doing?"

She knelt in front of him, saw the shock as his gaze widened and she smiled. "Spread your legs. I want to touch you more."

He hesitated but his legs parted to allow her to inch closer to him. She noticed his hands remained gripping the edge of the cot as if it were a lifeline. He looked unsure and uneasy all of a sudden with their positions switched. Lauren reached for him, deciding he looked cute and sexy at the same time. Her hand closed over his rigid cock. Her fingers didn't touch her thumb—she couldn't enclose him with her hand all the way. He softly growled.

Her other hand closed over him higher up, realized he was definitely a two-fisted hold, and smiled. Her hands explored his hard length. His skin felt satiny soft but under that skin he was so hard that there was no give to his erection. He growled again, deeper. Lauren's gaze flew up to his face to find his eyes closed and his sharp fangs revealed as he breathed heavily.

"I can see how you'd be afraid you'd hurt me," she said softly. "You are larger and thicker than anyone I've ever seen. I haven't seen many naked men though but you definitely are impressive."

"Your hands are so soft. There is no roughness to them," he groaned. "You feel so good."

Roughness? She didn't understand that and paused stroking him. His eyes opened. Something in her expression must have told him she wondered at his meaning. He held out his hand and placed it palm up on the top of his thigh.

"Our females have hands like mine."

She released his cock to feel his hand. His palms had rougher skin, almost like light calluses. Her fingers traced upward to his index finger. She rubbed the inner tip and felt the rougher skin there was well. She understood. Her hands were soft all over.

"I don't suppose you have lotion, do you?"

"Inside the top drawer of the nightstand." He smiled at her. "We have high sex drives. You will always find lotion in our bags. We need it to find sexual release often."

She smiled back, amused that he was so honest about masturbating. She'd never met anyone like him. Most men would die before they admitted to something like that. He candidly discussed it and smiled. She opened the drawer and found a big bottle of baby-oil type lotion. She grinned and uncapped the lid.

"You were being ambitious when you bought this."

"I don't understand."

"You thought you'd need this much lotion. That's ambitious. Do you understand?"

"I go through that in less than a week. We really do have high sex drives. I'm canine. I'm always turned-on."

She arched an eyebrow. "How many times do you use lotion in a day?"

He was still grinning. "At least a dozen times."

She almost dropped the bottle. "How old are you?"

He shrugged. "I don't know for sure. The doctors guess as best as they are able from our bones and teeth. We lost track of time inside the testing facilities. The doctors think I am in my mid-thirties. Don't your human males do this?"

"Yes, but not as much. The younger the men are, the more they do it. They slow down when they get older. At least that's what I understand but I'm no expert."

Wrath nodded. "I thought human males were the same about this."

"Now women are opposite or at least I am."

His eyes narrowed. "What do you mean?"

"My sex drive wasn't so good when I was younger. I'm reaching thirty now and my sex drive is really moving these days."

"So you *have* slept with Bill." His eyes narrowed and his mouth tensed.

"No." She frowned at him. "I take care of myself."

Surprise widened his stare. "You touch yourself?"

"Often. It's why I don't need to worry about sleeping with men."

"I did not know normal females did this. Ours don't. If they need sex, they just find a male to care for them."

"Normal females?"

He paused. "That isn't the right word. You aren't one of the humans who work making videos for sexual stimulation. I thought only they touched themselves to coax males into being interested in sex because they are paid to do so."

Lauren set the lotion on the floor and tried to hide her surprise at his answer. She wasn't sure how to respond to that and decided to let it pass. Teenage boys probably didn't go through as much lotion as Wrath did. She was impressed. Maybe New Species didn't slow down as they got older. She rubbed her hands together and reached for his hard shaft again.

His smile died and a growl rumbled from his throat. His gaze locked with hers. "Your touch feels so much better than anything I have ever felt."

She smiled, hoping he meant it. She caressed him from the crown of his cock to the base, her hands exploring every inch, and watched his expression trying to see what he liked best. More soft growls.

"Faster," he urged. "Please."

Lauren tightened her hold on his cock, massaging him faster. She felt his body tense and the flesh in her hands grew thicker. She couldn't help but stare as the girth of his shaft expanded in her hands. He didn't get longer but he got noticeably thicker near the base. He growled louder and his body jerked. Lauren managed to put her hand over the crown and warm heat spread across her palm. The guy had strength even with that. She felt pressure as his semen shot out.

It fascinated her, watching his facial expressions as desire cooled and his body relaxed. He breathed hard, his nipples were pebbled and once again she deemed him the sexiest guy alive. A tiny bit of pride swelled inside her at getting him off and having him seem to enjoy her touch so much. He smiled when his eyes opened and the look he gave her melted her heart. Tenderness was there and such warmth that she wanted to kiss him.

He suddenly came closer and she held her breath, thinking he might just do that, but his face stopped inches from her own as he reached down to the floor. He grabbed the shirt she'd worn and lifted it. Disappointed, she lowered her gaze to hide it as he gently cleaned her hands of all traces of the lotion and his release.

"I will want you to do that again if you keep touching me." His voice came out husky, soft, and sensual.

He discarded the shirt, gripped her hips, and she gasped from the shock of his strength as he lifted her. Her hands grabbed his biceps to keep from pitching face first against his chest and he turned her in his arms. Her back hit the mattress and Wrath suddenly released her to grip her thighs. He growled, his gaze dropped to her pussy and he slid off the bed to bend over it.

Lauren could only gasp as his mouth sought her out, his tongue going right for her clit, and he sucked. She threw her head back, clawed at the bedding just for something to grab and pleasure rolled through her. It felt like an attack of the best sort as his mouth mercilessly drew her to a fast climax.

Wrath released her thighs, slid his hands under her ass and back and lifted, to put her on her side facing away from him. He climbed onto the narrow cot with her, pulled her flush against his big body and made her lift her head to put his arm under it to be her pillow. He spooned her tightly, his other arm hooked around her waist, and his hard cock found a home in the seam of her thighs. Warm lips nuzzled the side of her neck.

"Is this comfortable for you?"

"You're turned-on again."

He chuckled. "I'll always be hard when you are this close to me. Sleep, Lauren. You are tired and I need rest too."

Wrath's body was hotter than hers or maybe she was just still flushed from what he'd done to her. Either way she fell asleep quickly. It had been a long, stressful day but she felt safe in his arms. As she drifted to sleep, Wrath sniffed at her, his hold tightened, and he whispered, "You fit so perfect in my arms and I want to keep you. If my life were different perhaps our time wouldn't have to be so short."

* * * * *

Wrath knew when Lauren drifted to sleep—her breathing slowed and her body relaxed against him. Having her in his bed seemed right and she fit perfectly there. The desire to keep her became so strong he had to resist the urge to wrap his body around hers protectively.

His heart rate spiked and his breathing increased when he thought about losing her. It would happen when the team located Bill. She'd be set free and he'd no longer have a reason to keep her with him. She'd be returned to her world where he'd never see her again.

A snarl threatened to surface but he choked it down. She was little and he could easily force her to stay with him. No way could she get away from him if he decided to prevent that from happening. Part of him wished to do just that but the logical side of him rallied against those crazy urges. She deserved her freedom, wasn't something he could just keep, and she'd grow to hate him if he caged her. He didn't want that.

A shiver ran through his tall frame at the memory of her hands touching him and he breathed her in. Each slow inhalation through his nose accumulated more of her scent and it seemed to reach his soul. The possessive feelings he suffered were bad. They were wrong. He was damaged inside and this was just more evidence of that fact. No sane male would be considering the things he was.

He'd set her free when they captured Bill. There was no other option. Things between them hadn't advanced to the point of no return. He'd avoided causing her any harm, something he took pride in, and the apprehension eased from his corded muscles. Lauren wasn't his to keep. He just needed to remind himself of that often.

Chapter Seven

ꟻ

Lauren woke on her stomach to the sound of running water and the shower door shutting. Her eyes opened and she turned her head to peer at the empty space beside her. Wrath stood inside the shower stall. She could see him since he'd left the bathroom door open and she watched as he tipped his head back in the spray of water. A smile curved her lips as he washed his hair.

The urge to join him made her sit up, push away the blanket he'd covered her with and rise to her feet. The sight of his lathered hands scrubbing down his chest drew her closer. It was fascinating to watch his nipples harden. The palms of his hand slide lower to his flat, firm stomach and desire shot through her as he soaped up his cock. He was hard again, a sight she enjoyed, and she entered the bathroom.

Wrath turned his head, his eyes opened and he smiled at her through the clear glass. She smiled back, used the bathroom quickly, and decided to join him as he rinsed the soap from the small amount hair he had on the top of his head. He looked surprised when she opened the door to step into the tight stall with him. He backed up to make room but his eyes seemed to darken.

"You shouldn't come in here with me."

Humiliation hit her hard. "Oh. Sorry." She spun, shoved at the door and tried to flee. Her feelings were hurt. She'd assumed he'd welcome her. Obviously she'd been wrong.

A soapy hand shot out and grabbed her arm before she could flee. Lauren turned her head and stared up at his frowning face.

"You have an expressive face and I saw pain, as if I rejected you. That's not the case. My control isn't very good in the mornings until I shower and eat. Never think I don't want you, Lauren. I just don't think it's safe for you to be in here with me right now."

"Why not?"

He hesitated. "I may pick you up, pin you against the wall and take you." His voice deepened as he spoke. "I need more time after I wake until you are naked near me. It was difficult enough leaving the bed with your body against mine."

Lauren turned to face him. "We could do other things besides have sex." Her gaze lowered down his body. "Let me touch you."

He hesitated but growled. The sound made her smile and his cock grew longer and harder as she watched him physically respond. She inched closer to reach the body wash, opened it and dumped a handful into her palm. One hand fisted his cock while she put the bottle back. Two hands gripped him as she leaned in closer. Her mouth opened and closed over his nipple.

He snarled. It probably would have scared the hell out of her before but she wasn't afraid of Wrath now that she knew the louder he got, the more he seemed to be turned-on. He pressed his back against the tile, arched his hips and gave her full access when he spaced his feet farther apart. She released his shaft to run one hand between his thighs and gently massage his nuts.

His chest vibrated against her lips as she sucked on his nipple, pressed her breasts against his belly, and scored him gently with the fingernails of both hands. He sucked in air, growled loudly, and his hands gripped her hips.

He didn't push her away but instead clutched onto her. His hips rocked slowly and she stroked his shaft with one hand, continued to use her other hand to tease his body, and her mouth left one nipple to taunt another. She glanced up to watch him in the throes of passion. His eyes were closed, his fangs showed and he moaned as he rolled his head against the tile.

His body tensed and stayed that way. He looked almost like a sexy flesh-and-blood sculpture to her. She flicked her tongue over his nipple and then nipped him with her teeth. His entire body jerked and he suddenly thrust against her hands so hard it almost knocked Lauren into the wall and probably would have if his hands weren't gripping her. His shaft swelled in her hand and she used both of them to fist him, stroke faster, and knew he was on the edge of coming hard. He groaned before jets of hot semen hit her stomach. Wrath stopped moving except for his heavy breathing.

Lauren smiled and released him. She reached for the body wash to clean him. Her gaze appreciated Wrath's relaxed features and the small smile that played at his lips. She started to wash his chest with her hands, loving touching him and that he wasn't protesting anymore.

His eyes opened. "I want you in all of my showers."

She smiled. "I wouldn't mind you being in my showers either."

He suddenly turned her in his hold until her back pressed tightly to his stomach and chest. He leaned over and his hands slid down her hips to the front of her thighs. His fingers gripped her inner thighs and softly applied pressure.

"Spread open for me and grip the wall in front of you. Bend," he whispered in her ear.

Excitement hit her that he'd take her from behind. The idea of being fucked by Wrath did things to her, good things, and made her instantly hot all over. She'd never wanted anyone more in her entire life or felt so drawn to someone so quickly. She shoved her hands under the water to wash off the soap, flattened her palms on the wall as she bent over in front of him, and braced. Her legs parted to make room for him.

His hands caressed the inside of her thighs, one hand cupped her pussy and she moaned as his fingers rubbed against her clit. Water hit her back but she barely noticed as he continued to stroke her, build her excitement, and she waited for him to enter her from behind. His fingers left her clit and she gasped when one finger suddenly slid inside her. He growled behind her when he found her ready to take him, withdrew it, and she squeezed her eyes closed, ready for him to fuck her.

It wasn't his cock that penetrated her pussy but two fingers breached her instead. The wonderful sensation of being slowly stretched by him caused her to moan and press back against his hand. Wrath bent over her more, pressed his body against her, and tormented her by finger-fucking her.

"So tight," he rasped next to her ear. "So warm and wet for me. Am I hurting you?"

She couldn't speak but shook her head. She parted her feet more until the edges of the shower stall prevented her from spreading them farther. Her back arched and she rocked against his fingers, urging him to take her. Words finally came.

"Fuck me, Wrath. Please?"

He growled but his fingers withdrew. She bit her lip, expected his cock to press up against her, but instead both of his hands gripped her ribs. He was strong enough to jerk her away from the wall and he spun her in his arms. Her eyes widened as she stared up at him in surprise as they faced each other.

"Wrap your arms around my neck."

She didn't hesitate. He bent enough to make it easier for her, one of his arms locked around her waist and he lifted her off her feet. Her back pressed against the wall as his body pinned her there. Their gazes locked as they studied each other.

"Wrap your legs around me."

His voice came out gruff, harsh, and sounded more animalistic than human. She didn't care. She just lifted her legs. It was hard to wrap around him with their bodies wet but she had help when he gripped her thigh to hoist her higher. She gripped him just above his hipbones and hooked her ankles together.

The hand under her thigh played with her clit and she threw her face against his shoulder, moaning, and cried out when two fingers drove into her pussy, fucking her fast and deep, while his thumb tapped against her clit. The pleasure became so intense she couldn't think and he pinned her so tightly she couldn't even move.

Lauren came screaming but her mouth pressed against his skin, muffling the sound. Her body jerked and her legs began to slip down his waist when she wasn't able to hold on to him anymore. Wrath didn't let her fall. He twisted his fingers inside her and she cried out again. She jerked hard, still climaxing, as he tapped his fingers right against her G-spot. He kept doing it until she begged him to stop, unable to take any more. His fingers slowly withdrew and she lifted her head until she could stare into his sexy eyes.

He lifted her up in his arms until their faces were level. He growled and suddenly buried his face in the crook of her neck and sharp teeth gripped her skin. He didn't bite into her but she wasn't alarmed at feeling them. She trusted Wrath. Her arms wrapped tighter around his neck and she wrapped her legs around his hips again once she recovered from the intense climax. His cock was pinned between their bodies but he shifted her higher in his arms until it was free, lowered her until the hard length of him rested against the seam of her pussy, and he growled again.

"Talk to me," he rasped.

"What would you like me to say? That was amazing."

"Tell me not to enter you."

"I want you to."

He groaned. "I'd hurt you."

Lauren squeezed his hips with her thighs and used the leverage of his body to move against him erotically. "I want you."

He snarled and gripped her thighs. Lauren was startled when he forced her to unwrap her legs from his hips. His hands pushed her legs together. His erection was trapped between her thighs.

"Hold on to me. Do you have your weight?"

Lauren held on tighter around his neck. "Yes."

He stared at her and suddenly bucked his hips up. His cock didn't enter her but the force of him driving up between her thighs would have thrown her if he hadn't had such a strong hold on her. She gasped and he growled.

"I'd take you harder. Do you understand? Once I enter you I'd be too rough. You're too small inside. I'd cause you pain and I won't do that."

"Be gentle. We'll go slow."

He turned his head away and closed his eyes. "I have issues you don't understand." He stepped back and she had to try to regain her footing when he wiggled his hips enough to force her legs to slide down his.

"Go." He released her, shoved open the shower door, and gently pushed her out of the shower stall.

Stunned, Lauren found herself dripping on the bathroom floor. Wrath slammed the shower door between them, held it closed, and fisted his own cock. She backed away, barely managed to grab a towel in her bewildered state but didn't miss it when he released the door and grabbed the soap.

He jacked off in front her, a near brutal show of muscles and strength, and fear inched up her spine. If he took her as roughly as he handled his body it would hurt. The fact that he wasn't hurting left her reeling as she backed out of the bathroom and finally turned away from him and she stumbled to the bed.

* * * * *

Shadow glanced at Brass, then at his watch. Brass frowned when he looked at him again. Shadow sighed.

"It's after eight."

Brass nodded. "It is."

"Should we check on them? Wrath usually is here to eat at six when breakfast comes. Their food has grown cold."

Brass shook his head. "I heard sounds as I passed the room. Leave them alone."

"What kind of sounds?" Shadow arched his eyebrow.

Brass grinned. "He wasn't force breeding her if that's what you're worried about. They were sharing sex for sure from the sounds but it was mutual. I heard the female moaning his name."

"I don't know if I should be very worried or very happy right now."

Brass frowned. "We should be happy. She is attractive and they are having a good time together."

"It's Wrath. We both have reasons to worry."

Brass hesitated. "It is a different experience with humans but nothing to be worried about. We have control of our bodies and strength. He will be fine and so will she."

"You have never had to endure what we have." Shadow's voice lowered. "We've been conditioned against human females. The sight of their bodies drives us into rages when we remember what was done to us. Sex isn't appealing but shameful and painful. We're both terrified that we might snap if we were to have a female in our beds. We've discussed it at length."

"I'm sorry about what happened to you but I'm sure he's fine. He's a reasonable male, he's protective of her and I believe he cares."

"Seeing one naked would be reliving what they did to us. You have never been forced to ejaculate your semen—the machine doesn't stop and it hurts. Your dick remains hard because we are designed that way and hours of pain pass with only short bursts of pleasure when your body is forced to come. Images of human women are what they showed us to keep our dicks hard with the help of the drugs."

Brass paled slightly. "I had forgotten the extent of your abuse."

"Wrath was afraid last night to take her to his room. His attraction to her was very strong."

"She is attractive."

"You have no idea. After you left to talk with Vengeance I asked her to take her hair down. Wrath dropped a plate of food."

Brass grunted. "Long and beautiful?"

Shadow nodded. "Definitely hair a man would want to spread out in his fingers and rub on his body. It looked very soft."

Brass glanced at his watch. "If he is not here soon we will leave without him."

"We should check on them to make certain they are fine."

"They sounded fine. Perhaps his need to protect her is overriding his conditioning. She wasn't screaming for help when she said his name."

"I'm still worried."

"Have faith in the male. I do."

Shadow hesitated. "He was always stronger than I was. I have to believe he won't harm her. We will leave without him anyway. One of us has to remain behind to guard the female or we'll have to trust some of the human males to care for her here while we are gone."

Brass' fingers tapped the tabletop. "I was hoping to take her with us. I wanted to use her to bait Bill. We'll give them more time."

* * * * *

Lauren huddled on the bed with the towel wrapped around her when the shower ended and Wrath entered the room with a matching towel tucked around his hips. His dark gaze sought her out and he slowly approached until he lowered to his knees in front of her. Sadness showed in his expression and it tore at her heart.

"I'm sorry. I scared you, didn't I?"

"I don't understand. Are you into pain? Is that it?"

"No." He stroked the back of her hand with his fingertips. "Mercile did some things to me that make me afraid I will hurt you." He stopped rubbing and gripped her hand. "They used images of human females to cause me pain. I'm afraid I will lose control if I'm inside you because they combined pleasure with severe pain. I don't trust myself enough yet to risk taking the chance that I'd lose the ability to separate the experiences."

"You, um, were so rough with, um, you know." Her cheeks burned.

"They gave me a high pain tolerance while forcing me to give them my seed."

Tears filled her eyes but she blinked them back. "They forced you to masturbate? Do you like pain now with sex? Is that it? I read a lot of books and I know some people need that."

A soft growl rumbled from him. "No. I don't wish pain for either of us. I just am afraid if I enter you that I'll lose control because it will feel too good. I'm terrified I'll take you too roughly and I won't be able to stop."

She stared deeply into his eyes. "I don't believe that."

"It happened. They did vile things to me."

"I meant I don't believe that you'd be rough with me and cause me pain. You've been nothing but wonderful. I admit my sexual experiences aren't that vast but I wish you could see yourself the way I do now."

"Give me time."

The humor struck her and she laughed. "I can't go home, remember? We have plenty of that."

"I'm sorry you're stuck with me."

She squeezed his hand. "I'm not."

"We should get dressed and go eat. We're both hungry."

"Okay."

"I am sorry."

"It's okay." She meant it. There was a lot she didn't understand but he was a tortured soul, one who had experienced deep emotional pain as well as physical, and obviously actual intercourse was something he feared. "We'll work through this."

He released her hand, stood, and got them both clothes from his dresser. She was becoming accustomed to him seeing her naked, didn't hesitate to drop the towel, and made the best of the sweats he gave her. They were too large but he used a knife to cut off some of the legs and the arm length enough to free her hands and feet.

"This is not my most fashionable look."

Wrath studied her body. "You look very attractive to me."

That made her smile. "Thank you."

They both used the bathroom and Wrath insisted on brushing out her hair. She sat on the bed facing away from him while he tenderly removed all the tangles. It was nice, a bit too personal, and a new experience for Lauren. No man had done that for her but she enjoyed it.

"Let's go." He stood, dropped the brush and walked to the door.

He opened it and waved Lauren to step out into the hallway. Wrath gripped her hand in his and stayed at her side until they reached the main room. Lauren hesitated when she saw two of the men from last night seated at a table. Vengeance wasn't one of them.

"He's gone," Wrath said softly, as if he could read her mind. "Vengeance was sent back to Reservation early this morning."

Lauren felt relief. The two men at the table stared at them as they approached. Shadow was the one to speak.

"You both overslept and missed breakfast. I put your plates in the refrigerator for you."

Wrath nodded. "Thank you." He showed Lauren to a seat. "I'll warm them. You relax. You're a guest."

Lauren glanced at the two men to discover Brass openly staring at her hair. It was still wet from the shower. She watched the large man until his gaze flicked to hers.

"It is beautiful hair. I imagine when it is dry it is breathtaking."

"Thank you." She smiled.

"How are you today?" Shadow drew her attention next.

"Better."

"Vengeance caused you no injury?"

"I have a few bruises but I'm fine. Wrath said he's gone now."

Brass nodded. "Yes. A helicopter and some of our people came to take him home. We apologize again for what he tried to do to you. Forced mating is forbidden and so is forced breeding."

"Wrath explained the difference to me."

Shadow blinked. "He did?"

She nodded. "I was curious and asked him. I didn't understand what Vengeance was talking about."

Shadow glanced at Wrath before meeting her gaze again. "I wondered how the subject came up."

Brass shook his head and the two men frowned at each other. Shadow turned back to Lauren.

"We would like to ask you a favor."

"What do you need?"

Brass spoke. "We would like you to take one of us into your work and see if you can find out where Bill is."

Lauren was stunned at that request. "You plan to just grab him if he's at work?"

"We have the right to arrest him for his crimes against New Species," Brass assured her softly. "I doubt he will be there but he's made friends at work, hasn't he? Perhaps you could find out from them where he is."

Lauren glanced at their black clothing. "I guess I could do that but one of you would definitely have to change clothes and wear…" She studied their eyes. "Sunglasses. Otherwise if Bill is there he's going to spot you right away. The black clothing will draw attention and if Bill worked for Mercile Industries he's going to be alarmed to see a New Species."

"We're sure he's the correct human male. We thought of this already." Brass hesitated. "We thought we'd have Wrath dress up however you think he should. He could pretend to be a client of yours and walk inside the building with you. Would it be appropriate for you to take a client to work?"

"Sure. I'm due in to work at ten today." She glanced down at her clothes. "Could we stop by my apartment first? I can't go to the office wearing this and my boss would have my ass."

Brass shrugged. "That would be fine. What would be appropriate for Wrath to wear?"

Wrath sat a plate of warmed scrambled eggs, bacon and toast in front of her. She gave him a smile and picked up her fork. She glanced at Wrath, who took the seat next to her and noticed he had two large steaks on his plate. That was all he had. He didn't reach for his silverware.

"You may not want to watch him eat," Shadow suggested softly. "We enjoy our meat barely seared on the outside and raw on the inside. We find it easier to eat with our fingers than with your utensils."

Lauren glanced at Shadow before purposely smiling at Wrath. "Eat up."

Wrath shrugged and dug into his food. He grabbed hold of one of the steaks with both hands and bit into it. His dark eyes met hers as he tore a section of the meat off. Lauren wasn't horrified but she was more than a bit curious. Blood dripped onto the plate and the interior of the steak was raw, red meat. She wasn't repulsed in the least. She glanced back at Shadow.

"Have you ever seen kids eat? I am from a large family. At least you guys don't shove peas up your nose and shoot them out."

Brass laughed. "No. We don't."

Shadow laughed. "Did you do that as a child?"

She shook her head. "No. But I used to gross my cousins out by telling them my spaghetti was worms and sucking them up. I was always kind of a tomboy."

Brass smiled at her and asked, "What should Wrath wear to your job?"

Nothing. That was her first thought but she didn't say it aloud. She'd love for Wrath not to wear a single thing ever again since he looked so good naked. "Nice jeans and maybe a casual dress shirt. Good shoes. Realtors notice those things right off the bat to judge if a client can really afford to buy a home. It's how we try to root out the looky-loos from the real buyers."

"What are good shoes?" Shadow questioned.

"Real-leather, casual dress shoes would work nicely. Do you happen to have any around?"

"No." Shadow shrugged his broad shoulders. "We have military boots and running shoes."

"Military will work. I could tell my boss that Wrath is in the service. We sell homes to them all the time. They always have good credit and the ability to get financing. I don't suppose you could get your hands on a military uniform of some sort, could you?"

Brass stood. "That we can do." He left the room.

Shadow continued to watch Wrath. "Brass and I had some time this morning to make plans while we waited for you to come out here."

Wrath finally looked up from his food to meet his friend's stare. "Good."

Shadow and Wrath seemed to be having a stare down as the silence in the room lengthened. Lauren darted her gaze between them, watching their facial expressions change just slightly.

"You two are doing that silent mind communication thing again."

Wrath turned his head, winked, and gave his full attention on his remaining steak.

"Eat quickly, Lauren," Shadow ordered softly. "We want to leave here soon since you need to get clothing from your apartment."

Lauren dug into her food. It wasn't good but she was starving. Reheated scrambled eggs tasted rubbery, the bacon was greasy and the toast a bit soggy. She ate it all anyway since she wasn't sure where her next meal would come from. The thought of Brent actually being at work when they arrived wasn't a good one. Wrath and his friend would grab her coworker and set her free. She wouldn't have a reason to spend more time with Wrath and that concept left her depressed.

Wrath excused himself to go change his clothing and left her with Shadow at the table. The blond one waited until his friend was out of sight before he spoke.

"He likes you."

Lauren knew which him he was talking about. Wrath. "I like him too."

Shadow's blue eyes were intense and he frowned.

"What?"

"We are not similar to the males you know. I just want you to understand that."

"What does that mean exactly?"

"I'm just warning you. You're playing with fire with Wrath."

"I'm not playing anything."

His blue eyes narrowed. "It was just a warning. Wrath is very intense and we have had difficult lives." He stood. "Let's go."

Chapter Eight

ꟍ

Lauren got to her feet, wanted to ask Shadow what he meant by that, or why he'd accuse her of playing some kind of game with Wrath but he didn't give her the chance. His long legs moved fast as he crossed the room and stopped at the elevator. She had to scramble to catch up with him as the doors opened after he punched in a code on a keypad.

"Aren't we waiting for Brass and Wrath?"

"They are either already upstairs or will be along shortly. This isn't the only elevator."

"I don't have keys to my apartment. They were in my purse."

"Your car and your possessions are being stored above. We had them moved here last night. Your purse is in your car."

"Someone drove my car?"

Shadow nodded, stepped into the elevator and pressed a button. She followed him before the doors closed.

"Yes. We were not going to leave it in the parking lot to draw suspicion. We weren't sure if you were Bill's girlfriend or not. We wanted him to find nothing wrong if he sent someone looking for you. Finding your abandoned car would have been suspicious."

Lauren couldn't fault the logic. "I can see that."

Shadow smiled. "We know what we are doing. This isn't our first hunt and capture."

"You didn't know I wasn't Brent's girlfriend. Sorry—Bill. You thought I was that jerk's lover. No offense but you were way off the mark on that one."

He shrugged. "You are the one who came in his place and you smelled of the perfume he gifts females he shares sex with. We have interviewed many of them as we've tracked him."

Shock tore through her. "You have more women locked up down here?"

He shook his head. "We knew he had abandoned the females we spoke to before we reached them. They had all filed criminal charges against him for stealing from them and that's how we were able to track him. He uses their money to fund his living but victimized women in this area recently. We used their photographs of him—ran them through the driver's license database—and his false new name showed up."

"He's a thief too? What a loser."

"He is a bad male." Shadow sighed. "We told the women he had deserted the Army when he was younger and that he would serve many years in prison for this. Those females were very willing to give us any information we asked for to help track him down. Most of them were very pleased to learn he was wanted by us."

"I bet. He's batting a thousand for winning the scum-of-the-decade award."

A comical look passed Shadow's face as he gawked at her when the elevator doors opened. "There is such a thing?"

"No." She laughed. "It's a saying but it gets the point across. He'd win, wouldn't he? I've only been around him three months and I know I could live with him being locked up for a while. The man is a first-rate creep."

"That is what most of them said about him. They had other names for him as well but none were flattering."

"I can imagine."

He motioned that she leave the elevator first and she hesitantly entered a parking structure. It was dimly lit and had concrete walls. Her car sat within sight about twenty spaces away from the elevator and half a dozen black SUVs were parked with it.

"We did not damage your car."

The elevator closed behind them and Lauren didn't see Wrath as her gaze continued to study her surroundings. She started to feel nervous about being alone with Shadow. She knew he and Wrath were close but after Vengeance, the only one of them she trusted was Wrath. The driver's-side door opened on an SUV and a guy dressed in all black climbed out. He approached them quickly, his gaze locked on Lauren.

She tensed but immediately identified him as human since his face wasn't covered by sunglasses, and his features were clearly shown. He had short brown hair, brown eyes and was almost as big as the New Species she'd met, minus a few inches in height. The uniform was the same that Brass and Shadow wore.

"Who's the woman?" He glanced at Shadow.

"She's helping us track our target."

The man grinned and offered his hand. "I'm Brian. How are you?"

Lauren shook his hand firmly. "I'm Lauren. I'm fine."

The elevator doors opened and Lauren turned to see who entered the parking level. Wrath and Brass stepped out of the elevator. Brass was dressed in black like Brian and Shadow but Wrath had changed into green fatigues. Wrath growled suddenly and lunged at Lauren.

She gasped as his arm hooked around her waist. He jerked her off her feet and spun her until his body blocked her from Brian. Another snarl came from him as he eased her back to her feet but kept his arm anchored around her middle. She twisted her head to look up at him but he glared at Brian with a scary expression.

Brian stepped back and put his hands up. "What's wrong?"

Shadow sighed. "You touched her and were standing too close. He's protective."

Brian put more distance between him and the angry New Species. "Sorry, man. I didn't know it would upset you. I was just introducing myself. It's a normal human interaction."

"Don't get near her," Wrath warned. "Are we clear, Brian?"

"Perfectly clear, sir."

Wrath relaxed. "You know my name is Wrath. Don't call me sir."

The man nodded. "Sorry. It's just that you're the boss when I'm assigned to escort you guys. You've got the rank. 'Sir' is what I usually call the team leader. It's just how Tim runs the ranks." He paused. "What's our game plan today?"

Brass stepped forward, taking charge. "We are driving the female to her apartment for her to change her clothing. She's going to be taking Wrath into the target's workplace while we monitor them from a distance. The female will talk to Bill's coworkers and see if she can locate him."

Brian nodded. "Good." He glanced at Lauren. "Do you think they will talk to you?"

She nodded. "They should. I work there too."

Brian's eyes widened in surprise. "Okay. Good. Are we ready to go? I assume I'm driving since I know the area?"

"Yes," Shadow sighed. "Let's roll."

Wrath slowly released Lauren's waist but gripped her hand quickly. She noticed he still appeared slightly upset over her shaking Brian's hand and wondered if that was taboo with his kind. Maybe it was rude to touch an unknown male in Species culture. She wasn't too sure about the reasoning but she made a mental note not to do it again. Wrath led her to the SUV and opened the back door.

"Get in. You sit in the middle."

"What about my purse and keys? I need them."

"I've got them," Shadow called out, rushing to catch up.

Lauren scooted across the seat to the middle and Wrath climbed in after her. Shadow opened the other door and took a seat next to her, while Brass and Brian entered the front. They all reached for their seat belts and she did the same.

The New Species all put on dark sunglasses before Brian even started the engine and Brass shoved a cap on. It made her really notice the tight braid at the back of his head for the first time. Her eyebrows arched but she didn't ask why he had long hair when the other two New Species had cut theirs so short.

Wrath was careful not to touch her and it became more apparent as the miles passed that he avoided her on purpose. He leaned away from her when the vehicle swayed through turns. She studied his features, hated the dark glasses that hid his eyes and leaned into him until he turned his face in her direction.

"Are you mad at me?"

"No. I'm preparing for the mission. I like to go over all possible scenarios we may encounter and plot my reactions."

"Okay." She wasn't sure what that meant but it must be a man thing.

Shadow laughed. "We all do that. This is your world and not ours. Everything is strange to us and we try to make sure our responses are as smooth as we can make them."

She could see how out of place they would probably feel in the big world. She'd read about the NSO Homeland and the NSO Reservation. They were massive properties that housed all New Species and were run by the New Species Organization. They had their own civilizations on those two properties but little was known beyond bits and pieces of information that the press got wind of. No one really knew what was true or not.

Curiosity piqued her. "What is it like where you come from?"

"I lived at Reservation for over a month before I took this assignment. Wrath and I both agreed our time would be better spent tracking down our enemies than learning how to play sports. Reservation is a big, forested area with few buildings. They have a hotel, just opened a movie theater, and we have a bar where our social events are held. We don't enjoy drinking alcohol but a lot of us like to dance. It is a good place to live."

"Do you miss it?"

Shadow hesitated. "What we do is important and we had less to lose than most since we were so recently freed. We volunteered for this duty and we're honored to represent our people."

Wrath growled. "Enough."

Shadow frowned, shot him a dirty look and continued. "We not only hunt criminals who harmed Species but some of our people are still being held captive. Wrath and I are examples of that. We were not rescued in the raids of the original testing facilities that were located. Before that even happened, we were stolen by some of the staff and taken to new locations. They used us to make money to begin new lives in other countries and escape justice."

"Shadow, enough." Wrath's voice came out a growl now.

"She needs to know and I don't hear you telling her." Shadow paused. "We are hoping that anyone we capture who worked for Mercile will have information to help us locate other Species."

Lauren turned her head and stared up at Wrath. He frowned at his friend and once again she wished she could see his eyes. "What is wrong with him telling me that?"

His lips parted but then he sealed them in a tight line.

"He is probably worried that you might think he is cruel to go after humans despite the harm they caused Species."

"I don't believe that." Lauren reached out and placed her hand over Wrath's. "I think it's very brave."

He didn't pull away and she relaxed in her seat. She turned to Shadow again to get more answers since he was talkative. "I thought all the New Species had been found and freed."

"We didn't know a fifth testing facility existed but it was located. There is evidence there may be more and who knows how many others were stolen away in the manner Wrath and I were."

"That's horrible."

Shadow jerked his head in agreement. "Yes. That is why we live away from our kind and sacrifice so much to do our duty." His chin lifted and he stared at Wrath. "We must not forget the commitment we have made to our people."

Wrath growled, his head snapped in Shadow's direction and his fangs flashed in a scary show of temper. "Enough."

Lauren glanced between the two men, wondering what she was missing.

"What's your address?" Brian's gaze met hers in the mirror. "It's hard to drive there if I don't know where I'm going."

Brass gave Lauren's home address before she could. He turned in his seat to meet her surprised stare. "We learned everything we could about you the second you showed up at that warehouse. I could tell you how much money you made four years ago and what you charged on your credit cards if I wished."

The silence in the SUV stretched on until she realized they were near her home. "It's the tan building with the big bushes. You can take the driveway to the left and park in the back. I have a visitor's parking space."

Brian parked where she indicated and Wrath helped Lauren climb out of the SUV. She spotted her neighbor and waved at Mr. Adams, flashing him a big grin. Amusement made her chuckle at the way his eyes widened behind his glasses as she passed him with her four large escorts.

"What is funny?" Wrath handed her purse over when she paused in front of her door.

She unlocked the door, pushed it open, and stepped inside. "Sorry if my place is a mess. I wasn't expecting company."

Wrath paused next to her. "Why did you find it amusing when the old man gaped at us? You are still smiling."

Lauren chuckled. "Mr. Adams is a gossiping busybody with a wild imagination."

"I don't understand." Brass spoke. "What is that?"

Brian laughed. "It means he's very nosy. He's always talking to everyone and makes things up." Brian turned to Lauren. "They don't understand some of our terms."

Lauren chuckled. "By tonight he's going to be telling everyone in the complex that I brought four big guys home and he'll probably say we had an orgy."

Brian grinned.

Wrath inched closer to her side. "Is that a party?"

Lauren laughed. "Kind of. An orgy is..." She looked at Brian for help. "Do you want to explain that one?"

He laughed. "The old man will tell everyone that Lauren had sex with all of us at once. An orgy is where a group of people all strip down naked and have sex together in a pile of bodies."

Wrath growled as he turned his head to Lauren, his lips pressed in a tight line from anger before he shot a warning look at every other male in the room. "I'd hurt anyone who touched her."

Shadow's mouth twitched with a near smile. "Easy, friend. She wouldn't survive four of us at once and we don't share well."

"Um, okay. I'm going to go change clothes so we can get this over with. Make yourselves at home." Lauren spun and walked down the hallway.

Wrath followed, his presence something she couldn't ignore, and both of them paused inside her bedroom. She glanced at him to watch his face as he peered around her room. She really hated that he wore the dark glasses that hid his eyes, more than a bit curious what he thought about her large four-poster bed and feminine décor. It was a far cry homier than what he was used to if his own bedroom was an indication.

Her cat leaped up on top of the bed, startled them both, and Wrath shot his arm out. His hand flattened on Lauren's stomach and he knocked her back roughly, against the wall.

The cat stared at Wrath and suddenly tensed, his back arched and he hissed. Wrath bent slightly, snarled and showed his own teeth. Lauren was stunned as both of them continued to hiss and snarl at each other.

"Wrath?"

"Don't move," he rasped and reached for his weapon.

"No!" Lauren shoved the hand pinning her to the wall and lunged for his body, put hers between him and the bed, and caught his wrist as he raised the gun. "That's my cat! Don't shoot him."

His head snapped down. "What?"

"That's Tiger. He's my cat. My pet."

Tiger hissed again behind them but Lauren didn't spare him a glance, too worried the man in front of her would shoot her cat. Wrath slowly holstered his weapon at his waist and frowned.

"That is your pet? It's not some wild creature that managed entry inside your home?"

"I know he probably needs to go to the groomer but he's not wild. He goes outside since I hate litter boxes but yeah, he's my pet."

He relaxed, the tight muscles bunched under her hand softened just slightly, and Wrath lifted his head.

"Your pet doesn't appear to be friendly."

She glanced at Tiger. "He's usually not like this. Stop it, Tiger. Bad kitty! Stop hissing at Wrath."

The cat bolted, rushed out the door, and Lauren laughed at the situation. "I take it you don't like cats?"

"I don't like cats who are small and don't talk."

A loud growl sounded and glass broke. Lauren cursed and darted around Wrath to rush toward the living room. Tiger yowled loudly and a deep, scary growl quickly followed. She halted just inside the entryway where Brass and Shadow had cornered her cat. The poor, terrified cat had his claws extended, his hair stood on end and he hissed at the men.

"Stop that!" Lauren lunged, getting between the men and her pet.

"What is that?" Shadow snarled.

Brian laughed. "They are canine. Dogs and cats don't get along. You should have warned them you had one."

"It's not an animal that got into your home?" Brass stopped growling and straightened to his full height.

Lauren turned and dropped to her knees. "No. Come here, Tiger. It's all right. They didn't mean to scare you. Come here, baby. Come here, Tiger."

"Tiger?" Brass laughed. "You named him Tiger? I have a friend by that name. I can't wait to tell him about this."

Lauren scooped up the shaking cat and used her body to shield it from the men in her living room. She moved, keeping her cat from seeing them as well and walked back down the hallway. Wrath stood inside her room at the foot of her large bed. She walked in and placed Tiger in the bathroom away from her guests, closing the door so he didn't rush back into danger.

"You sleep here in that?" Wrath turned his head to face her.

"Yeah."

He walked to the side of her bed and shocked her by tearing back the covers, exposing her sheets. She stood there mute as he bent over, pressed his nose against the pink material and sniffed loudly. He straightened and smiled as he adjusted the blankets back to where they'd been.

"What are you doing?" It was weird but she wasn't about to state that aloud.

"I only smell you and the cat. No one has slept here with you."

Anger stirred. "I live alone. I told you I haven't dated in a while and I wasn't lying about that. I've told you the truth. You didn't have to do that to check up on me."

He closed the distance between them and one hand raised to cup her cheek. "I'm sorry. I was curious. I do believe you." His hand dropped to his side. "You need to get ready. Is your animal safe in the bathroom? I won't snarl at it. I was startled and I thought it would attack you."

"He's fine in there. He's an indoor and outdoor cat and I keep the window open in there for him since I don't have a pet door. He's probably already fled after the way you and your friends scared him."

"I am sorry."

She shrugged. "I should have told you I have a pet. I take it that you aren't around too many cats?"

"Not small, domestic ones."

Lauren let that one slide. He wanted her to get ready for work and the team waited in the living room for her. She spun around, jerked open her closet, and grabbed clothes off the hanger. Tiger was gone when she opened the bathroom door and stepped inside. She closed the door while she changed, washed her face, and applied light makeup quickly. Wrath was touching things on her dresser when she stepped back into her bedroom. He spun to face her.

"You put your hair in a bun," he rumbled. "I enjoy seeing it down more."

"I have to put it up for work to appear more professional. It's too curly and tangles too easily otherwise." She bent by the door, grabbed a pair of black pumps and put them on. "I'm ready."

Wrath slowly stalked closer to her. The way he moved once again reminded her that he wasn't a normal guy, and it was kind of hot. She still wished she could see his eyes. He stopped inches away from touching her body.

"You look nice but I prefer you naked."

Her heart raced and heat warmed her cheeks. She couldn't help but trail her gaze down his body and then back up. He looked sexy in the military fatigues. The outfit complimented his fit body but she wanted to be honest as she stared at his glasses.

"I like you naked better too and definitely without those glasses. I hate not being able to see your eyes."

Wrath reached up and removed them. Desire darkened his already deep-brown eyes and instantly made Lauren feel hot all over. He moved closer and her heart rate increased.

"We need to leave," Shadow called from the doorway.

Wrath tensed and put his glasses back on. Lauren wanted to curse. She was pretty sure Wrath had planned to kiss her but the moment had been killed. She turned her head to shoot Shadow a dirty look but he'd already started walking back down the hallway.

Lauren spun, refused to glance at Wrath, and followed his friend back into the living room. The two New Species turned their heads her way. She wished she could see their eyes but presumed they were looking over her outfit. Brian was the only one not wearing the sunglasses she was growing to hate and he grinned openly at her as his gaze lowered down her body.

"You clean up damn nice, Lauren." He winked. "You are one attractive woman."

Wrath growled behind her, probably only inches away. "She didn't clean up. She changed clothes, bound her hair and put stuff on her face. Don't stare at her that way."

Brian's grin died and he shot Brass a worried look. "He growls at me a lot."

Brass nodded. "They haven't been free as long as most of us have been. He's protective of the female and you need to stop flirting with her immediately. That's the second warning he's given you and you should be real careful not to push his patience too far. He will attack you."

Brian paled and backed a few feet away from Lauren, his wary gaze fixed on Wrath. "I got it. I won't look at or even speak to her if that's what you want."

"Good." Wrath reached out and grabbed Lauren's hand. "Let's go."

Mr. Adams was outside still when they left and Lauren made sure she waved at him. *Yeah,* she thought, *the neighbors are going to be talking about me tonight.*

Wrath helped her into the SUV. The drive to her work was only five minutes away. Brass twisted in the seat to address Wrath.

"No growling. You're fully human. Remember that." Brass turned to face Lauren. "We can hear everything near Wrath. He's wired. Just act normal when you talk to the humans you work with and find out if anyone has seen or heard from Bill. Find out if they know where he is."

"I got it." It sounded easy enough to her.

Lauren and Wrath climbed out of the SUV half a block down the street from the office and watched it park across the street. She faced Wrath. "Let's call you Paul Williams, okay?"

He nodded. "My name is Paul Williams."

"You're interested in buying a two-bedroom condo. I have a ton of those listed and they would be in your price range with what you should be making in the military. You are single since you don't have a wedding ring on. I'm sure no one will really talk to you but just in case it's better to have our ducks in a row."

"Ducks in a row?" He arched an eyebrow.

"It's a saying meaning…well, having your shit together."

He grinned. "Why didn't you just say that?"

She smiled. "I'm trying to avoid cussing in front of you. It's not ladylike."

His smile died. "I don't care if you're a lady or not. I like you."

She felt heat spreading through her at his words. "Let's go."

Chapter Nine

ꟹ

Lauren fought down nervousness as she opened the door of her work for Wrath. He'd tried to open it for her but she'd shaken her head no. "You're a client. I'm supposed to impress you instead of the other way around. I appreciate the gesture but now isn't the time to be a gentleman."

He said nothing as he stepped into the office. Lauren smiled at Kim, the receptionist, and hoped it didn't appear forced. Her heart raced, she didn't want to let Wrath or his team down and catching Bill was important to them.

"Hello, Kim. This is Mr. Williams. We're going back to my office so I can pull up condo listings. Is anyone else in yet?"

"Mel was here when I arrived, John B and John T are here too, and Gina is in her office having a meltdown with a bank manager who is giving one of her clients some grief about their loan." Kim winced. "Avoid her. She's pissed."

"Thanks for the warning." Lauren took a few steps but paused. "Oh, last night Mel had me show a property for Brent. The guy was interested but he had some questions I couldn't answer. There are some ugly, large cargo containers inside the warehouse and he wants to know if those are staying or going. Is Brent coming in today?"

"I don't know. I could page him if you want and find out."

"That would be great. The man had some other questions so if Brent calls you back, please transfer his call to my office. The buyer is really interested in the property."

Kim nodded, reaching for the phone. Lauren smiled at Wrath and led him through the archway to a larger room.

Lauren spotted John T at one of the computer stations and approached him.

"If you'll just take a seat here, I'll be right with you, Mr. Williams." Lauren directed Wrath to take a chair close to where John T worked.

Wrath sat and Lauren focused on her coworker whom she knew spent time with Brent. They liked to go barhopping together and she figured he might be her best bet at locating the missing monster Wrath hunted.

"Good morning, John. I got a call last night from Mel to show one of Brent's properties. The buyer is really interested but he had some questions I couldn't answer. Do you know where Brent is? The buyer wants the warehouse but he wasn't thrilled seeing huge cargo containers on the property. I don't know if the owner plans to remove them or if it's an 'as is' deal."

"He got a call yesterday after work and took off out of here like a bat out of hell." John shrugged, still typing. "I haven't heard from him since. He was supposed to show up at the Bugle last night."

"What's that?"

He grinned. "It's our favorite strip bar. We go there a few times a week."

She tried to appear nonchalant. "Oh. Well, if you can reach him, will you have him call me?"

"Sure." He reached for his cell, picked it up, and turned in his chair. He spotted Wrath, appeared startled, and dropped his phone on the desk. He fumbled, grabbed it and spun to face the screen again. "I'll call him now."

Lauren turned, smiling at Wrath. "This way, Mr. Williams. I'll pull up those condo listings."

"Lauren!"

Lauren jumped, turning. Mel stood in her office, staring at Wrath with an odd expression on her face.

"Hi, Mel. This is Mr. Williams. He's interested in condos."

Mel smiled but it looked forced. "May I speak to you for a moment?"

Lauren nodded and motioned Wrath toward an open door near the front by the reception area just around the corner. "This is my office. Go on in and I'll be back in a second." She moved toward her boss, wondering if she was in trouble for trying to argue the night before over showing the property. "What is it, Mel?"

Mel waited until Lauren was inside her office before she spoke. "Who is he?" She kept her voice down.

"That's Mr. Williams. He was just stationed in this area and plans to stay a while."

Mel chewed on her bottom lip for a few seconds then frowned. "He called you and set an appointment?"

Lauren nodded and hoped her boss wasn't planning to screw her over by trying to steal a client. It wouldn't be the first time. Of course Mel didn't realize Wrath wasn't a real client and she worried what would happen if her boss wanted to show him listings instead.

"How did the showing go last night?" Mel changed the subject.

Lauren managed to hide her relief. "Good. Mr. Herbert is interested in buying the property but there are these large cargo containers left inside the warehouse that he wasn't interested in. He asked me about them but it's not my listing. I didn't know if they stay or if they'll be removed. He wanted to talk to Brent."

"I'll pass that along." Mel studied Lauren. "Okay. Go ahead and deal with Mr. Williams but I called a meeting in half an hour. You can set him up with some coffee while he waits for you. It won't take long." She glanced at her watch. "My office in half an hour and it's mandatory. You can go show him the properties he's interested in right after the meeting."

"Is everything okay? We usually don't hold meetings when clients are here."

A smile curved Mel's mouth. "Everything is fine, Lauren. We had some parking issues come up with the landlord and I swore I'd talk to all the employees. The man is a pain in the ass but we don't want to lose our lease. It won't take more than a few minutes. I just want to address everyone at once so no one feels singled out but we both know who the two worst offenders are. Both John T and John B know better than to use the alley. The other tenants complained."

"Okay." She left Mel, returned to her office and smiled at Wrath. She sat down at her desk and glanced at the open doorway, lowering her voice. "We'll be here for at least half an hour. My boss called a meeting and she said it was mandatory. That should mean that he has to show up for it too. He could walk in at any time."

"Did you hear that?" He seemed to be listening to his earpiece and gave Lauren a slight nod, keeping his voice low too. "They heard."

"I'll pull up listings while we wait. We'll just pretend to look at them to pass the time."

Lauren had him scoot his chair closer so both of them could view her computer screen. "While we look at condos, we can watch who walks in the door. I never get tired of looking at these. Some of them are kind of cool."

"I like the curved stairs and the big bathtub." He pointed at the computer monitor but his other hand brushed her thigh and rubbed before he leaned back in his chair.

They had viewed several listings when Lauren's phone rang about fifteen minutes later and she answered. "Lauren Henderson."

"Hello, Lauren. It's Brent."

Her gaze flew to Wrath. "Hello, Brent."

Wrath tensed in his seat and leaned closer. Lauren tilted the phone, hoping he could hear both sides of the conversation.

"I heard you were looking for me."

"Yes. I had to show a warehouse property for you last night. The guy is interested but he doesn't want the cargo containers. He had some questions about the roof, well, you know the drill, but I didn't have any answers for him. He wanted me to get the answers and meet with him today."

She looked at Wrath for direction and held up her hands questioning about what else to say. He nodded at her. He mouthed "at the warehouse at noon".

"He wanted me to meet him there at noon today to show it to him during the daylight hours. I told him I'd try to send you instead so you can answer his questions since it is your listing. He seems really hot for the property."

Brent chuckled. "Great. I'll meet him instead. Thanks, Lauren. I know we don't get along but this was really nice of you to call me. You could have screwed me out of the whole thing."

"It's your listing, Brent. One day I could have an emergency and you might have to show one of my properties. I would hope you'd do me right." She refrained from snorting. The guy would have no qualms over stealing a deal right out from under her.

"Thanks. I'll meet him at noon." He hung up.

Lauren grinned at Wrath, happy that she'd been able to help him. Brent was a bad guy who needed to be arrested. *Bill,* she corrected. He was an ex-Mercile employee who had hurt people like Wrath and that just pissed her off.

He smiled and lowered his voice. "He's going for a noon meeting at the warehouse."

Lauren suddenly realized how close she was to losing Wrath. "Well, what happens next?" Her gaze fixed on his dark glasses. She whispered, hoping the pain she suddenly felt didn't sound in her voice. "Is this where you just leave me and go back to your life while I go back to mine?"

"We haven't captured him yet. You're coming with me."

Lauren silently admitted she wasn't ready to say goodbye to Wrath. He leaned closer to her and his hand inched up her skirt, caressing her leg. The desk hid them from anyone walking past her office and she stared at the sunglasses she hated, knew he watched her back, and could feel the desire they both shared sizzle between them.

She decided to tell him the truth. She'd miss him and hoped they could see each other after they captured Bill. "I—"

"Lauren?"

Lauren jumped, startled by her friend's voice. Wrath jerked his hand away from her leg as Amanda stepped into the office. The other woman's eyes widened as she openly gawked at Wrath and licked her lips.

"I'm with a client, Amanda. Mr. Williams, this is my best friend, Amanda Davis." She hesitated, giving her friend a frustrated look. "This isn't a good time. I'll call you later."

Amanda didn't budge but she did puff out her chest. "Hello, Mr. Williams."

Lauren gritted her teeth. Amanda was eyeing Wrath's body as if he were a pork chop, which she loved.

"Please tell me that you're single." Amanda sat in the chair by the door, crossed her legs and seemed to get comfortable.

Wrath smiled. "I am."

Amanda glanced toward the ceiling. "There is a God." She laughed and batted her eyelashes at Wrath. "I'm single too. And looking."

Wrath kept his smile in place. "Okay."

"Amanda," Lauren said in a tight voice, "Mr. Williams is a client. What are you doing here so early?"

"I was bored and thought I'd come to see if you could have dinner with me this evening before the movie."

"I'm busy. As a matter of fact I'm going to have to cancel our movie plans. We'll go tomorrow instead."

Amanda pouted.

"I'm showing Mr. Williams some condos."

Amanda grinned. "I have a condo to show you. Mine." She winked. "I think you'd particularly enjoy my bedroom."

"Amanda," Lauren warned. "Stop."

Amanda ignored her. "Want to go home with me and see my bedroom, gorgeous? Why buy one when you could just move right in with me? I think you'd cheer my place right up. You work out a lot, don't you?"

"Amanda!" Lauren was getting pissed.

Amanda flashed her a smile. "This is why you're single. I'm trying not to be. Hush. He's all big and single. How many chances do I have to try to lure him home with me?" Amanda grinned at Wrath. "So, what do you say? Want me to show you my condo today? We could leave right now."

Wrath stopped smiling. "I appreciate the offer but Lauren is going to show me condos today."

"I want to show you more than just a condo." Amanda smoothed down her shirt, shoving her chest out again. "And I know I want you to show me more than a condo." Her gaze dropped to his lap and stayed there.

"Amanda!" Lauren gasped.

John T came to the doorway. "Meeting time, Lauren."

Lauren stood, shaking with anger. She turned to Wrath. "I shouldn't be long." She spun, giving her friend a glare. "Amanda, knock it off and behave."

Amanda grinned. "But I don't want to be good." She winked at Wrath. "I want to be bad. Verrrry bad."

Lauren stormed out of her office, silently swearing to kill her best pal later for hitting on Wrath. Amanda should never hit on one of Lauren's clients but she could have laughed that off. What wasn't funny was that she'd gone after Wrath. Her anger burned.

Mel's door was open so she just entered. Her boss stood by the desk facing Brent and both of them turned to stare at Lauren. She tried to hide her shock at seeing him there. They'd somehow missed him passing by her office and she wished she could signal Wrath. She schooled her features, she hoped, and tried to appear calm. It was rough, knowing she was in the same room with a killer and someone who had abused New Species.

John T and John B entered the office behind her and closed the door. Gina was absent. Mel quickly walked forward and gripped Lauren's shoulders.

"You need to tell me right now how that man in your office contacted you and when."

Alarm shot through Lauren. Her heart pounded in her ears and she stared mutely at her boss. She finally managed to get her brain working. "He called yesterday and set up the appointment. Why? What's going on?"

Brent glared at her. "Didn't you notice something off about him?"

Lauren shook her head. She hoped Wrath's good hearing could detect what was going on in the office. Fear gripped her that they suspected the truth but she didn't understand how they'd know Wrath wasn't exactly a normal guy. Brent hadn't seen him and he was the one who might recognize a New Species.

"No. Why?"

John T frowned. "He's got glasses on. How the hell would she know unless she's seen one of them, seen the facial differences? I doubt she ever has."

Oh my God. Lauren panicked but tried to control her features to hide her fear. *John T knows for sure what Wrath is, but how?*

Mel nodded. "You need to leave now, Lauren. That man in your office is...a rapist. He gets realtors to show him properties and he attacks the second they're alone. We'll handle this."

"But..." Lauren was at a loss for words. She studied the people in the office and felt chilled to the bone. They were lying and all four of them knew Wrath was a New Species. "Okay but my purse is in my office. I'll get it, make an excuse, and leave." *Warn Wrath.*

"Just leave it." Brent suddenly grabbed Lauren. "Go now." He shoved her toward the back door of Mel's office.

"But..."

Lauren was pushed out the back door and into the alleyway before she could protest. It slammed in her face, the bolt slid loud enough for her to hear, and shock washed through her at being locked out.

They knew Wrath was a New Species, had gotten rid of her, and they were protecting Brent for some reason. Terrified for Wrath's safety she spun and ran down the alleyway to get to the SUV to tell his team what was going on. They needed to warn Wrath to get out or they needed to go in there.

Amanda was with Wrath. More fear drove her to run faster. She almost broke an ankle in her haste, the high heels impeding her, but she was grateful when she spotted the SUV. A car nearly hit her when she forgot to look before crossing the street. The driver hit the brakes, honked his horn and flipped her off.

Brass opened the passenger door, climbed out and caught her when she practically slammed into his big body. Firm hands gripped her arms.

"What is wrong? Where is Wrath?"

"I think they know he's New Species. They fed me some bullshit about Wrath being a rapist before they shoved me out a back door. Brent is in there, they were all acting weird and my coworkers seem to be protecting him."

Brass cursed. "Stay here." He lifted her off her feet, pressed her against the side of the SUV and let go. "We're going in."

Lauren tried to catch her breath. "The alley." She panted, swearing to buy a treadmill in her near future to get more in shape. "They can get out the back if they try to make a run for it."

Brass turned to Brian—both he and Shadow had exited the SUV. "You take the alley and make sure they don't escape that way." Brian took off at a run in the direction Lauren had just come from.

"You stay, Lauren." Brass checked the guns strapped to his hips. "You're safe here."

"My friend Amanda is in there too. She's a blonde wearing a blue shirt and a black skirt."

"Understood," Shadow said.

Both men jogged across the street and down the sidewalk toward her office building. Lauren finally caught her breath and frowned. She didn't want to wait with the SUV, too worried about her friend and Wrath to be that patient. They might need her. She pushed away from the side of the vehicle and quickly followed them.

She was so worried and distracted by what could be happening to Wrath, his team, and Amanda that she nearly fell on her butt when she spun to face the voice that called out.

"Hey!"

Amanda waved at her from the street, standing in front of the open driver's door of her car, which was parked a few away from her at the curb. "God, that man was hot. I want to strip him down and sprinkle him with salt so I can take tequila shots off his body."

"I thought you were inside."

"Your boss ordered me to leave. She said she had sent you on an emergency call to let in a plumber at a property. That woman is such a bitch she probably wanted to take a shot at him herself but I'm not letting it go down. Tell me you have Mr. Williams' number and what in God's name, is that man's first name? He wouldn't tell me."

Lauren twisted her head to stare at the office building. "Stay here. Just…stay here. Don't move!"

"Okay! Bring me his number."

Lauren nodded, turning her attention back on the office, dying to know what was going on inside it. Amanda was safe. That was a big relief but she wouldn't calm down until she saw Wrath. She walked across the grass and avoided the front sidewalk, which could be seen from the reception area. Kim's desk was empty when she inched up to the window and peeked. Lauren frowned.

Lauren eased around the side of the building and crept toward one of the windows of the office area. She hesitated, lifted her head and peered inside. What she saw made her gasp. Brass and Shadow were facing a wall and John T had a gun pointed at their backs while Mel and Brent stood close by, arguing. She could hear their raised voices but couldn't understand the words. *Where's Wrath? Where's Kim, Gina, and John B?*

Lauren ducked and kept low to prevent being seen through the windows. She practically crawled toward the back of the building until she reached the alley. She gasped. Brian was sprawled on his back on the ground next to the back door. She ran for him. Fresh blood was smeared on his forehead. Someone had hit him with something but he was breathing. Her hands shook badly as she searched his pockets and located a cell phone, glad he had one.

The top number said BASE when she checked recent outgoing calls and she pressed it to have the cell dial it. A man answered on the first ring.

"Hello?"

"This is Lauren Henderson. Is this headquarters?"

The man hesitated. "Who is this and how did you get Brian's phone?"

"He's bleeding on the ground." She rattled off the address and name of her work. "They have Brass, Shadow and Wrath inside. My coworker has a gun pointed at Brass and Shadow. I haven't seen Wrath yet but he was inside. Should I call 9-1-1?"

"No," the man ground out. "We're on our way. Stay with Brian. Is he breathing?"

Lauren checked Brian over again, verified his chest rose and fell and took a calming breath, trying to control her panic. "Yes but he's out cold. He was hit in the head by something but it's not here next to him and I don't see anything with blood on it. We're in the alley behind the building."

"Don't move and stay on the phone. Do not hang up. We will have teams out to you in minutes."

Lauren left the phone line open and tucked it into Brian's vest so it wasn't in sight but the guy could still hear what was going on. She had no intention of just standing there to wait for help to arrive when Wrath could be in danger. She got to her feet, rushed to the other side of the building and crawled past the windows until she reached her office.

Lauren listened, heard nothing, and raised her head enough to stare into her office through the window. Wrath remained in the same seat he'd been sitting in when she'd left her office but it appeared as if he'd fallen asleep—his head was tipped back and his arms dangled limply over the arms of the chair. A red-tipped dart stuck out of his chest. She could see it move as he breathed, which assured her he was alive but obviously drugged.

Adrenaline rushed through her. Wrath needed help. She had no idea how long it would take for someone else to arrive. No way was she going to just stay there and do nothing. The screen came off easily and she gently rested it against the side of the building. Her gaze lifted to the inside lock, knew that window well since it stuck often when she opened it, and gripped the metal side with her fingers. She wiggled, tried to be quiet about it, and focused on her open office door. There was no movement but she'd have to hide if someone came.

The lock popped and she paused, straining her ears for any sign that someone inside could have heard it. She faintly heard yelling but couldn't make out what was being said. No one rushed into the room so she eased the glass along the track to get it all the way open. Wrath was so close. She had no idea what to do once she reached him, but maybe she could barricade her office door to lock them both inside until help arrived.

The voices were loud enough with the window open that she could distinctly make out her coworkers' angry shouting. She lifted up to the waist-high opening, raised a leg and jerked her skirt out of the way. Climbing in wasn't easy but she managed and dropped to her knees to crawl behind her desk to hide.

"What the hell are we going to do?" Mel demanded.

"Just calm down," Brent said. "I keep telling you that I'll think of something."

"It's probably your fault!" Mel yelled. "Did you get drunk and tell someone who you really are? Damn it, Bill. I told you that you were putting us all at risk but would you stop being such a selfish prick? Hell no!"

"I didn't." His voice dropped and she couldn't make out the rest of what he said.

"They found us!" Mel shouted. "You said no one would be able to trace us here and I trusted you."

"They did find us." It was John T speaking and he was obviously mad. "Let's just think of what we're going to do now. I say we kill them and get the hell out of here."

"And go where?" Glass broke, Mel was so irate, she'd probably thrown something. "We sank all our money into this place for our cover identities. They probably froze our account at the bank. We're screwed! I'm going to have to call my sister and you know how much I don't want to do that. I wanted away from this shit. I never wanted to see one of those bastards again and now we have three of them. In...our...offices!"

"Enough!" John B roared. "They offer reward money for them. We have three. Everyone calm down. I can't think when you're shouting. We can use them to get fast cash and start over somewhere else."

"Who is going to exchange them? Huh?" Brent yelled. "Not me. That's stupid. They'll just set a trap and we'll go to prison forever. They aren't really going to pay us."

"We'll get them out of here and it will buy us some time to think of a surefire way to get paid by the NSO to return these three. We're smarter than those bastards. We just need to get out of here before more arrive."

"Don't move or I'll shoot you!" John T yelled.

"Calm." Brass' deep voice barely reached Lauren since he wasn't shouting. "The NSO will pay for us. Just don't harm the women."

"See? I told you they were sappy enough to protect innocents. You move and I slit the receptionist's throat. She isn't a part of this and she's two months pregnant. Fight us and she dies. I can take out Gina too before you reach me." John B snorted loudly. "The NSO will pay us. We just need to get out of here. Bill, where are more darts? We'll tranquilize these two, tie up the women, and split." His voice rose. "More of them could be on the way. These three could be scouts or something. They are hunters, right? Shoot them with darts, we'll carry them out and figure the rest of this out when we're safe."

"Please," Kim begged. "Let me go."

"Shut up. I didn't bring enough darts." Brent sounded furious. "You told me there was one of them. Not three."

"He came in alone!" John T yelled. "If I'd known there were more, I would have told you on the damn phone."

"Don't move!" John B yelled. "I swear he'll shoot you both and you won't get another warning. These women will die too. Do you want their blood on your hands?"

Lauren's heart pounded and she knew she had to do something. She lifted her hand to call 9-1-1 from the phone on her desk but memory of the phone system stopped her cold. Every phone would show a line in use by flashing red. She couldn't risk making a phone call but her coworkers were planning on taking Wrath and she couldn't allow that to happen.

She pushed on her desk to test the weight of it but it didn't budge. It was the only thing big enough in the room to keep them from breaking down the door if she barricaded it. That plan wouldn't work though because they could as she had—go around the building, and come in through the window.

"Move," John T ordered. "In that back office now. Keep your hands above your heads, move real slow. If you even twitch, I'm going to shoot you."

"Yeah," Brent said, "do that. We have phone cords. We'll tie them up, take them out the back and grab the last one after we get them settled in the van." He paused. "Go get the van."

"My minivan?" John B gasped. "Everyone will see inside it."

"The company van, you idiot!" Mel shouted. "It's bigger. It's got the cargo area and tinted windows. Just dump the signs out of the back."

"Fuck," he shouted. "Move, Gina. You too, Kim. You're staying close to me. If they attack, you're both dead."

"Keep moving," John T ordered. "Keep your hands up. Mel, go rip out the phone cords. You have three in there. Use the ones to the fax machine too."

Lauren glanced around her desk, saw no one, and crawled forward until she could peek out the door. Her coworkers weren't in sight and she leaned out enough to see

Mel's office. John T's back was to her and he blocked most of the doorway, preventing her from seeing what was going on in Mel's office. All of them seemed to be in there.

Pure terror gripped her but she moved, shoved up to her feet and grabbed Wrath's chair by the arms. The back of it dug into her belly as she pulled. As the wheels moved over the carpet his boots dragged, making it tougher on her. She pulled, prayed he wouldn't slide out of the seat. He would be too heavy to put back if he did.

She paused, listened, and heard her coworkers arguing in Mel's office. She glanced around the corner again, saw John T's back was to her, and she frantically pulled. The chair left her office, she bit back a groan, and kept pulling Wrath toward the front. She just needed to make it about ten feet to the reception area. She made it without anyone spotting her. Guilt ate at her over leaving the New Species and her coworkers being held at knifepoint. She couldn't help them though. Wrath was the only one she could save. She needed to get him to safety first and just prayed the man she'd spoken to on Brian's phone arrived in time to help them. It would be suicide to rush into Mel's office to attempt to rescue anyone else.

Her back hit the exterior glass door but it didn't push open when she pressed against it. She hit it with her ass but the glass just barely moved. She twisted her head, realized someone had locked the door, and fought to turn the deadbolt. The glass door opened and fresh air filled her lungs as she sucked in a deep breath. She pulled, dragging the chair and Wrath out of the building.

No one was on the sidewalk. Gravity helped move the chair since the building was higher than the street. She turned it, pulled frantically, and kept going. Her eyes remained on the building. She expected her coworkers to come out after them at any second when they realized they were missing a New Species but she made it to where she'd left Amanda.

"Open the back door now." Lauren pulled harder, moving faster.

Amanda saw Wrath, the chair and Lauren. Her mouth dropped open and her eyes widened.

"Open the fucking door," Lauren snapped at her. "Now! Move it. Back door. Get it the hell open. Now, Amanda. Now!"

Amanda moved. She hit the button to unlock the doors and almost tripped on the curb as she ran around the car to open the back door but she swung it open just as a panting Lauren dragged the chair there.

"Help me get him in."

"What the hell?" Amanda's eyes were wide and she looked unusually pale.

"I'll explain later. Help me. He weighs a ton. We've got to get him out of here before someone sees us." Lauren grabbed the protruding dart from Wrath's chest and dropped it inside her skirt pocket. "Hurry."

Amanda grabbed Wrath's other arm and Lauren positioned the chair facing the backseat of the car. She gripped him firmly and they lifted to maneuver his limp form out of the chair.

"Jesus," Amanda grunted. "My back is breaking. He's got to weigh at least two hundred and fifty pounds."

The two of them managed to dump the unconscious Wrath into the backseat. Lauren bent his legs up to make him fit. Wrath didn't look comfortable but he was in and his face wasn't pushed against the seat. She slammed the door and yanked open the passenger one.

"Get in the car," she panted at Amanda.

Amanda ran around the car and jerked open the driver's door, collapsing into the seat. The engine started and Lauren's pounding heart threatened to explode from exhaustion and fear. One glance at her office assured her no one had rushed out yet and she twisted in her seat to duck down in case that changed.

"Drive, damn it. Get us out of here."

Amanda punched the gas. "Oh my God," Amanda babbled. "You're going to get us both arrested. I know I keep complaining about being single but have you lost your mind? You can't just kidnap a man. He's really hot but what were you thinking? Are you on drugs? Let's just call the police and tell them you had a breakdown. We could take him to a hospital and have them admit you for an evaluation."

"I didn't kidnap him, damn it. This isn't what it looks like. We need to go. Drive! I'll explain it all to you later but he's in danger."

"You know how friends tell friends when they've lost their mind?" Amanda licked her lips. "This is that time."

Lauren lifted her head enough to see her friend's flushed face and glared up at her. She opened her mouth but just closed it. She was too tired to yell at that moment. She decided to just be honest.

"You need to trust me. Please drive, Amanda. This really isn't as bad as you think."

"Where do we go?"

"Your place."

Amanda nodded. "Okay. Oh man, are we in deep shit. You better have a hell of a reason. I can't believe I'm doing this."

Lauren wanted to use Amanda's cell phone to call the police but didn't dare after being ordered not to. She prayed the team arrived but wasn't willing to stick around to make sure help came in time. Getting Wrath out of there was the priority, the only thing she could do.

Chapter Ten

ℵ

Lauren had managed to stop shaking by the time Amanda pulled into her garage. The electronic door sealed them inside and the interior light stayed on. Amanda turned off her engine and stared at her best friend.

"Do you think he'll press charges? Forget that. Of course he will. You knocked him out somehow and kidnapped him. What were you thinking? We'll get you help. Let's go inside and call someone. It's not too late to fix this, okay? We'll get you the best attorney. Insanity is a great defense. I never meant for you to do something so drastic to get me a man."

"Stop that," Lauren sighed. "It's not like that."

Amanda frowned. "Then why did you drug him and bring him to me?"

"I didn't drug him." Lauren shook her head, tired, frustrated and wondering if her friend needed some therapy. "It's a long story. How are we going to get him inside your place? Any ideas?"

Amanda turned in her seat and studied Wrath, frowning. "I don't know. He's a big one. Did you have to lose your mind and kidnap the biggest guy you could find? I know I said I was desperate for a date but Jesus, Lauren!"

"Stop it!" Lauren shot her a glare. "He's not a sex toy that I stole for you. I haven't lost my mind and I didn't do this in some misguided attempt to get you a man. His name is Wrath and he's in danger."

"I thought you said his last name was Williams."

"I don't think he has a last name. His real name is Wrath. It's a long story."

"I guess we have time for you to tell me what is going on since we have to think up a way to get him out of the car and up those steps."

Lauren hesitated. "Did you notice his features?"

"Who cares about his face when he's got that great body?"

"Look at him, Amanda. Look at his nose and think of your ultimate hero on television, the one you drool over. Here's a hint. Justice North."

Amanda turned in her seat so she could get a better view of the man behind her. She stared, tilted her head slightly and the color slowly drained from her face. Her mouth dropped open and she gaped at Lauren.

Lauren nodded. "He's New Species."

"Holy shit. What have you gotten me into? He's like an endangered species, right? They have really strict laws about them. Lauren, what were you thinking? We're going to get the electric chair if something happens to him. If you kill one of them, even accidentally, it's the death penalty for a hate crime."

"I didn't do this. The people at my work shot him with some kind of drugged dart and it knocked him out cold."

Amanda blinked. "Why? Did he have bad credit or something? I know your boss is a bitch but that's even harsh for her."

"Very funny," Lauren snorted. "It's complicated and a mess. I guess I worked with some jerks who used to work for Mercile Industries. They saw him and did this to him. They planned to take him away but I got him out of there first. We need to hide him in your condo until I can get him some help. His team and two of my coworkers who aren't involved in this mess are back at the office. I could only save him. I didn't know what else to do."

"Who are you going to call? The police?"

Lauren shook her head. "No. The people Wrath works with told me not to call 9-1-1 so I guess I'll have to leave them out of this." Lauren climbed out the car. "Let's get him inside."

Amanda climbed out of the car and frowned at Lauren over the roof. "How? I don't have a crane handy in here to lift him out of the car and up the steps. He's heavy."

Lauren studied the steps leading into Amanda's condo and had a thought. "Do you still have that twin air mattress you use when your niece comes to visit?"

"The princess one?"

"Yeah. We could inflate it, put him on it, and drag it into the kitchen."

Amanda sighed. "I'll go get the electric pump and fill it." Amanda's gaze drifted to the backseat as she stared through the window. "I wouldn't do this if he wasn't hot. He'll owe me." Amanda suddenly grinned. "He really does look hot in those clothes. Once we get him inside it would only be kind to take some of them off him."

Lauren groaned. "Amanda!"

"What? Just his shirt. Be a friend. I was the getaway car driver and hell, I should get some kind of reward after we drag him into the house. I think I already got a hernia from getting him in the car."

Lauren shook her head. "I think you would benefit from taking drugs and I worry about you."

"You should be worried. If I don't get laid soon I'm going to shrivel up and die."

"The things I put up with," Lauren mumbled.

"You? I just helped you dump the body of a hunky New Species guy in the back of my car and I'm harboring an endangered species in my home!"

"Good point. You're the best friend ever." Lauren smiled. "Go get the mattress. Don't you have some tarps in here somewhere from when we painted your bathroom last month?"

Amanda pointed to the corner. "Somewhere over there."

Lauren turned to search for one while Amanda entered the condo. Lauren found a few of tarps folded under a shelf and opened the back door of the car, checking on Wrath. He remained heavily drugged. She spread out the tarp on the floor next to the open door and was grateful that Amanda had a double car garage with only one car so they had plenty of room to work. Amanda returned, lugging a big pink inflatable mattress she dropped on top of the tarp.

"He is really heavy."

"I know," Lauren agreed. "I'll get his feet and pull him out. You climb in the other side and watch his head. I don't want to bump it when we get him out of the car."

"Okay." Amanda laughed. "Are you sure we can't take his clothes off? It would drop a few pounds off him."

"I'm sure."

"Damn. I always wonder if they have tails or any fur hidden anywhere. You know there's talk that some of them could have those. They could shave their arms and faces to hide some hair issues. We could totally find out."

Lauren gripped Wrath and tried to ignore Amanda. She was glad the boots were solidly on his feet as she straightened his legs and pulled on him by the ankles. Amanda gripped his arms, kept him from falling out of the car when his ass slid off the seat, and both of them struggled to get him flat and centered on the mattress.

"I should get to keep him since I think I just threw out my back and I'm going to need someone to take care of me."

Sweat trickled down her body and she knew it would only get worse when they had to lift him up the stairs. There were only three steps but it seemed an impossible task. Lauren kicked her shoes off and out of the way. She leaned down and grabbed the sides of the tarp and lifted.

Amanda grabbed the other ends and stared down at his face. "He's really good-looking. What color are his eyes? Do you know?"

"Dark brown and beautiful," Lauren grunted, pulling on Wrath. "Don't get attached. He's taken."

"He's got a girlfriend? Damn! Why is it that all the good-looking ones seem to be taken or gay?"

They managed to get Wrath up the stairs by protecting his back with the mattress and turning the tarp into a hammock. Both of them collapsed to their knees when they reached the living room, after dragging him from the kitchen into the bigger room.

"I'm not taking him upstairs," Amanda swore. "Stick a fork in me. I'm done."

"Me neither. We'd never make it."

"He looks good right there next to the coffee table. The wood matches his tan."

Lauren struggled to her feet, got them bottled water from the fridge and passed one to her best friend. It was a warm day and lugging around Wrath had exhausted them both.

"I have an idea," Lauren announced. "I'm going to use your phone."

"Help yourself. Forget taking off his shirt. I'm too worn out." Amanda lay back on the carpet. "I'll just die here for a while."

Lauren walked to the bar that separated the kitchen from the living room and sat down on the barstool. She reached for Amanda's phone and dialed information. She groaned when the automated voice answered.

"Damn automation," she muttered. She gave them the city she thought was right and the state. "NSO," she said clearly. She repeated it. She was put on hold for a person.

Lauren asked for the number of the NSO. They didn't have a listing. She asked for the number by their full name.

"It's the New Species Organization." They found the number and she wrote it down and dialed.

A man answered. "NSO Homeland. How may I direct your call?"

Lauren took a deep breath. "Hello. My name is Lauren Henderson. I didn't know who else to call but I have a New Species man in my friend's living room about ten feet from where I'm sitting. He's been shot with some kind of dart and he's out cold. I need you to send help for him."

There was silence on the other end of the line for a few seconds. "It's against the law to make crank calls to us, female."

"This isn't a crank call. His name is Wrath and he's living at headquarters. That's all they referred to it as. I was taken by him yesterday because he said I was working with someone who used to be an employee for Mercile Industries. We went into my office today to try to find the person he's hunting but it turned out that almost everyone in the office seemed to work for Mercile. They shot him with some kind of drugged dart. I got him out of there but I—"

The man cut her off. "You said his name is Wrath?"

"Yes."

The man growled. "I have a list of all New Species right in front of me. There is no one named Wrath. Female, if you ever call here again I will send the police to your home. We have your address right here. Any incoming calls are immediately traced." He recited Amanda's address. "Never call here again." He hung up.

Lauren clenched her teeth. She turned her head to stare at Wrath. He was definitely New Species. She dialed again and the same man answered.

"Listen to me, whoever you are. I'm looking at him. He's right here in the living room. Please send someone to arrest me because when they get here they are going to take one look at him and know I'm not lying. He's been shot with a dart and he's unconscious. He needs help, I'm worried about him, and have no idea what was in that dart. I was told not to dial 9-1-1 so I haven't. They took two more of your people, are holding two women hostage and hurt a man named Brian. He was bleeding in an alley."

"Who did this to the male and those others you mentioned?" He sounded bored.

"My boss and some of my coworkers. They took two of your people at gunpoint and were going to put them in the courtesy van my company owns. They—"

"Don't call here again, damn it. Call a head shrink." The man hung up.

"Fuck!" Lauren hit the top of the bar.

"He didn't believe you?" Amanda lifted her head.

Lauren was pissed. "No. He hung up on me again. I wish I knew where headquarters was but I wasn't paying much attention when we left there."

"Well, all you can do is hope that whatever they shot him with wears off soon and then he can tell us what to do."

Lauren pushed off the barstool and walked toward him. She sank down on her knees and put her hand on his chest while she studied his face. She removed the glasses with gentle fingers, stroked his cheek and hoped that he'd wake soon.

"I hope it was just a sedative. What if it wasn't?"

"We'll watch him and if he stops breathing or something, we'll call for an ambulance."

Lauren nodded. She shifted her body, getting comfortable, to stay by Wrath's side. She wasn't about to let anything happen to him.

* * * * *

Saturn shook his head, trying to shake off his anger. Didn't humans have anything better to do than screw with him? He got a bunch of crazy calls every day. An hour before a female had called to see if she could hire a Species to be present at her child's birthday party as if one of them would visit just to entertain children. The call before that was from a man saying he wanted to marry a Species female. Now a female was calling to tell him someone in a courtesy van was kidnapping his people and she had one of them in her living room. He snorted.

"Bad day?" Tiger, his supervisor, smiled.

"I hate phone duty," Saturn admitted. "Humans are crazy."

Tiger nodded. "I know. I can never decide if the ones who call to tell me to die are worse than the ones who call and ask me if they can get a ride back with us to our home planet."

"Direct line, Tiger," a female Species called out. "It's Tim Oberto and there's a problem."

Tiger cursed. Four—no, three—of his Species males were working with Tim's task force. He prayed there wasn't another issue. One of the males had already turned out to be unstable and unfit for duty. He hoped another one of them hadn't cracked under the pressure. He walked to the phone and lifted it to his ear.

"What is wrong?"

"We have a big fucking problem. One of my men and all three of yours have been taken. We're tracking two of your men and our man at this moment. They had their uniforms on and they are tagged. We're in pursuit and we should have them at any time unless they are stripped of their clothes. Unfortunately one of your men wasn't wearing his uniform and didn't take a tracker. We have no idea where he is, Tiger. He's off radar unless he's with the others."

"Son of a bitch. Which one is missing?"

"Wrath."

Tiger frowned. "Who?"

Tim sighed. "You called him 919. I ordered them to pick names and that's the one he chose."

"Wrath?" Tiger pushed back anger that something had gone wrong and fear for the safety of his males. "What happened?"

Tim quickly explained what the mission had been. "The woman called in on Brian's phone to alert us all hell was breaking loose. Brian is one of my men assigned to your guys. She's in the wind too now, wasn't on scene when we arrived, and to be honest, I'm playing catch-up. Your men didn't run this by me first or I would have sent more backup, Tiger. I just pulled the damn notes Brass made so I know what the hell was going on and who this woman is. No one was there when we got to the address. The entire office was abandoned. We found our SUV around the corner and some blood on the ground where she said Brian was injured."

"You think the woman stole them?"

Tim sighed. "She alerted us to something being wrong. Otherwise we wouldn't have known to activate their tracking devices until they didn't report in. That would have been a few hours. We're assuming she's friendly at this moment and was taken with the team."

"Got it. So a human female is missing too? What is her name? Did 358 pick a name too?"

Tiger wrote it down. "I'll alert my people. Maybe whoever has them wants a ransom. Call me back the second you close in on those signals." He hung up.

Tiger spun and raised his voice. "Everyone, we have a situation. We have three missing Species males, a human male and a human female. Our males were on a retrieval mission with the human male driver from the task force and a human female who was helping them locate the target. Our men missing are Brass, 919 and 358." He paused. "Sorry. They picked names. 919 is going by Wrath and 358 is going by Shadow."

Saturn suddenly cursed and stood. "Did you say Wrath?"

Tiger fixed his gaze on Saturn.

"Would the human female's name possibly be Lauren?"

Tiger strode across the room toward him. "Yes. Lauren Henderson."

"Shit. She called us but I thought she was a crackpot. I hung up on her twice. She's got Wrath and wanted us to help him but I didn't believe her."

* * * * *

Lauren grew more alarmed as time passed and Wrath didn't wake. She had borrowed clothes from Amanda, changed into something more comfortable, and stayed by his side. Amanda had tried to convince Lauren that he'd rest easier if they removed Wrath's shirt. Lauren shook her head at her best friend.

"Give it up. We're not stripping him down."

"But he'd be more comfortable."

"Not when he woke up and needed a shower from you drooling all over him."

"I'll get a drool rag and tie it around my neck."

Lauren laughed. "For the last damn time, no! You aren't taking his clothes off."

"You removed his boots."

"Well, that's just his feet. He's sleeping. No one should do that with their boots on."

"He's got big feet and hands. Think that saying is true?" Amanda grinned.

"It is in his case."

Amanda's eyes widened. "You peeked when I was changing, didn't you? God, you're such a bitch. You are supposed to do everything with your best friend."

Lauren hesitated and decided to just tell her friend the truth. "I didn't peek while you were changing. I've showered with him."

"No! Get out! You're lying just to make me jealous."

"We spent last night together."

Amanda let her eyes roam up and down the man on the pink inflatable mattress. Her gaze returned to Lauren. "You are my hero, girlfriend."

Lauren stood and entered the kitchen. "I'm getting hungry. How about you?"

The doorbell rang. Lauren instantly felt fear as she spun and her gaze flew to Amanda's. "What if it's the jerks from my work?" she whispered.

Amanda hesitated, paled, and whispered back, "How would they know where I live?"

"We work in real estate. Duh! We do title searches all the time."

"Do they know my last name?"

Lauren shrugged.

Amanda rose to her feet and tiptoed closer to the door. "I'll peek."

Lauren grabbed the largest knife in the kitchen and a rolling pin. She ran for the door too, ready to do battle if they tried to break down the door to steal Wrath. Amanda frowned and glanced at the things Lauren gripped in her hands, before rising up to peek out the tiny hole in the door. Amanda jumped back, spun, and looked terrified as she met Lauren's gaze.

"Two really large men wearing all black with sunglasses are out there. They look huge," she whispered.

"Lauren Henderson?" The male outside spoke loudly. "You called the NSO. We are here as you requested. We know you aren't a crazy female anymore and we've come for our male. Will you please allow us in to see Wrath? We mean you no harm."

Lauren eased closer to the door, rose on tiptoe and peered through the tiny hole. The two men were really large but the glasses and prominent bone structure assured her they weren't trying to trick her. She dropped back.

Amanda gave her a questioning look.

Lauren nodded at her. "Let them in."

Amanda shook her head. "Did I mention they are really badass looking and huge?"

"Open the door. Damn it, Amanda. Wrath needs help."

"Fine but I am going to annoy the shit out of you in the afterlife if you get us killed."

Lauren rolled her eyes. Amanda unlocked the door and slowly opened it. She jumped back, almost tripped, as two very tall, wide men wearing all black stepped into the room. They had long hair, down past their shoulders, and were wearing identical sunglasses. They closed the door behind them.

One of them frowned and slowly reached up to remove his sunglasses. Lauren was shocked when she met a pair of catlike eyes. He blinked at her before his attention dropped to her hands.

"Are you going to cut us or try to beat on us with those?"

Lauren realized she was still holding the knife and wooden rolling pin. She flushed and put them down on the nearest table. "I'm sorry. We were afraid you were the men from my work. Wrath is over there." She pointed.

They had to walk around the couch to see the unconscious Species. The man who'd spoken to Lauren suddenly laughed. "Is that a pink castle?"

"It's my niece's," Amanda admitted. "She loves to sleep in my room so I bought her that. It's got a princess under him."

The man grinned. "I'm Flame and this is Slash."

Slash was as tall as Flame, about six foot three, but he had streaked, light-brown hair with silver highlights. He removed his glasses. He had the same catlike eyes and they were an odd shade of blue. The man nodded at Lauren and Amanda.

"What happened?" Flame focused on Amanda.

"Talk to her. I'm just the getaway driver. I didn't know what he was or I might have at least bitched more on the drive here but she's my best friend so what else could I do? She said to drive and I put the pedal to the metal."

Flame turned to Lauren. She quickly explained everything that had happened and retrieved the dart she'd saved, handing it to Flame.

"This was what they stuck him with. I kept it in case you could test it to tell what drug they used."

Flame took the dart and sniffed it. He cursed. He dug out a cell phone and quickly dialed someone. "We need a helicopter out here now. Wrath has been tranquilized with a heavy dose of sedative and a paralyzing agent. There's a park half a block from here. We'll meet it there." He hung up and stared deeply into Lauren's eyes. "You did really good, human female. The sedative lasts longer with the paralyzing agent. It's a trick those bastards discovered to stop our bodies from working through their drugs as quickly. His heart could stop if they overdosed him."

Lauren nodded. "Will he be all right?" She was worried.

Flame nodded. "I believe so. His breathing is steady and strong. Grab some clothing quickly. We are taking you with us."

"But—" Lauren started.

"Let me grab my bag," Amanda said at the same time. Amanda shot Lauren a dirty look. "They want to take us with them. Be a friend, shut your mouth and let's grab some clothes."

Lauren frowned.

"Duh! Hunky guys. Move your ass, Lauren." Amanda was already turning, running for the stairs. "Don't leave without me!"

Lauren glanced at Flame and couldn't miss his shocked expression or widened eyes.

"Did she say hunky guys?"

Lauren sighed. "She's single and looking."

Flame frowned. "Looking for what?"

"She doesn't have a man in her life and she wants one. You're both men."

Flame relaxed and laughed. "Oh."

Slash made a weird noise. "What does she want one of us for?"

Flame grinned. "She's looking for a mate."

Slash shook his head. "Not me. Females are trouble and I don't want a mate."

Flame chuckled. "One wouldn't want you either." He stared at Lauren. "The helicopter will be arriving in fifteen minutes and we must leave here in seven to meet it. You may want a spare set of clothing."

Lauren ran upstairs to find Amanda in a fit of packing. Lauren shook her head, staring at three open suitcases on the bed and her friend tossing clothes at them.

"Put the cocktail dress down. We're leaving in a helicopter and that means one bag."

"But I have to look good. Did you see the both of them?" Amanda fanned herself. "So hot."

"They either fit you inside the helicopter or all those bags you're packing. How badly do you want to leave with them?"

Amanda hesitated. "Right. I can do one bag." Her voice lowered. "Who knows. Maybe I won't need any clothes." She winked. "Dibs on the talker. He's got the deepest, sexiest voice, and did you see those eyes? Meow! I totally want to rub him."

Lauren lowered her voice too. "They have really good hearing and he probably just heard what you said."

"Then he knows how I really feel. Life is too short not to go after something you want. I've learned that."

"I know you have. Let me help you. One spare outfit, something to sleep in and we should be good."

"You can borrow whatever."

"Thanks."

They returned downstairs and Lauren immediately went to Wrath's side to check on him. He was breathing slowly and deeply, his coloring was good, but he still didn't rouse. She was really worried about him. She turned her head to find both Flame and Slash a few feet away watching her intently.

Flame stepped forward. "I'll take Wrath. Please don't try to run. You will be safer with us than staying here. The people who shot him may be looking for him."

"Oh, we won't run," Amanda assured sincerely as she smiled up at him. "Try to lose me—it won't happen. I don't want to leave your side."

Flame grinned. "I like you, female. You are direct."

"That's me." Amanda winked. "Direct and single but you could change that."

Lauren stood and allowed the other man to bend down where she'd been. It stunned her when the large New Species just lifted Wrath as if he weighed nothing, shifted his body, and straightened with the other New Species draped over one broad shoulder.

"Let's go." He turned and his partner opened the front door.

"Holy shit," Amanda gasped.

Flame turned, eyeing Amanda silently. Amanda stared at him.

"He weights a ton and you just lifted him like he's a body pillow."

Flame wrapped an arm around the back of Wrath's legs to keep him secure. "We are strong."

Slash walked forward and put Flame's glasses back on his face, hiding his eyes.

Slash put his own glasses back on. "Let's go."

Flame nodded. "Females, let's go."

Amanda grinned at Lauren. "We're females."

Lauren shook her head and sighed. "Really? I thought you were a drag queen."

"Bitch." Amanda chuckled, elbowing her.

"Geek," Lauren mouthed back. She noticed the two New Species men were watching them silently. "We're ready."

"So..." Amanda smiled. "Where are you taking us?"

"We're returning to Homeland," Flame informed them, leading them out of the condo.

A black SUV waited at the curb and the driver opened the doors and the back. He wore sunglasses too but Lauren just knew he wasn't New Species since she could see his nose clearly. He reminded her of Brian and worry ate at her.

"Did you guys find Brass, Shadow and Brian? Did you save the two women I work with? They were being held hostage."

Slash shrugged. "That is not our mission. We don't know. We were sent here to pick up Wrath and whoever was with him."

Flame put Wrath in the back of the SUV and then he, Lauren and Amanda sat in the backseat. The driver and Slash took the front seats. Lauren turned, watching Wrath. She reached over and touched him to make sure he kept breathing.

"Why are you keeping your hand over his chest?" Flame asked.

Lauren turned to him, not knowing what to say.

"Oh, they spent last night together," Amanda chuckled. "She's seen him naked."

Lauren blushed. "Shut up, Amanda."

Flame chuckled. "Really? You and Wrath?"

Lauren ignored him and Amanda. She turned her attention back on Wrath. *Why isn't he waking up? If the drugs were going to kill him, wouldn't they have done that by now?* She kept her hand on him, feeling him breathe, as they drove down the street.

Chapter Eleven

ꕥ

The NSO Medical Center wasn't like anything Lauren would have imagined. It was a large building with a glass front. Inside were chairs lined along the wall, a long counter, and behind that were desks and open space. She saw hallways on each side of the room. Wrath had been wheeled down the one on the right and Lauren waited with Amanda. Slash left with their bags, stating that they needed to be searched, but Flame sat down with them in the chairs by the windows.

"What is your association with Wrath?" He removed his glasses and studied her.

"I met him yesterday. I was kind of taken against my will to where they were staying. Headquarters? Whatever that is. Wrath was assigned to take care of me and watch me. I had an incident with one of your kind. There was a fight between him and Wrath. I spent the night in Wrath's room with him."

"Tell me you did something with him," Amanda urged. "Please tell me you didn't let an opportunity like that go."

Flame frowned as he stared at Amanda. "What opportunity? To share sex with one of my kind?"

Amanda smiled at him. "Your kind? Hell, I'm talking about a cute guy."

Lauren wished a hole would open up under her. "Amanda has been single for a long time. She thinks if a good-looking man is interested that I should be interested too."

Flame nodded. "I see. It is not a race issue but just a male issue?"

"I don't care what race you are," Amanda flirted. "You're hot."

Flame laughed. "Thank you. You are attractive as a female too." He glanced at Lauren. "Have you shared sex with Wrath?"

Her face warmed more. She was totally uncomfortable where the discussion had headed. "That's none of your business."

"She admitted to seeing him naked." Amanda chuckled. "She had sex with him if she's smart. She's been single a long time too and she'd really be dumb if she had the chance and didn't take it."

"Amanda, stop. He's going to think you're nuts."

Amanda smiled at Lauren. "Shut up. I'm flirting."

Lauren pressed her lips together and was grateful Flame seemed amused by her friend's outrageous behavior. Lauren tuned them out while she stared down the hallway where they'd taken Wrath. An older man with white hair entered the hallway and walked toward them. Flame stood.

"How is he?"

"919 will be fine."

Lauren frowned. "919?"

"That was his testing-facility name." Flame nodded at the doctor. "Thank you, Dr. Treadmont. Is he awake?"

"He is. He's showering." He paused and studied each of the women. "Would one of you be Lauren?"

Lauren's heart did a somersault. "That's me."

The doctor met her gaze. "He asked about you. He wanted to know where you were."

"She's here." Flame hesitated. "He has taken the name Wrath."

The doctor nodded. "I'll update his files. It's good that he chose a name."

"Tell him the female is here and safe." Flame shifted his stance. "He'll rest easier knowing that."

Dr. Treadmont walked back down the hallway and Lauren felt Flame's gaze on her. She turned and lifted her head to look at him and found him grinning.

"What is that look for?"

"You shared sex. For him to ask about you right after waking up tells me this."

"That's my girl," Amanda laughed. "Good for you. You're not as dumb as you look."

"Please stop embarrassing me," Lauren almost begged.

"She doesn't look dumb." Flame gave her an up-and-down run with his gaze, looking confused.

"It's because she's blonde." Amanda winked. "We tease blondes about being dumb but she's actually really smart. She's just kind of a prude."

Flame chuckled. "I see. I know what a prude is. It was my word of the day not too long ago." He turned to stare down at Amanda. "We are learning new words so we get a word of the day. Are you a prude too?"

"God, I am so not," Amanda admitted.

"Should I leave the room so you can attack him?" Lauren was only half kidding.

"Attack me?" Flame frowned. "Why would she want to do that?"

"I meant it to mean making a pass at you. Do you know what that means?"

Flame grinned. "I do."

Wiggling her eyebrows, Amanda grinned at him. "Would you be interested?"

Flame growled. "I would be."

Lauren couldn't miss the way her friend's eyes widened when he made that slightly scary sound. "When they make noises like that, it's a good thing. It means he's interested."

"Hot damn!" Amanda chuckled. "Way cool!"

"Please get a room first," Lauren pleaded, not wanting to see her best pal in action with a guy, up close and personal.

Flame moved closer to Amanda. "I have a room. After my shift is over I will show it to you if you want to see where I live. It's a one-bedroom apartment located in the men's dorms. Females are allowed to visit there."

"I'd love to see where you live." Amanda smiled up at him.

"You will be assigned somewhere to stay if my people plan on keeping you here overnight or for a few days." Flame pulled out his cell phone. "Let me call and see what they want done." He walked away from them and across the room.

Lauren eyed Amanda. "Are you sure you want to go to his room? You shouldn't tease a man like that."

"Who's teasing? Look at him. I'd love to get him out of his clothes."

Lauren sighed. "He's definitely not a puppet type."

"Definitely not." Amanda agreed.

Lauren lowered her voice. "They growl when they get turned-on and have sharp teeth he might show you. No tail or fur so please don't ask him about those." She shot a glance at Flame, saw his back was turned and he seemed intent on his phone conversation, before taking Amanda's hand. "Just don't get your feelings hurt if this doesn't work out. I hope it does though. He seems really nice but try to take it slow, okay? I can't handle seeing you with a broken heart again."

Amanda squeezed her hand and released it, suddenly very serious. "I can't let what happened to me ruin the rest of my life. I just hope the scars don't turn him off if I get him to that point."

"I'm really proud of you for being so brave. Have fun but be safe."

Lauren studied her friend and remembered getting that horrible call five years ago. Amanda's live-in boyfriend had shot her and she was in critical condition. He'd turned out to be a real piece of shit who'd duped her best friend, taken out a hefty life insurance policy on her and then tried to kill her after making it appear as if a robbery had gone wrong. Amanda had fought him off long enough to reach help before succumbing to her injury. Lauren had stayed at her side for three days in intensive care until Amanda had started to recover.

Flame returned to them. "You were assigned a visitor's cottage. It's a two-bedroom. I hope you don't mind sharing. We have some other human guests and the housing is full except for the one."

"We don't mind," Lauren said softly. "Thank you."

"I was told to escort you there now."

Lauren glanced at the hallway. "What about Wrath? I'd like to see him before we go."

Flame nodded. "I'm in no rush. It shouldn't take him long."

They waited until Wrath finally came walking down the hallway. Lauren stood and took a few steps toward him. Wrath smiled and walked right up to her, their gazes locked together. He'd changed from the camouflage fatigues into jeans and a formfitting T-shirt. Lauren didn't miss noticing his well-defined muscular arms and wide shoulders.

"Thank you, Lauren. I was told what you did to get me out of there. You risked your life for mine."

"You fought Vengeance to save me. I guess we're even."

He cupped her face. His gaze left hers to study her hair and he sighed. "I hate seeing it like that."

She smiled. "I'm sorry. I could take it down."

His hands rose to the top of her head. He pulled the pins out one by one and unwound her hair. Lauren felt the weight of her hair falling down her back. Wrath's fingers brushed through it. He smiled and his hands rested on her shoulders.

"Much better."

"Are you all right? I was worried when you didn't wake up after a few hours."

"I'm fine." His fingers were playing with her hair. "What you did was very stupid but brave. They could have captured you too or just killed you for trying to save me."

"I'm sorry you didn't capture Bill."

Wrath blinked. "He was captured. We captured Bill, two other males and the female as well. We are trying to identify them. Shadow, Brass and Brian were recovered. They are well, along with the two innocent females they used to control our males."

Lauren let that information sink in. Her boss and coworkers were arrested and that put her out of a job. Of course on the whole, it was a good thing. They were monsters who'd worked for Mercile. "I guess I'll be sent home."

He nodded. "Tomorrow."

Swallowing, Lauren hated the twinge of pain and loss she felt. "I guess I won't see you again, will I?"

He leaned closer. "I would like to spend time with you while you are here."

"I'd love that."

Wrath nodded and his hands dropped. He glanced at Flame over Lauren's shoulder. "I will go where you take her."

"They have been assigned human housing. You can meet them there when you've been cleared."

"The doctor said I am fine to leave."

Wrath took Lauren's hand and tucked it over his arm. Flame opened the door and offered Amanda his arm. They walked toward a golf cart that was parked at the curb.

Flame drove with Amanda next to him while Lauren and Wrath sat in the back. Flame took them to a cute yellow cottage-style house next to a large lake. He parked in the driveway.

Lauren just wanted to be alone with Wrath but came to terms with the fact that the other couple would be with them. Flame led Amanda into the house first. The living room was spacious with an open floor plan to a dining room and kitchen. Down a hall were two bedrooms that had their own bathrooms.

Flame pulled Amanda aside after the house tour but his words carried. "I am off shift now that I've brought you home. Would you still like to go see my apartment?"

Amanda smiled. "I'd love to." She took his hand. "Is this going to be an all-night tour or am I coming back here tonight?"

"It's your choice but I would like to keep you all night."

Amanda reached down, grabbed her bag and waved at Lauren. "Don't wait up. I'll see you in the morning."

Flame took the bag from her hand. "Allow me to carry it. Are you hungry? I'd like to take you to a bar. We can eat and dance before going back to my apartment."

Amanda smiled up at him. "You're perfect. Has anyone ever told you that?"

"No, but I like hearing it."

Lauren watched the couple walk down the hallway and out of sight. She heard the front door close. She turned her head to peer into Wrath's dark gaze.

"Tomorrow is goodbye." Lauren felt depressed instantly. "Will you stay the night with me?"

He nodded. "I hoped you would ask me to sleep with you one last time."

Lauren backed up into the bedroom, tugging on his hand. He closed the door behind them. Lauren released his hand and reached for her shirt. She shoved it over her head, dropped it and kicked off her shoes before she reached the bed. Wrath advanced on her, following her step for step. She stopped and unfastened her bra, let it drop and smiled at him.

Wrath growled. Encouraged, Lauren reached for her borrowed stretch pants. She hooked the waistband with her thumbs, making sure she caught her panties as well. She pushed them down her legs and stepped free of them. She stood in front of Wrath completely naked.

"This is our last night since I'm going home tomorrow." Lauren moved, putting her hands on his chest. "I want to go all the way."

His features tensed. "You want me to enter you?"

"Yes."

The look in his eyes baffled her. He almost looked sad. "I can't." His voice came out raspy.

"Why not?"

"There are things you don't know about me. I don't want to risk hurting you. I have been damaged, Lauren. I could lose control and that would be a dangerous thing."

She shook her head. "I know you won't. You will be very gentle with me. I know that from the way you touch me. I trust you. Have some trust in yourself."

"I—" He closed his mouth.

"You won't if you're afraid of getting me pregnant. I'm on something that prevents it. I have a clean bill of health."

He shook his head. "That is not my fear. I have been harmed in the past and it makes me afraid I might revert to that conditioning. It could make me dangerous."

Lauren sat down, ignored her naked state, and tugged on him until he sat next to her. She turned to face him, stared into his eyes and licked her lips.

"There's nothing you could tell me that would change how I feel about you. I've done some reading on New Species and I heard rumors that sometimes some of you would end up killing the jerks who held you. Is that it? Did you kill some of them? If that's it, I'd award you a medal. They deserved it for everything they did."

The pain reflected in his eyes tore her apart.

"That isn't it."

She took a deep breath. "Just tell me. The worst thing is keeping a secret. Once it's out, we can deal with it."

He gripped her hand and his gaze drifted away from her to stare at the carpet near their feet. Lauren waited patiently, didn't want to push him, and wondered if he'd really talk to her. She was hopeful.

"My life in the testing facility was rough."

She squeezed his hand but remained silent, waiting for any details he wanted to share.

"But then they moved a few of us to a new place. There was Shadow and another male we didn't know. He had a mate but the humans killed her."

Tears filled her eyes at the horror of what he must have seen and endured but she kept silent, waiting. He refused to look at her and she saw his mouth tense, a coldness seep into his stare, and his voice deepened with emotion.

"They drugged me to make me aroused, hooked me to a machine and showed me videos of human naked women touching themselves to force my seed from my body. They would do it for hours until the pain became too much and I would pass out. I grew to hate the sight of human females." He paused and finally lifted his gaze to hers. "I feel rage, thinking about what was done to me, the humiliation I suffered, and I know you aren't responsible but I'm afraid of losing control. I might have a flashback and cause you pain."

Lauren blinked back tears. "I'm so sorry, Wrath. You're a victim and you're right—I wasn't there and I'd never be a part of that." She gripped his hand tighter. "They can't hurt you anymore and we don't have to have sex if you aren't ready. We could hold each other. I'm okay with that. I don't believe for a second that you'd hurt me though. You're the gentlest man I've ever met."

His eyebrows arched.

"I mean that. The way you touch me is special and you make me feel that way too."

A soft growl rumbled from his throat. "I never believed I'd be attracted to a human female but you're all I want."

"I'm right here. We can do whatever you want or what you feel comfortable with."

"Do you see me as less now?" There was a catch in his voice. "Less male now that you know what was done to me? I should have been stronger and resisted more. They took my seed by force."

Her heart broke. "No. God no, Wrath." She moved, released his hand and climbed onto his lap. He let her and she wrapped her arms around his neck, pressed her face against his throat and clung to him. "You're amazing, strong, determined and brave. You hunt down those assholes that hurt your people. That's so noble and yeah, brave. I admire you and think you're the sexiest guy ever. I'm so glad you came into my life."

His arms wrapped around her and he clung. "I want you but I'm afraid."

Her lips pressed against his skin and she kissed him. "I'm not afraid of you. Why don't you get naked? I love holding you."

"I want that." His voice deepened again.

She leaned up enough to see his eyes and smiled. "We'll just take everything slow and see how it goes. You're highly overdressed."

He chuckled and suddenly lifted her off his lap, placed her in the middle of the bed and rose to his feet. "Give me a moment to fix that."

He stripped out of the shirt, revealing that wonderful array of perfectly sculpted abs first then his broad shoulders. The discarded shirt hit the floor. He bent, tore off his shoes and straightened. Lauren held her breath as he reached for the front of his pants and opened them. She loved the expanse of skin that assured her he was going commando.

"No boxers?"

"They didn't have the kind I like. I'd rather do without."

"I like you without."

He chuckled and shoved the pants down, freeing his cock, and impressing her by revealing how thick and hard he was. He might not be ready for sex but his body said otherwise. He stepped out of the jeans, kicked them away and hesitated.

"I don't want to just hold you."

Her gaze lingered on his hard-on. "I see that. I'm all for anything you want to do with me."

A soft growl came from him as he slowly took a step toward the bed. Lauren stretched out on her back, hesitated then spread her arms and legs apart on the bed. Wrath's eyes widened and he put a knee on the mattress.

"What are you doing?"

"You're in charge." She held his gaze. "I'm all yours."

The color of his eyes seemed to darken as they widened but he put his hands down flat, crawled over her, and a deep snarl came from his parted lips. "Don't say that."

She wasn't afraid. "That you're in charge or I'm all yours?"

His gaze lowered down her body and he licked his lips. "That you are mine. I might believe it and you wouldn't want that."

"Why?" Her heart raced.

He lowered, his face hovered by her throat and warm breath fanned her there. "You have no idea what I want from you."

"Tell me."

Dark eyes stared into hers. "Right now I want to touch you."

"Go ahead."

He leaned in and brushed a kiss over her throat. Lauren turned her head and exposed it to his wandering mouth. His tongue traced a pattern, sharp teeth gently brushed too and she resisted the urge to reach up and grip his shoulders just to have something to cling to.

He lowered down her body slowly, teasing and awakening her desire with each caress of his hot mouth. She moaned when he sucked on one taut nipple and her restraint broke. Her hands lifted, opened on his chest and she stroked him.

A deep growl came from him, his hot, rigid cock brushed her leg and she spread them wider apart. Wrath suddenly pulled away and their gazes met.

"I want you. I hurt for you."

"Take me. I said I'm yours."

One of his hands opened on her belly, slid downward and Lauren moaned when his thumb rubbed against her clit. His fingers tested to see how turned-on she was, found how sleek and wet he'd made her with his mouth, and just the sight of his body.

"You're so ready for me."

"Always."

His eyes closed and his head hung a little. Lauren's hands left his chest to cup his face. Wrath looked at her then, his gaze tortured with longing and something else…maybe fear. She hated to see it and lifted up until their mouths were mere inches apart.

"Kiss me, baby. It's okay."

An eyebrow arched and his lips curved upward just slightly. "Baby?"

"An endearment. I could call you sexy. You really are."

"So are you."

"Please kiss me?"

His focus fixed on her mouth. He paused and glanced back up. "I've never kissed someone before on their lips."

She tried to hide her shock. "Never?"

His gaze slid away as he avoided hers. "My experience is limited to breeding experiments. Mercile enjoyed testing pain drugs on me more. The few females who were brought to me didn't want that kind of intimate personal contact since they didn't know me."

"Look at me, Wrath."

He did and she identified his pain for sure then. "I'll kiss you. Everyone has a first time. I'm honored that I'll be yours." *And I wish I were your last.* The idea of him touching someone else, being with them, made her chest hurt. "Just relax and put your mouth over mine. I'll show you."

Wrath wanted Lauren, wanted to experience everything she offered and so much more. Fear of losing control gripped him but he breathed through the worst of it. She was waiting for an answer.

He allowed all the feelings he experienced to surface and quickly determined that he'd do anything to avoid causing her any harm. It gave him confidence to face down his ultimate fear of having a flashback to his abuse strike at an intimate moment.

He was a strong male. He needed to have faith in his ability to control himself. He refused to allow the past to ruin his future. Lauren stood before him, willing, ready and eager to share sex with him. Nothing had ever tempted him more.

He took one deep breath and made a decision. *I can do this. I'm stronger than my conditioning. Lauren isn't someone I'd ever harm and that will keep me from losing control.*

He leaned in closer, closed his eyes and Lauren fused her lips to his. Her tongue darted out, licked the seam of his mouth and entered to explore. He was hesitant at first but caught on quickly, devouring her with passion as they stroked each other.

His weight pinned her down as he stretched out over her. Lauren lowered her head back to the bed, released his face and wound her arms around his neck. She only paused for a second before wrapping her thighs around the backs of his legs. With his height, he'd have to move up for him to enter her since his cock was below her pussy. She arched her back to urge him on. Her breasts pressed tightly against his chest and Wrath snarled.

Kissing her, the taste of her, drove him insane. He wanted more, needed it, and quickly knew he was about to lose control. The desire to take her nearly overrode everything else. *Calm,* he ordered his body. *You can do this. Focus on her desire…her desire…*

He knew they needed to slow things down. He was determined to be the male she deserved and that would be one who could take her with tenderness. It might kill him but he wanted her bad enough to face his own inner demons.

Wrath broke the kiss, breathing hard, and their gazes held. Desire made his eyes appear almost black as he stared at her. Lauren gazed back and ached for him to continue kissing her. Her lips parted but he spoke first.

"I want you."

"I want you too."

He braced his arms on the bed and pushed his chest off hers, put space between their bodies, and Lauren refrained from protesting. She unlocked her calves from behind his thighs to free him. She didn't want him to feel trapped by her in any way and prayed he wouldn't call their lovemaking to a halt.

"Will you roll over for me?"

Her mind worked. "You want to take me from behind?"

"Yes." His voice deepened.

She nodded. "I like doggy style."

He suddenly laughed.

Her face burned, realizing he might take that wrong considering he was New Species and had mentioned he was canine. "I mean—"

"It's fine. I knew you meant the position. It is my favorite." He chuckled again. "I wonder why."

Lauren laughed and rolled over, breaking eye contact with him. Wrath rose to his knees, his hands gripped her hips and he pulled her up to her knees.

"Spread your legs just a bit more," he urged. "I'm much taller than you. I need to put my legs on the outside of yours but you're so small I'm afraid I'm going to hurt you."

She looked back at him and arched her eyebrow. "Most people don't tell me that."

All humor left his face. "I don't want to hear about other males touching you. It makes me angry."

"I meant that people don't call me small."

"You are, compared to me."

She couldn't dispute that. Wrath was one big, tall, buff man. She spread her thighs, braced her palms flat on the bed and watched him shift his legs to the outside of hers. It made them more level in height that way. One of his hands settled on the small of her back and his gaze locked on the curve of her ass. He stared into her eyes finally.

"I will go slow. Tell me if I hurt you."

"I'm hurting already but it's because I want you so bad."

His tense features relaxed slightly. "I am in control."

"Yes, you are."

He smiled. "I was reminding myself of that, not you."

"You aren't going to hurt me, Wrath. You're large." She glanced at his straining cock. "But I can take you."

"I hope so," he muttered.

"I'm a lot of things but fragile isn't one of them."

Lauren turned away, lowered her head and waited. She knew he was worried about having a flashback to being abused but she trusted him. His hand pressed down and she lowered, tilting her ass higher, and he leaned in closer until the head of his cock touched the slit of her pussy. He rubbed her there, stroked her clit, and she moaned. The blunt head of his cock slid higher, pressed against the entrance to her vagina, and he slowly pushed.

Her body didn't admit him easily. She'd never been with someone so large and she spread her legs a few more inches to help him. He growled, pushed, and she moaned slowly at the feel of being parted and stretched.

"You're so tight," he snarled.

The sound turned her on more. Wrath sank into her slowly. She could feel her pussy stretched taut around his thick shaft and it felt amazing. She kept her body relaxed as he eased in. It allowed her to adjust to him as he bent over her. One hand braced on the bed next to her shoulder as he curved over her back, pinned her there, and his other hand reached around her to play with her clit. A louder moan broke from her lips.

"Am I hurting you?"

"Don't stop," she got out.

He growled in response, withdrew a little and pushed inside her deeper. His hips moved slowly, rocking against her gently until he was fully seated. He paused there and allowed them both to share that connected feeling before he started moving again. He fucked her faster, his finger tapped the bundle of nerves, and Lauren realized she wasn't going to last long. It was too much sensory overload having him inside her while he stimulated her clit.

"Yes," she panted and shoved her ass back at him, urging him to go faster.

He bent farther over her, his weight pinned her and his mouth opened on her shoulder. Sharp teeth raked her skin but didn't hurt. He turned his head, lightly bit the back of her neck and Lauren cried out as the climax struck.

Wrath snarled, jerked his mouth away as her vaginal muscles clamped down tightly and fluttered from her orgasm. Pressure suddenly filled her as his hips ground against her ass. He stayed buried deep inside her, his hand jerked away from her pussy and his arm wrapped around her waist to lock her in place.

His body tensed, shook violently and he cried out. It wasn't like any other kind of sound she'd ever heard—it was a mixture between a shout and a howl. His cock felt as if it grew even bigger. She felt pressure inside her pussy, and warmth.

Wrath leaned his weight to the right, kept a tight hold on her and they both fell over on the bed, hitting it on their sides. It surprised Lauren but she didn't protest as he wrapped around her more, spooned her tightly in his embrace and brushed a kiss on the side of her arm up near her shoulder.

"Did I hurt you?"

She turned her head as he bent his elbow and propped his head on his hand. Their gazes met and she smiled. "No. You, um, feel bigger."

"My dick swells. Are you sure it's not painful?"

She reached up, cupping his cheek. "I'm okay. It doesn't hurt."

"I can't stop it. I will hurt you if I tried to pull out right now. I'm locked inside you but it will only last a few minutes."

Shocked a bit, Lauren stared at him. "Locked inside me?"

He nodded. "It's part of my altered—"

"It's okay," she promised him, not really caring why it happened but just accepted it. "It's part of you." A chuckle escaped. "Don't move. Stay right where you are."

Shock filled Wrath's eyes. "You think this is funny?"

"Not exactly funny but it's kind of cool from my prospective. Most men just pull out and roll away from a woman after sex. You can't do that, can you?"

"No but I admit I have no urge to separate us. I'm where I want to be."

Lauren knew right then she had lost her heart to the big New Species.

Chapter Twelve

Lauren wiped at tears, feeling grateful Wrath hadn't been there to witness her sadness at leaving the NSO Homeland. Regret lingered too, that they hadn't gotten the opportunity to say goodbye but she knew it was probably for the best. It was hard to walk away from the man she was pretty sure she loved but they'd captured her coworkers so there was no logical reason for her to stay at his side anymore.

"Don't cry." Amanda handed her a tissue. "Then you'll get me started and I don't look good at all with red, puffy eyes."

"We didn't get to talk during the trip back to your condo since we didn't have any privacy." Lauren studied her best friend. "How did your night go?"

Amanda sat on the couch next to her in the living room. "Not exactly as I had planned. Flame took me to their bar, it's really cool there, but they don't drink alcohol. Kinda weird, huh? They are totally into juice and sodas. Anyway, we ate a nice huge steak dinner—he ate three of those babies—but he is a mountain on legs, in his defense. I swear, I feel downright dainty compared to that hunk of kitty love."

A smile curved Lauren's mouth. "God, please tell me you didn't call him that."

"I didn't. I thought it though. He can dance." Her eyebrows wiggled. "I mean, he can bump and grind with the best of them but he got called away on some emergency."

"I'm sorry."

"Me too. It was cool though. I didn't want to go back to the cottage since I knew you and super stud needed some alone time. I hung out with their women. Man, they are kickass fit. I got to go to the women's dorm for a sleeping party in the living room. They think it's totally cool to have slumber parties and I admit it was fun. There are a few little women too. They made me feel huge. You know?" She rested her hands on her stomach. "But we watched movies and they asked me a ton of questions. Now it's my turn to grill you." Amanda studied her. "You are in love with him, aren't you?"

"I'm that easy to read? I think so. He's amazing. I never thought I could fall so fast for someone."

"You don't cry often yet there you are sniffing and leaking. Is he going to call you?"

"I don't know. He had to leave for some kind of meeting early this morning. They needed to ask him questions about what happened. He kissed me, told me breakfast had been delivered to the living room and he'd be back as soon as he was able. Instead two guys showed up after I ate and told me it was time to go."

"I'm sorry."

"Me too. I wanted to at least say goodbye. I left him a note and my phone number."

"He'll call. I saw the way he looked at you." Her gaze dropped to Lauren's chest. "And you've got big boobs. Men always call women with those."

Hot tears welled again and Lauren admitted the truth. "I wasn't ready to let him go."

Amanda leaned closer, putting her arm around her best friend. "This is probably why we don't date. We suck at this whole one-night-stand thing."

"I had two nights with him," Lauren corrected. "How am I going to sleep without him tonight? He holds me so tight in his arms. I never felt so safe and so right with someone before. He's special."

Amanda suddenly snorted. "You slept? Shame on you. I would have stayed up to enjoy every moment with Flame if he hadn't had to leave. That's a man who needs a warning label tattooed across his chest that says 'a woman needs a strong heart to climb on this ride'. I'm really disappointed I didn't get to find out for sure but I gave him my numbers. He promised to call."

"I'm sure he will." Lauren took her hand. "What a pair we are."

"I just hope it wasn't something dangerous for Flame. The word emergency implies something awful, doesn't it? The women said it was probably something to do with those stupid protesters who are always giving them grief. I wanted to march out to the front gates and bitch-slap the lot of them. My poor Flame has already been through so much and having to deal with the worst types of human trash just pisses me off." She sighed. "Especially since it took him away from me. He's such a good man and I just wanted to kiss him and take him to bed. I think I'd make a hell of an ambassador to show him some real goodwill and human kindness."

Lauren laughed. "You're terrible."

"No. I fell for him and wanted to fall on a mattress with him too."

"You're such a slutty bitch."

"You're such a…oh hell, Lauren. I think I'm in love. You know how we used to snort at the love-at-first-sight thing? Not so funny now. I spend a few hours with him and he's all I can think about. It's not just because I'm horny and haven't had a date in forever. He's funny, sexy, and I know he would have rocked my world."

"Lucky you. I am pretty sure I'm in love with Wrath."

They sat there. Lauren yawned and caused her friend to do it too. They glanced at each other and laughed.

"Are you staying here or are you going home?"

"I need to go home and check on Tiger." Lauren pulled away. "I also want to be there in case he calls me. I don't want to miss it if he does. God only knows where my cell phone ended up…or my purse. I have keys though." She patted her pocket. "One of the NSO guys handed them to me and said my stuff would be delivered to me later. I don't even have a car until they bring it back."

"Do you want to borrow my car? I'd offer to drive you myself but I'm so tired I'm afraid I wouldn't make it back without falling asleep behind the wheel. I've got a hot redhead to live for."

"The walk will do me good and it's only a few blocks away. I hope Flame calls you soon."

"Me too." Amanda looked sad. "I'd so love to go visit him again but only when he's got a few days off because I don't want him called into work again. Want to go storm the gates of the NSO with me soon? That's my plan if he doesn't call me. I'm not letting this one go."

"Only if Wrath wants to see me."

Amanda nodded. "I'm sure he will. I saw the way he looked at you when we were in their medical place and he first walked out from the back."

"I hope you're right. I'd feel better about it if I'd gotten to talk to him before they took us away." Lauren stood, stretched, and another yawn passed her lips. "Call me later. Much later."

Amanda turned on her side, stretched out on the couch and waved. "Lock the door, okay? I'm too tired to go upstairs."

"Sweet dreams."

"You know who I'm going to be spending my snooze time with. He's total fantasy material."

Lauren let herself out, locked the bottom lock, and made sure the door latched well. The sun hurt her tired eyes but she trudged home and managed to avoid most of her neighbors since they'd already left for work. Walking inside her home reminded her of the last time she'd been there with Wrath and his team members.

"Tiger?"

He was stretched out on her bed. He raised his head and peered at her.

"No scary guys today, unfortunately, but hopefully at least one of them will be back soon. You're going to like him as much as I do once you get past that whole growling thing. It's sexy. Trust me." She kicked off her shoes, stripped out of her clothes and stared at her answering machine by the bed. It didn't blink, there were no messages, so she closed her eyes as she curled up under her covers.

He'll call. He has to call me!

* * * * *

Wrath was furious as he glared at Fury. "You had her escorted off Homeland and taken to her friend's home while I was gone? How could you do that? I planned to spend time with her after I was done with my duties."

The other male frowned. "Is she your mate? I wasn't informed of this."

"No."

Fury tilted his head, studied him closely, and Wrath shifted his stance. The scrutiny left him feeling nervous and meant he'd probably crossed a line. "Are you sure the female isn't your mate? You look upset, Wrath. Does she mean a lot to you? We need to discuss this."

"She means a lot." Opening up about his feelings wasn't easy to do except with Shadow. "Lauren is all I think about and I'm feeling anger that I didn't get to say goodbye to her. I hoped to see her again soon."

Fury smiled. "I understand. I felt a pull toward my Ellie from the first. We went through a lot but she was special to me. Perhaps you should take this time apart to do some thinking. You agreed to give the task force at least six months of your time and I know you're still struggling to come to terms with who you are."

The idea of not seeing Lauren for five more months sent panic shooting through his body. She could meet another male who might claim her in that time or she could forget about him.

"You are bad at hiding your dismay." Fury chuckled. "She left you a note." He withdrew it from his back pocket and held it out. "Read what she wrote and perhaps it will be something you wish to know to take that stricken look from your face."

Wrath lunged for it. He tried to ignore the way his hand trembled as he unsealed the envelope. It tore in his unsteady grip but the paper inside remained undamaged. He stepped back, ignored everything around him, and read the few short words. His heart slowed to a more normal rate and he glanced up to find Fury watching him.

"She gave me her phone number and wants me to call her."

"Poor bastard," Tiger sighed, stopping next to him. "I heard enough from my office to know you're going down too."

Fury frowned at his friend and shook his head. "It is not a disease or a bad thing to find a female who makes a male feel whole. Ellie is the center of my world and so is our son."

Wrath jerked his head up, his gaze leaving Lauren's neat writing to gawk at the male in front of him. "You have a son with your mate? I hadn't heard that."

Tiger gripped his shoulder. "You've been gone, you were with the task force, and they aren't allowed to know about our ability to have children. Only Tim knows the truth. Fury's son is a few weeks old and as cute as hell. I'm surprised to find Fury in the office. He rarely leaves his mate's side but I'm betting our females have swarmed his house again to visit and make funny noises at the baby. He tends to flee in case they snarl at him over how painful labor seemed. Our women are very protective of Ellie but of course, no one took it worse than

Fury did. Trisha threatened to Taser him and have Slade sit on his back if he didn't stop snarling at everyone when Ellie had a contraction. He acted as if everyone was the enemy because he got protective of her." Tiger laughed. "Are our females still threatening to neuter you?"

"Shut up," Fury snapped.

"They are." Tiger snickered. "None of our females want to do surgery on my nuts and that's another reason I don't want a mate." He released Wrath. "Don't allow our females to get attached to yours if you take a mate. Only threats can come of it and a lot of pissed-off Species females with grudges."

"Don't you have phone calls to make or someone else to taunt?" Fury glared at him. "I was talking to Wrath."

"He loves me. My man is just grumpy because he's not getting any loving." Tiger laughed.

"I am though." A smile curved Fury's mouth. "There are many ways to do that."

Wrath glanced between the males, knew they were friends, and wished he could escape their good-natured argument. "I have a phone call to make."

"Not so fast." Tiger shifted to block his path and all humor left his face. "You did agree to work with the task force for six months and we can't afford to lose you. We're already one Species down since Vengeance didn't work out. Whoever this female is, she can wait."

"You could keep her with you. You have your own sleeping quarters, correct? I can talk to Justice and he'll be able to smooth things over with Tim."

Excitement struck Wrath for a few heartbeats as he absorbed Fury's offer. "I don't know if she'd agree to that."

Tiger growled. "That's too risky. She'd have to—"

"Agree to remain there during the rest of your mission." Fury shot Tiger a warning look. "He has feelings for the female. You may not understand but I do. I'd live anywhere with Ellie and she'd live with me. It could be inside a cave in the woods but she wouldn't care as long as we'd be together. This female might return his strong feelings."

"Tim is going to pitch a fit. I know him better than you do. He will adamantly refuse to allow a human female to live with one of our males."

Fury shrugged off Tiger's assessment. "That's not his call to make since he works for us and we give the orders." He stared at Wrath. "You should find out how deep her feelings run for you. Justice and I both have mates and we understand how important they are to our happiness. He'll support me on this issue. Do you love her?"

"She is all I think about," Wrath confessed. "I've never been happier than when I'm with her."

"Sounds like love to me." Fury chuckled. "Stop wasting time with us and go call her. Find out if she loves you."

Wrath hesitated, staring at the other male. "What if she doesn't return my feelings?"

"It's her choice and her heart. You can't be mates unless the love and need to be inseparable flows both ways. It's what makes the mating bond alive. Just don't be surprised if she asks for time to figure out if she is willing to give up her life as she knows it to be with you. They are different from us and I've heard their males aren't as intense as we are. She may not take you seriously due to how some human males don't understand the true meaning of loyalty and commitment for life. It's your duty to tell her how we are, that it's for life, but you aren't allowed to share classified information about Species until after she is your mate."

"He means use condoms to prevent her from becoming pregnant and don't tell her there's a possibility of it until she's really yours. I'd wait until you live at NSO before you do that. We can't allow the humans to know we can have children. It's too dangerous and you getting her pregnant while living with the team would reveal our secret."

Wrath understood the importance of protecting his people and their future. "She is on the birth-control shot."

"Good. Make sure she keeps taking it. They assume we can't get them with a baby and might decide she no longer has to take it." Tiger spun on his heel. "I do have calls to make. Good luck."

Fury nodded toward Wrath. "Call her." He stepped into his office and closed the door.

Wrath hesitated and walked outside to find privacy under a shade tree before he pulled out his cell phone and dialed the number on the note Lauren had left him. His stomach twisted from the uncertainty of what she would say or how she would react. They hadn't started out on good terms when he'd taken her from that warehouse but emotionally they'd come a long way in such a small amount of time. He was willing to risk anything for her, even the pain of rejection.

* * * * *

The phone woke Lauren and she lunged for it. "Hello?"

"Lauren."

Her heart instantly squeezed at hearing that deep, wonderful voice. "Wrath."

"The briefing took longer than expected and then I was asked to be present while Bill was interrogated. I returned to the cottage to see you but was informed you'd been escorted to your friend's home." He paused. "I wanted to see you and was deeply disappointed that you were gone."

"I wanted to see you too but they didn't exactly give me a choice." She sat up and clutched the phone tighter, fully alert. "You got my note."

"I have it right here."

She only hesitated for a second before blurting out what she really wanted to say. "I miss you already. I know I shouldn't say that, it probably makes me seem kind of clingy but I just wish I was there with you."

"I miss you too and wish you were in front of me." He growled.

Her body instantly responded to that sexy sound. "Don't do that. It makes me miss you more and I'm remembering the night we spent together and how you would make that exact sound when we were making love."

He growled again and she closed her eyes, listening to him breathing, and hated holding the phone instead of him.

"I want to touch you so badly." It stunned her that those words had come from her but she didn't regret them. It was the truth.

"I will be returning to the task force headquarters tonight." He paused. "Would you stay there with me? It's too dangerous for me to stay with you since your place isn't secure. I have to stay where I've been ordered to live—at headquarters. I know my room is small. My bed isn't as big as yours and you have a pet." He growled again. "It sounds as if I'm trying to talk you out of staying with me but that's not the case. I'm just thinking of all the reasons you can use to say no but I'm hopeful you won't. I want to sleep with you in my arms."

"I'll pack a bag." Lauren grinned, opened her eyes, and excitement gripped her. "I'll make sure Tiger's food dispenser is full and I'll ask Amanda to check on him. I'll even put out extra for him and fill the bathtub so he's got plenty of water. Not that he really needs it since he roams outside a lot of the time and probably has his own ways of getting it. I don't have a job anymore so no worries about not going to work tomorrow." She laughed. "Is it just for tonight or should I pack for a few days? Where do I go to meet you? I'll drive there if they've dropped off my car. Just give me a place and a time. I'll be there."

"I'll pick you up. Pack a lot of clothes. Expect me between seven and eight."

"I'll be ready!"

"I will be there as soon as I am able, Lauren. I can't wait to see you."

"I can't either. Hurry up. I'll be ready! Goodbye, Wrath."

"It is never goodbye between us, Lauren. I'll see you soon." He growled again and hung up.

"Yes," she laughed, hung up, and dialed. Wrath wanted to see her, spend time with her and she needed to pack. First though, she needed to call Amanda.

"Hello?" The groggy voice assured her that her friend was still sleeping.

"Sorry I woke you up. He called me! He's coming tonight to pick me up and I'm going to spend at least a few days with him. Did you hear from Flame yet?"

"No." Amanda sighed. "But I'm happy for you. Run with scissors, Lauren. If there's ever a time to take a stupid and crazy chance where you know you could get hurt, well, he's the one."

"Thank you. I'm sure Flame will call you soon." She glanced at the clock. "He's probably still at work. It's only four o'clock. Most people get off work around five, right? You're a wonderful person and he'd be stupid not to realize that. He seemed pretty smart to me in the little amount of time I got to spend with him."

"I hope so. He did say he was sure I could make him roar."

"Roar?"

"He's part lion or something. He purred at me a few times while we were rubbing up against each other on the dance floor. It was the hottest thing. I swear it made me wet."

Lauren chuckled. "TMI, Amanda. I don't need to know that."

"We're best friends so there's no such thing. Give it up, besty. Does Wrath purr?"

"He's canine. He growls and snarls." She bit her lip. "His cock swells at the end of sex and he's locked inside me until it goes down. He snuggles with me afterward. It's wonderful but that information stays between us."

"No! Seriously? Wow. What did that feel like? The swelling?"

"Amazing."

"I wonder if Flame swells. I can't wait to find out. Of course now I'm a little frightened. He is seriously hung. I couldn't miss that when we were pressed together and I noticed it was 'ouchie' sized. I can't imagine it if he swells even bigger. I might take on more than I can chew." She chuckled. "Or suck. You know what I mean?"

"Way too much info."

"What about Mr. Hunk? Anything to write home about in that department?"

"He's more than a letter. He's worth an entire book."

Amanda snorted. "Maybe it's a New Species thing. Good thing they weren't mixed with horses. That would totally be scary, right?"

"No shit." Lauren scooted off her bed and dropped to her knees to dig one-handed under her bed for her suitcase. "I need to pack. I'm taking my cell if it's in my car—hopefully they've brought it back here by now—but if not, Wrath probably has a phone I can use. I'll call you in the next few days."

"You better. Are you going to the NSO? Tell Flame to call me."

"We're going back to that headquarters place. It's a secret so keep it hush-hush."

"I'm the queen of discreet."

"Right."

"What is it like there?"

"He lives there underground. A lot of people hate them so keep your lips sealed about that place. He says it's not safe for them to live where it isn't secure—I guess that means anywhere other than their compounds—or he'd just stay here with me. He's got a private room with a bathroom. They also have a big room with a kitchen and a living room. There's even a pool table."

Amanda laughed. "You could have him do you on it. Pool table sex is hot."

"It's in a room everyone uses."

"Even better. The thrill of maybe getting caught."

"I worry about you." Lauren laughed. "Go back to sleep. I need to pack and get ready."

"Don't worry about how long you're gone. I could pop in there and check on Tiger. I know where you keep the food."

"Thanks. That would be great."

"That's why we have keys to each other's places. Are you telling anyone else where you're going?"

"Nope. Just you. If my family happens to call, tell them I'm out of town or something. You know the drill."

Amanda laughed. "I'll tell them you joined a nudist colony that worships women with big boobs. I'll say a dozen sex-starved naked men grabbed you in a van and you're doing the whole free love thing. They'll enjoy that. When they start to bitch at me about how come I didn't try to stop you, I'll just tell them I was looking out for you by buying you a don't-come-a-knocking-if-the-van-is-rocking bumper sticker. I'll remind them how supportive I am."

Lauren laughed. "Don't you dare."

"I'll assure them that you'll come home as soon as someone knocks you up and with all that sex with a dozen guys it shouldn't be too long since you forgot your pills. They don't know you take the shots, right?"

"I swear, Amanda, if you do that, and I know you would just to freak out my bitchy sister, I'll personally call your grandma and tell her you're ready for her to introduce you to men again because you so desperately want to get married. Remember the last time she started sending men your way? I don't know which one was worse. The mortician she hooked you up with since most of her friends keep dropping dead or the horse jockey she met when she was dating that guy who liked going to the races. What was he? Four-nine? You had nightmares for months about those dates you suffered to avoid hurting her feelings."

"You wouldn't dare. It took me months to get Monty the creepy-ass mortician to stop calling me. He sent me flowers and I swear to God he stole them from graves. He missed one of the condolence cards once. He said he really wanted to have sex with me in a coffin and that was his version of tempting me to go on a second date with him. I refuse to talk about the jockey. He asked me if I'd ever worn a saddle while I tried to eat my dinner. I don't even want to go to that bad, ugly place, Lauren. That was just mean to remind me. You just forget Grandma's number and I'll make up something nice to tell your family if they call me."

"Love you. I'll call."

"You better. Love you too."

Lauren hung up, dropped the suitcase on the bed, and returned the phone to the cradle. It didn't take long to pack, shower and grab her e-reader. She downloaded a bunch of books while it charged, packed it, and prepared Tiger to be alone for a few days.

Wrath was coming! She glanced at the clock, only had a few hours to go, and time couldn't move fast enough.

Chapter Thirteen

ꟸ

Lauren grinned when the doorbell rang early and rushed for the door. Wrath must be as impatient to see her as she felt to see him. She'd already gotten dressed, had eaten an early dinner and was more than ready to leave when she threw open the door with a grin in place.

Her joy died instantly when a stranger stood on her doorstep instead. The tall, thin woman bore an uncanny resemblance to her boss, Mel Hadner. Her heart raced, she tried to hide it, and had a sinking feeling this person just might be related to the woman who had tried to hurt Wrath and his team.

"Hello," she got out. "May I help you?"

"I believe so. You work for my sister, Mel. I went to her office today after receiving an urgent message from her yesterday that she needed to speak to me but no one was there. Do you know where my sister is?"

"No," Lauren lied. "No idea at all. She was in her office when I left." That part was true.

"Today?"

"Yesterday. Today is my day off."

A frown curved the woman's thin mouth downward and lines appeared on her forehead. "I came here because I spoke to a few of the businesses near the office and they saw you pushing a man out of the office in a chair. They said he appeared drunk. My sister is missing and so are a lot of your coworkers. I've already been to their homes and they aren't there, didn't sleep in their beds last night, and haven't been seen." She crossed her arms over her chest. "Their cars are in the parking lot but they have just disappeared. Do you know anything about that?"

Shit! Think! "I had a man come in to see condos yesterday who had a bad knee. He injured it when he stood after sitting so long viewing listings. I had to push him out to his car."

The woman's arms slowly lowered and a cold look entered her eyes. "That was almost believable. Not bad. You're a fast thinker, aren't you, Lauren?"

Mel's sister lunged suddenly and grabbed Lauren's shirt with both hands, shoving her back. A large man suddenly stepped out from where he'd been hiding against the wall next to the door and entered the apartment. Two more came from the other side of the door and yet one more entered and closed the door firmly behind the five intruders who'd invaded the living room. It was the last guy who held Lauren's attention.

He wore a hat and sunglasses but his features were something she'd learned to identify with the wider cheekbones and flatter shaping of his nose. His full lips were sealed but she knew he was New Species. His big frame and tall height also pointed to him being one of them. Of course the three human men were no slouches in the muscle and sheer-size departments either. They all were bruisers.

"Where are they, Lauren? I'm not screwing around. I want answers."

"I don't know. Who are you?" She knew she was in deep shit. The only thing she couldn't figure out was why a New Species was with Mel's sister. She forced her gaze away from him to stare at the woman still fisting her shirt. "I haven't seen them since I left the office yesterday."

"140? Tell me what you smell right now."

The New Species lifted a hand, removed his glasses, and stepped forward. He inhaled, sniffed a few times, and his eyes widened slightly while he frowned. Lauren stared into his eyes. They were catlike—an amazing swirl of bright blue, rimmed along the outer edges with deep amber. They were beautiful, striking, and almost unreal. No one should have eyes that looked like that. His tan skin and black hair only added to how dramatic and exotic they appeared.

"Well?" The woman turned her head and shot him a glare. "Tell me, damn it."

"Their scent isn't here at all. Not on her or inside this place."

"What do you want to do, Mary?"

The woman shot a glare at one of the thugs with her. "She knows something."

She shoved Lauren hard enough that she hit the back of the couch but she was free. Lauren assessed her situation and knew it was grim.

Mary backed up a step, held her gaze, and it chilled Lauren to the bone. If the eyes were the windows to a person's soul this woman had a dead one. A shiver ran down her back.

"I know you brought a New Species into the office yesterday. My sister called me and told me that. She was freaking out and scared. I didn't get home until this morning to hear her message. Where the hell are they, Lauren? Tell me the truth and stop playing games or you're going to regret it."

"I don't know anything," Lauren lied. "Mel pulled me into her office and said the client was a rapist and she shoved me out the back door. That's all I know. She wasn't alone with him though. Brent and both John T and B were in her office with her." She paused. "I was sure Kim was still there when that happened and Gina should have been in her office. Ask them again because I'm sure they were there after I left."

One of the thugs snorted. "They can't talk. They had accidents."

Horror hit Lauren and she didn't need to ask. They were dead. She wanted to scream but managed to stay on her feet, a real victory since her knees wanted to collapse under her.

"I'm a real bitch," Mary admitted. "You're going to tell me where my sister and her friends are or I'm going to have

140 start breaking your bones one at a time until you tell me what I want to know I have my sister back. You took that New Species out of there in a chair after he was shot with a tranquilizer dart. My sister said they had one of them out cold and two more captured. All the witnesses couldn't be wrong and they know you. Kim and Gina were pawns who are no longer a threat." Her gaze raked Lauren. "A chubby blonde was pushing him out of the office and down the street. Tell me now or you're going to die a really slow, agonizing death. You are done lying to me."

Lauren stared up at 140, decided she'd be honest, but only with him. "Why are you with them? You're being called a number as though you weren't freed. Is that it? I've seen two New Species fight and you could kick these humans' asses. Your people have been freed and you don't have to stay with these people."

He growled. "They have my female."

Shit. Lauren swallowed. "Can't you just kill them and get her back?"

Mary struck hard and fast, backhanding Lauren in the face, and the blow threw her back against the couch where she nearly flipped over the thing. Pain made her curse, grab her injured cheek, and glare at her.

"I guess you weren't joking about being a bitch, were you?"

"Where is my sister and her men, Lauren?"

She figured out quickly it would be a death sentence the moment she confessed they'd been taken by the NSO. They'd already killed the other two innocent people who'd worked in her office. Kim and Gina hadn't worked for Mercile but they'd been witnesses to what had happened inside that office. Her only hope would be to stall for an hour until Wrath and his team arrived. If they arrived at seven. Otherwise there'd be two hours to drag out to give her any hope of surviving.

"I might let you live if you just tell me." Mary rubbed the hand she'd struck her with.

Lauren glanced at the New Species. He shook his head, telling her not to trust what she was told and she believed him. He was obviously being forced to be there but it didn't mean he liked it if he was willing to give her that tiny signal of warning.

"Okay. I'll tell you the truth." She remembered the conversation she'd overheard from her office. "I didn't know what he was until Mel told me. Brent and both Johns wanted to ransom the three guys for a lot of money."

Mary glared at her.

"Mel didn't want to cut you in on it. Brent said to throw you off the track and they'd just disappear after they got paid. Your sister doesn't want to give you any of the money. I'm sorry but that's the truth."

Lauren hoped her plan would work. Mel's sister should be mad, thinking Mel was trying to screw her out of a bunch of money. It might possibly make the woman buy the story enough to wait around for a nonexistent phone call.

"If I don't answer, they are going to be in the wind. That's what John T said."

Mary hit Lauren again, harder, and the taste of blood filled her mouth as she spun hard and sprawled over the back of the couch. It was the only thing that kept her on her feet.

"You're lying. My sister wouldn't do that."

"You didn't find the courtesy van in the parking lot, did you? That's what they used to transport the New Species. They don't want whatever phone they are using traced to my phone since I'm calling the NSO. They are having some stranger call and I'm supposed to answer with a code word. You're not getting that out of me because then I know you'll kill me." She watched her blood drip on the couch, stain it, and used her hand to wipe some of it from her chin. "It's Mel you should be pissed at. I'm just the idiot who lost her job and desperately needed money enough to do whatever she said."

"They wouldn't run like that," one of the men said. "Mel wouldn't do that. You know that, Mary. She's lying."

"You have five minutes to tell me where my sister is before I have the animal start breaking your bones. Do you know he can snap them in seconds? I won't have him kill you by breaking your neck. You'll lie there bleeding on the inside, in the kind of excruciating pain you can't even imagine, until you die of shock. It will be the longest minutes of your life. Tell me where to find my sister. You're going to die but it's up to you how painful you want your last moments to be."

Lauren saw the truth in her eyes and one glance at the New Species' grim expression assured her that he believed it too. She had to change tactics. Nothing was going to save her if she didn't think of something fast.

She allowed the tears to well in her eyes, not something difficult to do since the inside of her mouth hurt.

"Fine. I do have a number for them. I was supposed to call it when the NSO has the cash ready for the exchange but I'll let you talk to your sister. She will tell you not to kill me."

"What's the number?" Mary seemed to calm.

"I don't know it by heart. John T wrote it down and I hid it in case the NSO showed up here. It's in the top drawer of my desk."

"Get it." Mary jerked her head at one of the thugs.

The desk sat across the room by the hallway and Lauren's mind tried to figure out her next move. It was hard to think around the fear that gripped her but she wanted to live. She purposely stumbled, held her head, and hoped she appeared more hurt than she really was. Her cheek throbbed, the taste of blood lingered in her mouth, and she knew the inside of it was torn up a bit. One of Mary's men trailed closely behind her as she walked to her desk.

The desk was old, a hand-me-down from an uncle, and the drawer had to be wiggled to get it open. A stack of her bills were on top and she shifted papers. The thug moved to her side. She glanced at him, but he wasn't watching what she was doing. Instead he peered around the room.

Her fingers brushed metal under the papers, gripped it, and Lauren allowed sheer panic to lead her actions. They were going to kill her, she wasn't getting out of this mess alive, and there was only one thing to do. Her other hand gripped the small scrap of a fortune cookie message that had been funny enough to keep. She purposely dropped it on the floor.

"Sorry. I'm shaking. It's on there."

He bent to retrieve it and Lauren acted. It horrified her, she screamed inwardly, and knew her life changed forever in the instant that she plunged the letter opener as deep as she could into the back of the man's neck. Her hand fisted the handle of the sharp implement, she twisted hard to do more damage and heard his gasp of pain.

His body dropped to the floor, she dodged in the opposite direction and hit the side of the wall in her haste to flee toward her bedroom. She screamed, hoping to draw attention from the neighbors. It might scare off the remaining people in her living room if they thought the police would be called.

"Get her, 140," Mary yelled.

Lauren reached her room, spun around and grabbed the doorknob. She got a glimpse of the big, grim New Species coming at her as she slammed the door closed and locked it. The shelf full of paperback books next to it was only waist high but heavy as she had to strain to tip it over. It fell sideways to block the door. Another scream erupted as something big thumped against the door.

She spun and dashed for the bathroom, slammed that door too and locked it. She tore open the drawer that housed her makeup to block the door and scrambled to climb up on the sink. The window she always left halfway open for Tiger was her only escape.

The thing stuck, didn't want to open all the way, but desperation drove her to find that extra amount of strength to jerk it up. A loud sound in the other room assured her that the New Species had just burst through her barricade and now had breached her bedroom.

It wasn't easy to fit through the tight space and she silently swore to get on a treadmill as she wiggled and finally fell to the ground below the window. Pain shot up her arms as her hands braced the impact to protect her face from hitting the grass first. She fought to her feet and screamed again, sure some of her neighbors would hear her now that she was outside and ran for the front of the building.

Two strong arms grabbed her and tore her right off her feet. The body she hit was solid, big, and two thick, muscular arms were banded around her waist. Lauren twisted her head and stared up in horror at 140.

"Don't fight me. I don't want to hurt you," he growled.

"I'm not your enemy," she panted. "They are. Please let me go. You're New Species."

Confusion clouded his extremely blue eyes. "What does that mean?"

"It means they are bad people and you're not. New Species are good."

He refused to release her. "They have my female and will kill her if I allow you to escape. I'm sorry."

Hot tears filled her eyes. "Please let me go."

"I wish I could." He hesitated. "I smelled unknown males in your home and again in your bedroom. Some of them are like me, aren't they? Did you really help her sister kidnap others of my kind?"

"No. I rescued him and helped him get away from her sister. His name is Wrath and I love him."

His eyes widened and he frowned. "You don't scent as his mate." He sniffed. "I can't smell him on you. Where is her sister? Do you know? Tell me."

"I showered but he's coming for me. Please let me go. Her sister and the men with her were arrested by your people. They have them at the NSO. That stands for New Species Organization and they run it. A lot of your kind have been freed from Mercile. They'll help you if we get out of here and call them. You're one of them and they'll do anything for you."

"I can't allow you to escape. If Mary doesn't call the one who holds my female every hour, he's been ordered to shoot her in the head." He turned her in his arms, threw her over his shoulder as if she were as light as a body pillow and growled.

"Act as if I hit you hard enough to knock you out," he ordered. "Don't move or talk. I'm going to try to save you. I know you have no reason to trust me but I don't wish you harm. I will treat you as if you are the mate of another one of my kind. I would hope someone would do the same for my female if ever given the chance."

Lauren went limp over his shoulder, knew no amount of struggling would get her free of someone so strong, and closed her eyes. Regret swamped her over telling him the truth about her ex-coworkers' whereabouts. She shouldn't have trusted 140 but she wanted him to know how hopeless her situation was. She couldn't help Mary get her sister back, that was a lost cause, and now she was useless. That meant they'd kill her.

He moved fast, her body swayed with each step, and she knew when they entered her home again because, even with her eyes closed, she felt it when they stepped out of the sunshine.

"I didn't tell you to kill her," Mary snapped. "Fucking stupid animal."

"She's not dead. I struck her and knocked her out." Anger made his voice deepen. "The 'fucking stupid animal' will tell you how to get your sister back if you'll allow me to speak. I know where she is. I made this one tell me by torturing her with pain."

Lauren listened, confused over his lies, but willing to try to trust him. She was all for anything that would keep her breathing. The silence was long until Mary finally spoke.

"Where is Mel? What do you mean, get her back?"

"This one is mated to one of my kind. His scent is all over her and she told me that the NSO has taken your sister and her technicians. You can exchange her for them." Bitterness laced his voice. "You are very aware of how far we will go to protect our mates. Hers will get your sister safely back to you if you return his female safely to him."

"I don't know about this," one of the thugs grunted. "It sounds fishy."

140 growled now. "You remember how protective we are of our mates. You have me leashed like a dog to protect mine. Otherwise I'd kill all of you. He'll get your sister and her technicians to you, whatever it takes, to get his female back." He turned his head, his hair brushed Lauren's side where her shirt had ridden up and it tickled slightly.

"You keep your hands off her. Scent stays with a body for a long time and he won't want her back if another male mounts her. He'll insist on smelling her first before he accepts her back. I know your fondness for forcing females but leave this one alone. He'll know and reject her." His head turned again. "Order him to leave her alone if you want your sister and her technicians back."

Lauren felt sick at hearing that last part. Her skin crawled thinking that one of those guys obviously was a rapist but 140 was trying to protect her from that too. The fingers gripping her thigh slightly squeezed, almost a reassuring gesture. She guessed he could figure out how terrified she felt.

"How do you know for sure that her mate has my sister?" Mary had moved closer.

"Her mate has them. She was so terrified she confessed everything to me. Trade her for them. It will be the only way you will ever get your sister back."

The silence was lengthy. Mary sighed. "Fine. You better be right, 140. Since you're so damn smart, how do we set up this exchange?"

"Leave a note and a way to contact you here. He will come for her soon. You know we can't be away from our females for long without going insane."

Mates go insane if they are separated for too long? That bit of information stunned Lauren but of course, 140 could be lying. He was bullshitting a lot to try to save her butt. Gratitude filled her. The New Species was buying her time and trying to protect her.

"It had better work, 140." Mary sounded furious. The threat was clear that he'd pay if he were wrong.

"What do we do with Olson's body?" It was one of the thugs asking the question.

"Leave him. I don't want him staining my trunk." Mary sighed. "Write down my disposable cell number and leave it on the couch next to her blood. He won't miss it there, will he, 140?"

"No," he growled. "He will not."

* * * * *

Wrath waited impatiently for the team to gather and leave. He turned his head and stared at Shadow. The male met his gaze and smiled.

"You are impatient."

"I don't want to be late. I told Lauren I would be there between seven and eight o'clock."

"Brass and Tim are arguing again."

"I'm aware." Anger surged through Wrath. "He doesn't want a civilian staying in headquarters and he's still upset we had her there in the first place. The walls aren't thick enough to miss most of what is being said."

"He insisted that a background check be done on her and he's right for that. She did have a strong tie to ex-Mercile employees. She worked with them."

Wrath snarled. "Lauren is not my enemy."

"Tim is worried about the rest of us." Shadow suddenly grinned. "She's so dangerous."

"That is not funny. She couldn't hurt a fly."

"I'm aware. I saw her face when you were fighting with Vengeance. She's not used to brutality. She practically begged us to call an end to it. She worried about your safety."

He allowed that information to sink in. "She will worry about my duties with the task force. We put our lives in danger constantly when we go out to retrieve our enemies."

"I wouldn't mention that aspect to her. Let her believe you mostly do paperwork."

"I will not lie to her."

"I didn't suggest you do but I just wouldn't offer more information than necessary."

He thought about that. "Do you regret agreeing to work for the task force?"

"No." Shadow shook his head. "It's been good for me. You?"

"The same. I met Lauren."

Shadow smiled. "You seem more healed since she came into your life. I'm glad. Perhaps one day I'll meet a female who challenges me to face my fears."

"I hope so."

Tim stormed out of the office with Brass behind him. Tim refused to meet their gazes but Brass smiled.

"We're leaving to pick up your female, Wrath. Tim and his team are going to give us backup support. He's irritated that we've left headquarters so much without more of the human teams backing us up. It makes sense, especially after we were taken prisoner. We came to an agreement."

"Thank you." Wrath meant it. He turned his attention on Tim. "Lauren is no threat to us."

"Women are always bad news." Tim spun, stormed for the door and yelled over his shoulder. "Don't let her paint anything pink, damn it! It's still my building."

"Pink?" Shadow glanced at Wrath and Brass. "What does that mean?"

"I have no clue," Brass sighed. "No wonder their females seem to enjoy our company more. Humans are strange."

Wrath had to agree with that assessment. He didn't care if Lauren wanted to paint or what color she chose. Just having her at his side was all that mattered.

Chapter Fourteen

ꟃ

Lauren was scared and angry at the same time. The backseat was a tight fit with 140 sharing the limited space. She'd given up playing unconscious after her New Species protector whispered for her to sit up.

Mary and one of her men argued at the front of the car. The other man remaining followed in another vehicle. There was no way Lauren was going to get a chance to escape but she did glance out the windows to track where they were going. She'd learned her lesson to be more aware of her surroundings after leaving the task force headquarters but having no idea where it was located.

"I don't care what your opinion is, Marvin. Shut up. You're giving me a headache."

The thug driving shot the woman in the passenger seat a glare. "We should do some experimenting while we have her." He glanced back at Lauren and his gaze lowered to her chest before he turned to face the road again. "I'll warm her up before we hand her over to one of them."

Mary snorted. "You're so pathetic. You didn't work for Mercile for the money, did you? It was the opportunity to grope women who couldn't stop you. Forget her. You heard the animal about their sense of smell. You aren't fucking up my chances of getting my sister back because you're a pervert."

Lauren stared at the balding head of the man in front of her and hated him instantly. She had a sinking feeling this was the man 140 had warned off about touching her. He was gross and seemed to have the morals of an alley cat.

"Your sister is a bitch and none of them are worth risking our lives over. They got caught so I say screw them."

Mary reached over and pinched his arm. He howled, jerked away, and the car swerved.

"Don't do that. I could wreck the car."

"My sister is worth more alive to me than you are. Don't you ever forget that." She paused. "Plus she knows too damn much. She won't talk but give it a month or two if they lock her up and I bet she'd sell out our own mother. Prison is a nasty place and we all want to avoid it. She could screw us over if we don't save her ass and that goes for her team too. They know our names, we all worked together, and do you trust any of them not to turn us in to save their own asses if they are offered a deal?"

"Fucking hell," Marvin muttered as he hit the brakes at a red light. He turned his head and stared at Lauren's breasts again before frowning at Mary. "I need some stress relief. I won't take her pants off. Haven't I been loyal? Haven't I done all the shit you tell me to?"

140 growled. "Her mate will know. Do you want me to tell you what you ate for lunch? I can. She would also fight." He turned his head and fixed his gaze on her. "Would you allow him to make use of your body in any way? He likes to open his pants and order females to put their mouth on him."

Disgust made Lauren want to throw up and she snapped her head to meet the gaze of the man in the seat ahead of her. "I'd rather die and I can promise you, if you unzip near me you'll need a trauma surgeon after I am done with you."

Mary laughed. "I'm starting to like her just a little. The idea of someone biting your dick off is amusing." She reached out and pinched Marvin's arm again. "Stop being such a sick son of a bitch. Eyes on the road and shut your mouth unless it's not related to thinking with your dick."

"Bitch," Marvin grumbled. "Stop doing that to my arm. It hurts."

The light turned green and he stomped on the gas in anger. "Stop drawing attention to us, idiot." She turned in her seat and glared at Lauren. "And I'm watching you too. The windows back there are tinted but don't try to draw any attention. Got it? The car behind us will make sure we get away. If any cops show up he will do something to distract them."

"She's not stupid," 140 said and sighed. "She knows you need her and she will survive if she just complies to get you what you want." He shifted his gaze to the driver. "It is your own technicians you should worry about."

"He's getting damn mouthy," Marvin cursed. "Sounds as if we need to remind him of his place." He suddenly barked out a laugh. "Do I need to visit your mate again?"

"Shit," Mary snapped and her hand flew out and hit the thug in the back of the head as 140 snarled loudly in the confined space. "You are a fucking idiot. You really want to taunt him in this car? I don't want to die when he lunges across the seat and rips your head from your body."

"She said she'd prefer to die than feel your hands exploring her body again. I'd kill you if you had harmed her or ever do. She's mine."

Lauren saw the pure anger on 140's features, the way his hands fisted in his lap, and how his chest rose and fell harshly as he seemed to pant through a fit of rage.

"He isn't going to do shit to her," Mary swore, trying to keep the peace for once. "I took care of it when he molested her, didn't I?" She twisted in her seat and stared at 140. "Calm down now. That's an order. Remember our deal? You do as you're told and no harm comes to your girlfriend. Marvin is going to keep his big mouth shut from now on or I'll personally pinch something far more painful than his arm."

The glimpse Lauren was getting into 140's life made her angry enough to want to reach forward and break Marvin's neck herself. Of course she wasn't strong enough but she regretted he hadn't been the one she'd had to stab with the letter opener. The fact that she'd killed someone was pushed back. She couldn't deal with that now. Besides, the more time she spent with the arguing pair in front, the more justified it seemed.

"What is her name?" Lauren kept her voice down and hoped to distract the still-furious New Species.

He turned his chilly gaze on her and his nose flared. "Mine."

She let that slide, not really believing that the woman had that name. His gaze jerked to the driver and she knew that statement of possession had been for the driver's benefit.

"Is she feline like you or canine like…" She almost said Wrath's name. "My mate."

"She's primate."

"Oh." Lauren hesitated. "I don't think I've seen one of them yet."

"I thought you were mated to one." Mary frowned at her from the front seat. "A lot of them survived."

Lauren met the bitch's stare evenly. "I am. My mate is canine and all the people I've met at Homeland have either been that or feline."

"Primates aren't common." 140 spoke. "They didn't make as many of them. What is Homeland?"

"Shut up," Mary snapped. "Don't tell him a damn thing about the NSO. Got it, Lauren? Not a word."

She was tempted to keep right on talking but 140 shook his head. She sealed her lips together and clenched her teeth. She would bet that Mary didn't want 140 to know about any of his people being free. It would give him hope that he could be rescued too.

The car slowed and turned. Lauren glanced out the window and realized they'd entered an old part of town where a lot of businesses had closed due to the bad economy. It had really turned into a slum in the years since she'd frequented the area in her late teens and early twenties. Boarded-up windows became a common sight as they continued to drive down a few narrow streets.

"Do you know where we are?"

Lauren met Mary's calculating eyes and shook her head. "The east side of town. I am a realtor and I know my properties." They were actually on the border area of the south side and almost out of the city limits.

That answer made the other woman smirk. "Yes, you sure do know your areas." She faced the front of the car, dismissing Lauren.

They turned into a driveway blocked by an old security gate. Mary flipped down the visor and hit a remote. The gate shook and wobbled as it began to roll sideways to allow the car to pass through. Recognition struck Lauren instantly. The place had once been a popular nightclub. Jasper's had a new name painted on the back of the decrepit building, some restaurant name, but she was sure it was one and the same.

140 gripped Lauren's wrist gently when they parked and he kept hold of her as they exited the car. He faced Mary with a defiant glare.

"I have done everything you ordered and I have behaved. I want to see my female now."

Mary crossed her arms over her chest, lifted her chin and glowered at him. "Do you? You are sounding a bit too confident."

"Please," he hissed and lowered his gaze to the cracked tar.

That seemed to make the bitch happy and she dropped her arms to her sides. "Fine. Take her to a cage and you can go downstairs. I'll make the call."

"Thank you." 140 tugged on Lauren. "Come."

The back door was rusted metal. Marvin unlocked it with a key on the car ring and it squeaked loudly when it opened.

The interior was dark and the smell of mold, dust, and stale air assaulted Lauren's nose instantly. The floor felt uneven under her shoes as they walked through what used to be a kitchen. Outdated, stained, and broken cooking appliances indicated it hadn't been used in at least a few years.

Shock gripped her when they stepped out of the kitchen area into what used to be the dance area of the club. The windows were all boarded up and debris from parts of the ceiling littered the floor. Some broken tables had been shoved against the stained walls but it was the five large animal cages that made her stumble. They were about eight feet high, maybe six feet square and three of them were occupied. New Species males stood staring back at her from behind the bars.

They wore sweatpants, no shirts, and all looked as if they could use a bath. One of them growled—a dangerous sound—and his dark eyes fixed on Lauren. A chill ran down her spine at seeing the hatred directed at her as she glanced at each one.

"It is fine," 140 assured her.

He led her to one of the empty cages, putting her the farthest away from the men, and steered her inside. The floor was solid metal while the walls and ceiling were barred with inch-thick bars. He closed the door and Marvin moved close with the keys. The sound of it being locked was distinctive.

"Go, 140. Mark is expecting you. If you misbehave before you're locked in your girlfriend's cage, he's been told to shoot her in the head."

"I know." 140 spun, marched through another hallway that used to lead to the bathrooms, and was out of sight.

Marvin stepped closer to Lauren and lowered his gaze to her chest. "Do you want to eat?"

She said nothing but backed away from the door, not that she could go far.

"You do something for me and I'll return the favor."

"You're really pathetic and repulsive. I can totally understand why a troll like you would have to lock a woman up and threaten to starve her to try to make her touch your ugly ass. No thanks. I'd rather eat my shoe."

"Fucking bitch," he spat. "Wait a few days and say that then."

She turned her back on him to prevent him from ogling her breasts anymore and observed how much the old club had changed. The roof obviously leaked from the appearance of the yellowed and destroyed ceiling panels and the walls were stained. Someone had wallpapered near the boarded-up windows. It was peeling and blackened around the edges, which she figured was the source of the moldy smell that made her breathe through her mouth.

She glanced at the only light sources—the hallways from the kitchen and bathrooms. No lights were on in the open space. She doubted the overhead lights worked anymore due to the water damage.

The only thing inside her cage was a balled-up nasty-looking blanket in one corner.

"I'll let you use the bathroom if you open your shirt while you go."

Lauren spun and flipped him off. "I'd rather piss down my legs."

The guy's face turned bright red. He huffed and yanked the keys from his pocket. She tensed when he reached to unlock the door, knew he planned to hurt her, but someone walked out of the kitchen.

"Leave her alone, Marvin!" Mary yelled. "Jesus. You are a troll. Get your ass over here and follow me to the office. We have work to do."

Marvin hesitated but Mary turned around and disappeared. His voice lowered as he shoved the keys back inside his pocket.

"I'm going to hurt you, bitch. Don't get too smug. Just wait."

Lauren watched him go and figured he meant the threat. The creep was a total perverted asshole. She faced the three New Species when they were alone and felt fear at their hateful scrutiny. But they were locked up too. They couldn't get to her.

"I'm Lauren."

No one spoke.

She gripped the bars and gave them a firm shake but they were as solid as they appeared. She took a deep breath, blew it out and studied each one of the men. Two of them had feline traits while one had eyes shaped very similar to Wrath and Shadow's.

"Why are you looking at me that way? I'm locked up too and I am not with those assholes. I'm a good guy."

One of them frowned. "You're female."

"Yeah."

"A guy is a male."

Her mouth parted, stunned that he took what she'd said so literally. The blond one with catlike eyes sniffed the air. "She smells good. Maybe they want to do breeding tests."

"Breeding tests?" Her eyes widened. She understood they thought she might have been brought for them to have sex with and wanted to clear that misconception up immediately. "I was kidnapped so they could exchange me for other people. I'm not here to do any testing."

The dark-haired canine growled. "I want her. It's been too long since I had a female under me."

"It's going to be a lot longer because that's not happening." She frowned. "I'm hoping we're all found and rescued soon."

The one who'd been silent until then, a golden-haired feline, hissed. "By who?"

"The NSO. They'll be looking for me, well one of them will be, and if he finds me, he'll find you too."

"Who is he? What kind of name is NSO?"

"The NSO is the shortened name for the New Species Organization." She paused, realized by their blank stares that they didn't comprehend, and remembered they probably didn't know anything. Her guess was that they'd never been freed and she figured she was spot on about that since Mary had told her to shut up about the subject.

"New Species are like you, the people Mercile Industries created. My kind found out about what was being done to yours so they broke into the testing facilities and freed your people." She paused, expecting some kind of reaction, but their facial expressions never changed.

"They started the NSO. Your people have two large plots of land where they all live together and they search for New Species just like you who haven't been freed. Hopefully they will find us and we'll all be rescued."

The blond snorted. "She is here to taunt us." He turned his back, crouched down and sat on the floor. "Ignore her."

"That's rude and I'm telling you the truth. I don't know why you're in this place but I've heard enough to know the jerks who are holding you here used to work for Mercile Industries."

"They still do," the dark-haired canine snarled. "You are with them."

"I am not. Don't insult me like that. Mercile Industries no longer exists. They were exposed, put out of business, and everyone who worked in their research divisions and knew about the testing facilities are wanted by the police. They are facing serious criminal charges. I read that a lot of them are already serving extended prison time."

"Be silent. Lies." The canine snarled again.

He was starting to piss her off. "Don't listen to me but once I get out of here I'm going to do everything I can to send help back to you. You'll see then." She paced the small space. "Wrath will get me out of here." She had faith that he'd save her somehow, even if he did have to exchange her life for Mel and her other ex-coworkers.

The canine growled again. "I hope they brought her here to try to gain our trust and make us believe her lies. I will not be kind or gentle when I mount her."

The golden-haired Species growled. "Enough. She's human and they'd never hand her over to one of us. Did you see the way 140 treated her? The way he gently touched her? He implied she wasn't the enemy. He knows more about her than we do and I saw no rage in his eyes when he looked at her. I don't know why she is here but don't make threats until we know more."

"She's one of them." The canine growled again. "Our enemy. They are all evil and tell lies to try to fool us into doing what they want. She is planning something."

"I'm planning on getting out of here." She moved to the door of the cage again, gripped the bars and rattled the thing. Frustration rose. "I'll do everything in my power to send the NSO to rescue you."

"Human lies," the canine snarled.

"I resent that." She frowned, rattled the door again, but wasn't willing to give up just yet. Maybe she could shake the lock loose. "I get that you have been mistreated. I can't imagine all you've suffered but what I said is the truth. A lot of your people have been freed, they aren't locked up anymore and they will be searching for you just as soon as I tell them what I know."

"What does free mean?" The golden-haired feline squatting in his cage watched her with narrowed eyes.

"You won't be locked up anymore, no one will hurt you, and we're equal." She glanced at him.

"What does that mean?"

She turned away from the door to face him and sighed. "It means you have the same rights as I do. We're not enemies but instead friends. No one will test you anymore. You'll have homes instead of cages and you never have to deal with assholes like the ones who have you now."

The canine snorted. "Next she will say we will get to eat when we are hungry, get clean when we are dirty, and get access to females when we want one."

"That is exactly what I'm saying."

The blond turned his head and shot her a glare. "How many of us are a part of this NSO?"

"I don't know the exact numbers but hundreds at least."

"Lies," he growled, jerking his gaze away to give her the back of his head.

"Are any of our females there? Were they freed?"

Lauren met and held the curious gaze of the golden-haired feline. "Yes. There aren't a lot of them, from what I understand, but my best friend said she met a bunch of them."

"What is the bad news of this?" The canine was obviously the grim one of the bunch. "There is always a price. What do they expect for those privileges?"

"There is no they. I assume you think it's like here where they threaten you to make you do what they want or you're punished? I know they are holding 140's girlfriend over his head. The NSO are your people. They just want you to be happy."

"Lies," the blond hissed.

Lauren knew they didn't trust her, thought she was making stuff up, so she stopped trying. The only way to show them she wasn't full of shit would be to survive long enough to hopefully be exchanged and then she could tell Wrath about them. Maybe the NSO could arrive before they were moved.

Chapter Fifteen

ꟗ

Wrath strode quickly from the SUV and knew Brass and Shadow followed him. The sun had gone down, he was late—they'd been stuck in traffic—and he hoped Lauren hadn't given up on him and gone to bed. His excitement over seeing her could barely be contained.

He was about ten feet from her door when the smells filled his nose and he jerked to a halt. He sniffed loudly, knew the two males with him did the same, and he snarled. The smell came from Lauren's home and he could see that her front door hadn't been closed completely. He lunged, shoved it all the way open and alarm shot through him.

Brass moved to his side and sniffed. "Three human males, one human female, and a Species male."

"Do you smell that?" Shadow hissed. "Mercile."

"I do."

Fear shot through Wrath as another smell filled his nose. Blood, decay and death. He rushed forward, terrified he'd find Lauren's body as the source, but a human male lay crumpled on the floor in the darkness. It took only seconds for his eyes to adjust but one of the males flipped on the light.

"Lauren?" He yelled her name, rushed for her bedroom and halted again when he saw the destruction of the doorframe.

Shadow gripped his shoulder. "Someone broke through it."

A snarl tore from Wrath and he stepped over books that were spilled over her floor. The scent of the unknown male Species was stronger in her room, the only scent he could detect besides Lauren's, and he saw the busted bathroom door. The counter had damage from where a broken drawer had been ripped out. He was inside in seconds, stared at the open window and jumped up on the counter.

"The human is dead," Brass growled.

Wrath spun, pain shot through his chest, and he met the male's eyes.

"The male. Not Lauren," Brass assured him, yanking out his cell phone and holding it to his ear after he dialed. "I'm calling for assistance."

Wrath gripped the windowsill, had to fight to fit through it and saw signs on the grass of what must have taken place. He tracked the footprints, small ones and large ones, until he found where the male had grabbed her. Her footprints disappeared and the larger ones were deeper with the combined weight of the male and Lauren.

"He carried her," Shadow stated from behind him.

Wrath followed the tracks around the building and lost them when they reached the sidewalk near Lauren's door. He rushed back inside, crouched near the dead body and examined it with his gaze.

Shadow gripped the letter opener, jerked it out and sniffed the handle. He looked up and held Wrath's gaze. "Lauren killed this male. She had to be afraid. I can smell fear and it probably caused her to sweat, including her palms. Her scent lingers on the handle."

Brass' voice carried. "We're scenting an unknown Species male here and he's got the smell of Mercile."

"What does that mean?"

Wrath twisted his head and refrained from snarling at the task force male who'd driven them. He'd followed them inside. Lauren was gone and she'd had to kill someone. Wrath's worst fears filled his mind and he couldn't even speak around the lump that formed in his throat that she might be dead.

"A Species male has been here but he carries the smell of the soap Mercile always made us use. No free Species would ever purposely touch it." Shadow straightened. "Go outside and ask the neighbors if anyone saw anything. Bring them here if they did. We need to question them."

The man at the door turned, rushed out, and Wrath threw back his head. A howl tore from his throat. Lauren was gone. His gaze returned to the dead human on the floor. She'd killed him and that meant whoever had taken her would seek revenge for the death. They'd kill her as punishment.

"Keep calm," Shadow demanded. "You can't help her if you fall apart."

"They will kill her."

"We don't know that."

Brass cleared his throat. "There's blood and a note on the couch."

Wrath shoved him out of the way, leaned down and sniffed. Lauren's scent was the only one he could pick up on the couch and he knew the smell of her blood. There was only a little of it but it didn't ease his terror that she might be dead.

"They want the humans we captured yesterday returned to them and they want to trade Lauren for them," Brass said after reading the note.

Wrath turned slowly and glared at Brass. "We'll trade them."

Brass nodded. "We will. We'll get your female back."

"Our male chased her outside, captured her, and carried her. We found the tracks." Shadow said. "I don't understand. He could have allowed her to escape yet he didn't."

"I will kill him," Wrath swore.

Shadow gripped his arm and held tightly but Wrath refused to calm. He couldn't. Mercile employees had Lauren. He knew his ragged breathing was out of control but he couldn't get a handle on all the emotions warring inside him.

She was in danger, hurt, and every instinct inside him screamed for him to do something. Anything.

"Sir?" It was their driver, the human task force male.

Brass faced him. "Yeah, Ted?"

"One guy who lives in an apartment upstairs said he saw four men and one woman show up about two hours ago. He thinks one guy is still here since he never saw him leave." Tim's head turned and he stared at the dead body. "I'm guessing that's the one."

Wrath tried to jerk away from Shadow. He had questions for the human who'd seen something but his friend pulled hard enough to make him stumble.

"No," Shadow growled. "Calm down. You do her no good when you are in this condition. Take deep breaths."

He fought down his rage.

"They left a number." Brass studied Wrath. "Don't make a sound." He opened his cell phone, glanced around him and read the note again. "Not a sound." He dialed and put it on speakerphone.

"I see you got my note." The voice was female. "I don't know this number so I assume you're Lauren's mate?"

Brass arched his eyebrows at Wrath but spoke before he could. "Yes. When and where do you want to make the exchange? Don't harm Lauren or you will never see your people alive again."

"Is my sister still alive?" The woman's anger and distrust were easy to hear. "I want to talk to Mel right now."

"I am not at her location as you must know but it can be arranged for you to speak to her. I would like to hear my female to make sure she is alive."

"You're not talking to her until I get to talk to my sister. Call me back when you're with her. How long?"

"Give me an hour. I need to travel to where your sister is being held. She is well and so are the males who were captured with her. Her living arrangements are much more comfortable than the ones we were accustomed to while we were imprisoned."

She snorted. "At least we let you get laid occasionally. I'm mentioning that because Lauren is going to learn all about breeding tests and being passed from cell to cell if I don't talk to my sister in less than sixty minutes. I doubt your mate would survive since they haven't had access to a woman in months." She hung up.

Brass growled. "Did you catch that? She is either bluffing or she's got more than one of our males."

"She thinks Lauren is my mate." Wrath wished that were true. "Why?"

"I don't know." Brass shook his head.

"We need to go now to reach Homeland and place that call," Wrath said and tried to lunge for the door but Shadow jerked him back, still holding his arm. He twisted his head and flashed fangs. "Let go."

"No." Brass stepped closer. "We aren't going anywhere. Tim and the secondary team are on their way to us right now. They will find out everything they can about the dead human male. We can conference call with Homeland. We don't have to actually go there to allow this female to speak to her sister." He paused. "They can trace the call too. We have no assurances that they'll make the exchange in good faith. They could kill Lauren out of spite."

"They want their people back," Shadow reminded everyone. "They'll keep her alive since they know that's the deal."

Tim Oberto strode into the apartment, a few of his team members behind him, and quickly assessed the situation. "I was informed that Lauren Henderson has been kidnapped." He glanced at Brass. "We'll try to get her back."

Brass handed over the note. "We need to set up a conference call between Homeland and the kidnappers. They wish to speak to the female prisoner you captured yesterday. They want to exchange Wrath's female for the captured humans. We will do this to get his female back."

"But—"

"We will do this," Brass stated firmly, cutting Tim off. "We will capture those monsters again. The sister of the female has Wrath's future mate. Saving Species is our priority. Lauren is one of us because she belongs to him. I don't know if your men heard us but a Species male was also here and he helped kidnap her."

Tim gasped. "Why in the hell would one of yours betray the NSO?"

Shadow sighed. "He's still in captivity. We smell it on him. They might have found a way to control him or perhaps he doesn't know Mercile is his enemy. He is—"

"Dead," Wrath snarled.

"Confused," Shadow corrected, frowning at Wrath. "He knows no better."

Brass nodded. "Confused." His gaze fixed on Wrath. "He will be deemed unfit if he has harmed her with malice."

Tim eyed Brass. "Unfit?"

"Leave it at that. He will never be a threat again if he is deemed unfit."

Tim nodded at Brass. "We have that too for unfit humans. It's called the death penalty and I'm all for that in some cases."

"We need to return to your headquarters and set up this call. The faster we make the exchange, the better." Brass stared at Wrath. "I know this must be difficult but know that everything will be done."

"I want to be there," Wrath demanded.

"Only if you calm."

"I'll do whatever it takes," he swore, holding Brass' gaze, and meant it.

Tim spoke to one of his men. "Run that dead bastard. I want to know everything on him, including where he bought his last condoms and who he used them on. Call me as soon as you have info and have someone clean this mess up. We don't want it on the news."

"Yes sir." The guy saluted and stepped around them to reach the body.

* * * * *

Shadow sat in the SUV next to him and bumped his shoulder. "We'll find her."

"I'm afraid."

"I know."

"She could be suffering, hurt, or even dead. They could be lying."

"We have her sister. Humans care about family. They won't risk killing her if she's useful to them. We know how Mercile works."

Rage flooded through Wrath. "Yes. They lie and aren't to be trusted."

"We have what they want. Lauren is useful."

That had to calm him because nothing else did. Another fear gripped him. "She will want nothing to do with me if she survives this. Her association with me has put her in danger."

"Let's deal with one problem at a time." Shadow paused. "She would have gotten away if they hadn't had one of our males with them. She's smart and she killed someone trying to save her own life. She's strong, Wrath. She's a survivor. We have to keep hopeful that this will work out."

* * * * *

Lauren was scared, tired, and hungry. Someone had turned off the lights in both hallways, the sun had gone down and it was pitch dark in the room. Strange little noises kept making her jump as she huddled in the center of the cage, too afraid to go near the sides in case that creep Marvin tried to touch her. The room was growing colder by the minute.

No way was she using the blanket in the corner. It smelled like sweat, dirt, and ten-day-old, reeking laundry. She also needed to use a bathroom desperately. Another little noise sounded but it wasn't from the direction of the three men sharing the room with her. She hugged her chest tighter.

"Why are you afraid?" It was the unfriendly canine Species.

"I can't see anything. What is making those sounds?"

"There are rats. They are not near you and they leave us alone."

Shit. I don't want to know that. "Great. I'd like to eat something instead of being on the menu for rodents. Please tell me they aren't really big." She imagined cat-sized ones and shivered. "How do you guys go to the bathroom?"

He paused. "We call out and they bring us a bucket."

Ewww. She winced but she was desperate enough to do it.

The canine growled though. "We're males and it is easy for us. I wouldn't call out if I were you. The human will probably make you open your shirt to allow you to leave your cage. Use the blanket in your cage since you've refused to touch it. Toss it outside the cage."

A rat squeaked loudly as lights were flipped on in the hallway that led to the bathrooms. Mary appeared and held out a cell phone. Confusion filled Lauren when the bitch stopped outside her cell. "Here she is. Talk to them and watch what you say."

"Hello?"

"Lauren?" It was Wrath's wonderful voice. "Are you well?"

"Yes. I'm okay, Wrath."

"Has anyone harmed you?"

"No. I'm locked in a cage."

A snarl came over the phone from him. "I'm going to get you back no matter what it takes. Trust in me."

"I do." Hot tears poured down her cheeks and she opened her mouth, wanted to tell him she loved him in case she never got the chance, but Mary hit a button on the phone face, lifted it to her ear, and walked a few feet away.

"Very touching," Mary sneered. "Now you've heard for yourself that she's alive and well. You have your proof of life. You'd better do exactly what I say if you want her to stay that way. The meeting will take place at five in the morning and the location will be texted to you right before then. I'm not giving you time to set up a trap and if we see anyone, your girlfriend will die. You better make sure my sister and her friends are all there or your girlfriend gets a hole in her head."

Whatever he said made Mary pale. "I said we'd meet at five. Don't threaten me, animal. You'll get her back as long as you don't screw with me." She hung up and turned to glare at Lauren.

"Your animal needs to be put back on a leash. This is what happens when you give them a false sense of being people."

"They are people." Lauren gripped the bars as she rose to her feet, her legs a bit sore from sitting on the hard, cold surface. "May I use the bathroom?"

"Mark?"

A new man came down the hallway, this one smaller than the thugs who had shown up in Lauren's apartment, and he looked worn out with his tired expression and sagging shoulders. "You bellowed?"

"Unlock her door and take her to the bathroom."

He came forward, produced keys, and warily studied Lauren. "Don't give me any trouble."

"I just want to use the bathroom."

He opened the door and Lauren moved slowly, didn't want to give them a reason to hurt her, and noticed Mary placed another call on the cell phone. Mark pointed. "This way. It's close and you need to leave the door open. I won't watch you."

"They made the deal," Mary informed someone. "They agreed to the money too."

The hallway was a long one and boasted male and female bathrooms and other doors that Lauren had no clue about. They had locks on them.

The guy turned his back to her and blocked the doorway. She walked to a stall. The doors had long ago been removed. It hadn't been cleaned either and she quickly used the bathroom. He glanced at her once when she turned on water, splashed some on her face and used her finger to brush her teeth. She returned to him.

He hesitated, opened his mouth, but Mary shouted from down the hallway.

"What's taking so long? Hurry up!"

"Go," he ordered her, moving out of her way so she could leave the bathroom.

Mary gripped Lauren's arm the second they walked into the large room, gave her a hard tug and returned her to her cage. Mark locked the door and Mary glared at him. "Go get 140."

The guy fled, obviously afraid of his boss. Mary put her hands on her hips and stared at Lauren. "You really believe they are people?"

"Yes."

"They are nothing but animals who can talk. Do you enjoy fucking one? What's that like anyway? I'd never trust them enough not to snap my neck."

Lauren hesitated but couldn't refrain from answering. "I'd say you have a really good reason for that fear after meeting you."

Mary's lips twisted into an ugly sneer. "I would never allow an animal to shove his penis in me. I have standards. I'm not a dumpy blonde with bad hair who is so desperate she'll let anyone fuck her. I'm assuming with your weight problem that you don't have the luxury of being picky. You're just happy when anything is willing to bend you over."

Anger burned but Lauren clenched her teeth. She might be overweight but at least she wasn't a crazy, vicious bitch. Staying alive was the priority and it really sucked not being able to respond.

"Even them." Mary glanced at the three New Species in their cages before giving Lauren an amused look. "They'd probably fuck my grandma if I shoved her into a cage with them. You're kind of pathetic for hooking up with one. Nobody else wanted him and you were the only taker. Sad."

It was bad enough the woman insulted her but now she'd dragged Wrath into it. Lauren gripped the bars and stepped closer. "Wrath is as sexy as hell and did you want to know what it's like being with him? It's the best sex ever. He blows my mind and makes me scream. He touches me like no other man ever has, worships me, and I bet no man has ever been willing to do anything for you. I might not be gorgeous or have a model body but, lady, you're a cold-hearted bitch who no man could ever love."

Fury glittered in the other woman's eyes but at that moment Mark returned with a very tall, grim-looking 140. Mary spun, backed away and pointed at Lauren. "Put him in her cage. She loves spending time with animals."

Mark hesitated but walked over to the door, opened it, and stared up at 140. "In you go."

"No." He refused.

"Get in there," Mary snapped. "Marvin is watching your girlfriend. The longer you drag your ass, the longer he's with her. You know what a pervert he is."

A snarl tore from 140 and he stomped through the door. Mark locked it and put space between himself and the cage. He stared at Mary. "How did it go?"

"The animal swears he'll bring them to the exchange. Mel sounds scared but fine and mentioned they were going to prosecute her under New Species law."

"What's the difference?" Mark looked nervous.

"Since they are the ones who arrested her, she falls under their jurisdiction. Those fucking animals are allowed to kill her if they want."

"Fuck," he hissed. "You mean they can execute us?"

"Yes. I hate those fucking animals." Mary glared at the four New Species. "All of them. I need a drink. You stay up here and watch them. Got it? I'll be back in a few hours."

"Okay." He didn't look happy.

Mary stormed through the hallway and disappeared. A door slammed and the silence in the room was absolute as Mark just stood there. He finally turned and his gaze fixed on Lauren. It looked as if he wanted to say something but instead he glanced at 140.

"I'll go get your food." He rushed away.

Lauren was locked in a cage with 140. He slowly turned and studied her body, sniffed, and his body language changed from rigid to near relaxed. "Marvin didn't touch you. Good." He paused. "I smell your fear but I won't harm you."

"Thank you."

He nodded and turned, glancing at the other New Species. "How are you?"

The blond frowned. "How do you think? How is your mate? Is she better?"

140 shook his head. "No. She is still weak."

"What's wrong with her?"

140 snapped his gaze to Lauren. "What do you care?"

She flinched at the look of hatred in his eyes. "I am not the enemy."

He inhaled and some of his anger faded. "You aren't. I know this. You are with one of our kind. Tell me about him."

"He's a few inches taller than you and he works with a group of humans who are searching for those of your kind who haven't been freed yet. They track down people like those assholes holding us."

"You were telling the truth about the NSO, weren't you?" It was the dark canine.

Lauren met his eyes. "Yes. Everything I've told you is true. When places like this are found by the people Wrath works with they come in to rescue us. They take you home to the NSO and you are free."

"Tell us about them," 140 urged.

Lauren began to talk, sharing everything she'd ever read or seen in person during her brief visit to Homeland. They listened and shock showed in their eyes often. She finally stopped. She didn't let them know she was aware of exactly where they were in case Mary or any of her men were listening. She was afraid they'd move the New Species to a different location.

"I'm going to tell them about you when I get out of here. They'll find you." It was a promise she made.

140 sighed. "There is real hope of them coming for us, isn't there? That we could go live in peace with our kind away from our enemies?"

"Yes. I did mention the hate groups, right? There aren't many of them but they are annoying. Most people are good, not like the assholes you've dealt with, and they are as horrified as I am over Mercile Industries."

Footsteps sounded and Mark returned carrying plastic bags in his hands. He stopped near one of the cages. "Move back."

The golden-haired New Species edged to the back corner of his cage. Mark reached in and dropped a bag, moved to the next one and left another bag. He finally stopped at Lauren's cage. 140 moved, pressed against the back of the cage, while Lauren didn't budge. He set down two bags and backed away. His gaze fixed on Lauren.

"I was told you're dating a New Species. Is that true?"

"Yes. Are you going to insult me too?"

He glanced behind him and lowered his voice when he faced her again. "I want a deal. When you get out of here, will you talk to your boyfriend for me? I'm willing to give them the address of this place in exchange for a million dollars, total immunity against any crimes and safe travel out of the country. I didn't know they had their own justice system. They can make deals, right? I never signed on for any of this shit but they'll kill me if I don't do what Mary says. The only choice they gave me was to stick around Mercile to be arrested or go with them."

Lauren bit her lip, her mind working, and hope filled her. "To agree to your terms they'll want all the New Species back alive."

"We have four of the men and one woman. Mary and her sister were researchers at one of the facilities. They took these five and we helped get them out after the search warrant was served. We all thought it would blow over but it didn't. Mary just wanted to protect her research with these ones but now it's all gone to hell. Our place got busted. We're probably wanted by the police and I can't even contact my parents or sister. I'm sick of living in this dump and being treated like shit. I just want my life back."

Lauren felt zero pity for him but he was desperate and she was willing to take advantage of that. The bastard had worked for Mercile and was still holding New Species in cages. "I'm a mate," she lied. "I can negotiate a deal with you and they'll accept it."

Hope filled his eyes. "Really?"

"Yeah," she bullshitted. "A million dollars, immunity and a helicopter ride to the nearest border is a bargain for the lives of five New Species. I know they will agree."

"Okay." He nodded. "How can we do this? If anyone here finds out they'll put a bullet in me."

"Do you have a phone?"

"Yeah but I'm afraid to give it to you. They could trace that shit. I'm not stupid."

She plotted fast. "It takes at least three minutes to trace a call."

"I've heard that."

She had no idea if it were true or not, didn't care either, but he needed to get a message out. "Call Homeland, keep it under three minutes and tell them you know where five New Species are. Give them your terms and tell them I made a deal with you. My name is Lauren Henderson." She paused. "Tell them my code word is Jasper's. That will assure them it's for real and we actually spoke."

"Code word?"

"You know how parents give their kids a safe word? New Species use code words and mine is Jasper's."

He paced as he contemplated her offer and finally nodded. "Okay. Mary is gone for a few hours, the guys are taking off in a bit and I've got access to the office. They keep cell phones in there. Homeland, you said?"

"Yes. Call Homeland."

He walked away and Lauren began to pray he actually made that call and that someone got her secret message. It was a long shot but a lot of humans worked with Wrath. One of them might remember Jasper's. It had been a popular club once.

"Was that the truth?" 140 drew her attention. "Will the NSO make a deal to buy us?"

"They'll do anything to get you back."

140 smiled. "I like you."

Chapter Sixteen

ᖰ

Wrath paced, too worried about Lauren to sleep. He heard footsteps running down the hallway and spun just as his door was pushed open. Shadow burst into the room.

"Come with me now." He spun and bolted away.

Wrath was on his heels a heartbeat later, terrified something bad had happened. The NSO had assured him they'd meet whatever demands the kidnappers made to get Lauren back safely but humans were unstable. They could have changed the terms.

Shadow ran down the hallway into the main living area and slowed. Wrath paused at his side. Tim and some other humans were sitting at the table with Brass, who pointed at the phone that had been brought into the room.

"We will do that," Justice North stated from the speakers on the phone. "This female is very smart. We know they have five Species and now have a way to get them returned to us."

"He's talking about Lauren," Shadow whispered.

Confusion filled Wrath but Brass gave him and Shadow a signal to be silent.

Tim sighed. "Are you able to get that kind of money? The guy wants it in a few hours."

"That isn't a worry," Justice replied.

Tim was grim. "The exchange is going to happen in the middle of the night. Where the hell can we get that kind of money? The banks are already closed."

Justice laughed and so did Brass. Tim shook his head. Wrath wondered what was going on and why there was a meeting about Lauren. He also noted the mention of the exchange possibly happening before dawn and five Species were involved now.

"What is so damn amusing?" Tim slammed his palm on the table. "What aren't you telling me?"

Brass cleared his throat. "Lauren rescued Wrath when my team was captured and she called Homeland for assistance. One of males told her that they have the ability to quickly trace all incoming calls there. He didn't believe she really had an unconscious Species with her and accused her of being one of those humans who harass us. He identified her location to prove his point. She talked one of the humans holding her into calling Homeland directly."

Justice spoke. "She remembered and hoped we could track the signal. She went even farther to ensure that we'd be able to pinpoint the location."

"It just takes longer to trace a cell phone signal, which the human male used when he called to make his demands but we have bought the best technology there is. We were able to pinpoint the cell tower used where the call originated." Brass grinned. "Tell them, Justice."

"This human called and had to explain the deal Lauren made with him. She not only talked him into calling but convinced him we'd agree with any deal she made with him. To prove it, he told us her specially assigned Species code word." Justice chuckled. "Which we don't have and that tipped us off that it must be a message."

A new voice came on the line. "It's Tiger. I immediately called the local police authorities in the area of the cell tower and asked them if her code word meant anything to them. I had them pull in all their detectives to pool their resources and as soon as they heard it, one of them remembered a club. Her word was 'Jaspers' and do you want to know what the name of that club once was?"

"Jasper's." Tim smiled.

"Exactly," Justice chuckled again. "It was turned into a restaurant but eventually it closed down. According the police the building has been unused for a few years but they were kind enough to place a call to power and water for us. Someone is paying to keep the lights on."

Tim stood fast enough to almost knock his chair over. "I'll get a team ready immediately. We'll breach the building." He snapped his head in the direction of his men. "Find out if we can get the blueprints on it and I want current satellite pictures."

"Yes sir." The guy fled to do Tim's bidding.

"Is Wrath there?"

He stepped closer to the table and the phone. "I'm here, Justice."

"Your female is very smart. You should be proud of her."

"I am." He paused. "I just want her back safely. Wouldn't it be better to exchange her for what they want, rather than go in after her in an assault?" He glanced at Shadow, seeing worry in his friend's eyes too over that concern.

Silence stretched but Brass broke it. "We've interviewed the human female Mel. She's unstable and we fear her sister is more so. There's no guarantee she'll keep her word, Wrath. We think this is the best option. We'll hit them fast and hard. Justice is sending both helicopters our way with our people. It will be a joint venture."

"Her safety is as paramount to us as are our people," Justice swore. "We want to get them all home. We have two humans trying to make deals with us, both of them want different things, and that implies they aren't aware of it. They could figure out they are betraying each other and kill your Lauren. It would also give them time to move our people before dawn. We really thought this out."

"Okay," Wrath conceded. "I will be there." His body tensed. "I insist."

Brass gripped his shoulder. "We agreed you should be with one of the teams going in but you need to keep in control. Do you understand me? One sign that you're losing it and you're out of there."

"When do we leave?" He wanted it to be right then.

"We're set to go in an hour," Justice stated. "The helicopters should be setting down in the parking lot in about fifteen minutes. That should give Tim time to plan the mission. We don't want to rush in there without a plan in place. We're going to hit them hard and fast, but effectively."

Wrath grimly nodded. "Agreed."

* * * * *

Lauren watched the men eat and tried to hide her aversion. It wasn't cooked at all, just bags of totally raw chunks of meat. She declined when 140 offered her some.

"You need your strength."

"I can't eat that," she admitted. "Really. It makes me sick."

He frowned and offered it to her again after he used his teeth to tear off a small strip. "One."

She took it and popped it into her mouth. The metallic taste of cold blood was horrible and it was chewy. It took a while but she managed to choke it down.

"Eat another."

"Nope. That was it for me. Trust me on that. You don't want to see it come up." Her stomach churned. "I'm good until breakfast." *Hopefully I'll be out of here by then.*

140 sighed, appeared slightly disappointed with her, but didn't argue. He divided her portion of the food into fours, which he split among the other men. They didn't talk even after they finished their quick dinner and Lauren leaned back against the cage wall. She was tired and it seemed as if a lot of time had passed.

Footsteps drew her attention and Mark walked out from the hallway. He stopped about six feet from her cage. "I called them and they accepted the deal. They are getting the money and my immunity paperwork in order." He puffed out his chest. "I told them I insist on it being on paper so I have proof. They are planning on having it all done by three. I'm going to leave and they'll come right after I give them the address." He pulled out a small little camera and waved it slowly at the cages. "My proof that you are alive and well."

"Is that deal for all of us?" Lauren worried about that.

"Yeah. You, them, and the woman in the basement."

Lauren glanced at 140 and he seemed relieved his mate was included. She didn't blame him. He'd said the woman was sick and she hoped it would be something simple that a full medical staff could handle. The NSO would make sure she got the best doctors. They took really good care of their own.

"I'm going to go pack," Mark informed them. "I have to think of where I want to live."

He left quickly and turned off the lights. She wished he hadn't as darkness settled around them. The bastard no longer cared what happened to them as long as he got his deal. Hope swelled in her chest that he'd remembered to give her code word and that someone would run a search on it, figure out there used to be a club, or that they'd call Amanda to ask her what it might mean. Her best friend would instantly remember their old hangout.

Wrath was smart and he'd figure it out. She definitely had faith him. Time had lost meaning and she couldn't even estimate if it were still early evening or past midnight. All she could do was wait in the darkness. It sucked.

"Are you cold?" 140's voice startled her.

"I'm okay. A little chilled but I'm not touching that blanket. It reeks and who knows where it's been or what's been done to it."

He chuckled. "True. Come here and I'll keep you warm."

"No thank you."

"I have a female. I won't attempt to mount you."

"You're damn straight you won't. I have a guy and I love him. No offense."

"Come here. I will hold you. Our bodies are warmer than yours."

She hesitated. "You won't touch me in a sexual way?"

"No. I said I have a mate."

"And that means what?"

"I do not want another female. I only want to mount mine."

There is that mounting word again. She hesitated but nodded. "Okay. Where are you? I can't see a thing."

Big, gentle hands touched her waist. She gasped when he just dragged her closer, forced her to lie on her side, and he shoved an arm under her head. One arm tightened around her middle and jerked her closer to his body. She found herself spooned by a stranger. 140 just held her, didn't try anything funny, and his body heat was nice. She relaxed against him.

"Thank you. You are warm."

He rested his chin on her head. "You are chilled. Your skin is cooler than it was today."

"You remember my skin temperature?"

"I noticed everything. It's what we do."

"Are we alone in here with just the other New Species men?"

He lifted his head. "Yes."

"Can all of you hear me if I whisper?"

"Yes." His body tensed. "Why?"

"Will anyone else hear me? Do you know if they have listening devices or cameras?"

"They don't and none of them are nearby. I'd smell them." 140 sounded sure.

She whispered. "I tricked that man into calling the NSO. I am hoping they will send help to us really soon. Homeland traces all incoming calls and they might know where we are. They will come get us before any scheduled exchanges. I don't want any of you to be alarmed if that happens."

The arms around her middle tightened noticeably, almost squeezing her to the point of pain. "Will they kill us?"

She knew he meant him, his mate, and the three other men in cages. "No. They are your people, 140. They are going to rescue you. They work with my people and I don't want any of you to be alarmed if they show up."

His hold eased. "I am afraid to hope for freedom."

"I understand."

Time seemed to stretch on forever. Lauren yawned, the stress of the day getting to her. 140 wasn't Wrath but in the dark he reminded her of the man she loved. She wasn't afraid to have hope. *I'm getting out of here and I'm going to see Wrath soon.*

* * * * *

Wrath wanted to go into the dark building immediately but Brass gripped his arm, shaking his head.

"Wait. They are setting up now. We need to do this right, hit it at once from all sides and take over as quickly as possible to avoid any fatalities. The infrared is showing a lighter heat signature near the hot spots. That means it's a human."

Tim watched the portable tablet device monitor in his hands and spoke. "We found her." He looked grim when he lifted his head, seeking someone out in the group clustered around him.

Wrath didn't like the way Tim held his gaze with a look of near pity. He glanced back down at the screen.

Brass addressed the issue. "What is wrong, Tim? Tell us."

"We didn't detect Lauren Henderson's heat signature right off because another masks it. She's with one of yours and they are lying on their sides. He is right against her. She's smaller than him, at first it seemed a blurred image but we got a better angle. They are lying together real tight."

Rage filled Wrath. "They've forced bred her to one of the males."

Shadow gripped his other arm when he tried to spin around to rush to Lauren's aid. Brass' hold clamped down tighter as both of them held him in place.

"You don't know that for certain," Shadow rumbled. "Calm."

"Calm or leave," Brass agreed.

He took a deep breath to regain control of his anger. He nodded sharply to let them know when he had. "We need to go in there."

"We have to wait until the lesser heat signatures are farther away from the hotter ones. They could have guns. The problem is that we're picking up a human close to a Species." Tim touched his screen and turned it to show the men around him. "This is the blueprint of the building. There's a small storage basement and that's where one of yours is being held." He tapped the screen. "The human is damn close. It's harder to read the heat signatures belowground but we've got them here and here." He pointed.

"We need to create a distraction," Brass suggested.

"That's what I was thinking. We put an SUV in the parking lot to observe the back of the building. We could set off its alarm. That might pull the human to the back of the building to check out what is causing the noise. We can breach if they fall for it."

"Do it," Wrath urged, desperate to get in there and find Lauren.

Tim tapped his ear. "Trey?"

Everyone on the teams could hear any chatter on the coms and a male answered. “Yeah?”

Tim outlined the plan. “Everyone get ready to blow in on my command. We all go in at once, no delays, and remember we’ve got five victims in there. We’re assuming the four New Species have never been freed so wait for New Species assistance before you free them unless we hit a hot zone.” He released his ear and stared at Brass. “Are your teams ready?”

“We’re already prepared to fight for the freedom of Species.” He glanced at Wrath. “And for the females of our males.”

“What if it is a hot zone?” Wrath didn’t even want to think about someone taking the time to set explosives or other deadly precautions that would kill anyone inside the building in case of a breach. “We aren’t abandoning them, are we?” He wouldn’t leave Lauren.

“It’s a grab-and-go if it’s a trap.” Tim frowned and held Brass’ stare. “You sure he’s okay? This is personal for him.”

“It’s personal for all of us. There are Species in there as well. He’s got a right to try to save his female.”

“Shit.” Tim sighed. “I don’t think this is a good idea. We need everyone coolheaded.”

Brass released Wrath’s arm and leaned in closer until they were practically nose to nose. “You go for your female. Don’t hurt the male with her, Wrath. Do you understand me? We don’t know the circumstances and until we do, swear to me that he’s safe from you. I give you my word to personally lock you in a room with him later if he hurt her without justified cause.”

“I swear.” They were hard words for Wrath to say but the most important thing was Lauren.

Tim reached up and touched his ear. “Set off the alarm. Everyone get ready to breach on my mark. Remember the damn layout.”

Wrath's heart pounded and fear gripped him hard. He silently swore to get Lauren past whatever horrors she'd endured. They could deal with anything together, as long as he got her back alive.

Chapter Seventeen

ꟼ

A car alarm going off in the distance woke Lauren and she tensed, disorientated, but the arm around her waist reminded her quickly of reality. She was locked inside a cage with 140, her cheek pillowed on his arm and the sound she heard was a typical one.

"It is fine," he assured her. "We hear those sounds sometimes."

"Car alarm," she supplied. "Everyone seems to have one these days. I'm guessing it's windy outside or a cat jumped on it. My Tiger has set off many of them."

"Tiger?"

"My pet."

"Are you warm enough?"

"Yes. Thank you." He was keeping her warm, made sleeping bearable in the confined space, and she closed her eyes again, ready to drift back off.

140 growled, his body turned rigid and his head jerked up.

"What is it? Do you see a rat?"

"No. I smell humans."

"I do too," one of the other Species hissed.

"Unfamiliar," one of them growled.

"Thank God!" Joy hit Lauren as she tried to sit up but 140 held her against him. "Let me up. It's got to be the cavalry."

"Who?" 140 didn't release her.

"The NSO. They must have found us, got my message, and figured it out. Everyone remain calm," she whispered.

"These will be the good guys and some of your people should be with them." Tears filled her eyes. "Wrath must be out there too."

A male shouted and it was the start of rapid action that had Lauren screaming in terror and confusion. The boards over the windows blew apart, glass shattered and loud booms deafened her. Men's shouts, blinding lights, and smoke came with it.

Big shapes seemed to fly through the now-destroyed windows and the big body behind her was instantly gone. He almost stepped on her when he pinned her body between his calves, planting himself above her in a half crouch. He snarled.

She had to blink a few times to adjust to the flashlights bouncing all over the big room. Boots pounded over the old dance floor and she watched dark shapes rush past the sides of the cages. One of the big shapes hit the other side of the cage and snarled. Her head jerked in that direction and Wrath crouched down enough for her to see him clearly.

"Wrath!" She tried to turn on her stomach and crawl to him but 140's legs still pinned her.

140 spun, snarled at Wrath, and refused to let her go. Wrath showed sharp teeth but didn't make any scary sounds. He did lift his flashlight though, enabling her to see more of his features. It was the best sight Lauren had ever seen.

"140? This is Wrath. It's okay. Can you ease up on my legs and let me go to him?"

He moved, stepped away, and she crawled a few feet to Wrath. His hands came through the narrow bars, cupped her face and pulled her so close her skin brushed against metal. His eyes looked black as she stared deeply into them. The sounds of shouted orders from the task force faded away as all her concentration centered on him.

"Did he force breed you? Hurt you? I can't smell right now from the way we had to come in."

"No."

She shoved her hands through the bars to touch him. He was warm. He let her caress his jawline on both sides and even lowered to make their faces level.

"You're telling me the truth? You haven't been harmed?"

"I'm okay. I'm great. You're here. You came for me."

"Always," he swore.

He pulled back to stare at something behind and above her.

She turned her head and saw 140 watching them quietly from the other side of the cage. He frowned, his eyes narrowed and he shook his head.

"I have a mate of my own. She is downstairs. I was only keeping yours warm. Her skin is colder than ours. Please find my mate."

Lauren glanced at Wrath. "She's sick. I don't know what they've done to her or why but they are keeping her in the basement."

Brass was suddenly there. "I'm on it. I'll get her." He rushed away.

Wrath released Lauren and moved to the door of the cage. A human member of the task force met him there. The man dropped to his knees, aimed a flashlight on the lock and withdrew a small kit from one of the pockets on his pants.

"This is a piece of cake," the man chuckled, glancing up at Wrath. "Can I let them all out? Is it safe?" He turned his head to warily stare at 140. "We are here to rescue you and your people. We'd appreciate it if you didn't try to attack me. You boys would kick our asses."

140 nodded. "We know you are not our enemies." He turned his head to the other three New Species. "Relax. They are here to free us."

"Let them out," Wrath ordered. "I will handle it if one attacks."

The human on the floor went to work on the lock. In thirty seconds he managed to pick it. He stood, pulled the door open and stepped back. Lauren rushed into Wrath's open, welcoming arms.

He lifted her off her feet, his arms almost crushing her to his chest, until their faces were level. She threw her arms around his neck and wrapped her legs around his waist. She clung to him and buried her face against his neck, thrilled to be able to touch him again. The lighting in the room growing stronger finally caught her attention and she lifted her head to peer around.

Members of the task force who had come in with battery-operated lanterns stood watching them calmly and Lauren chuckled when Wrath began to sniff at her.

"I need a shower. You might want to hold off on that until I smell better."

He chuckled. "I don't care. You're safe."

"I knew you'd come." She stared deeply into his eyes. "I had no doubt about it."

He growled. "I am not letting you go again."

"My mate," 140 growled. "Can I go to her?"

Wrath tilted his head to peer around Lauren, his hold eased, but he refused to put her down. "Wait here where it's secure. They will bring her to you as soon as they deem it safe to move her. She will come to no harm from us."

140 paced the cell and Lauren didn't understand why he stayed inside it when the door had been left wide open. She glanced away, realized the other cage doors had been unlocked by the task force member, yet not one of those three had stepped outside their enclosures either. Her gaze swept the room to search for a reason, realized at least ten humans and five New Species were watching the newly released men and wondered if fear kept them from venturing out.

"You can come out of your cages," Lauren informed them.

The golden-haired feline male stepped carefully out of the cage, looking uncertain and prepared to attack if necessary. Movement from the corner of her eye had her head turning and she gaped as a tall, long-haired New Species female came striding into the building. She wasn't wearing a uniform, just jeans and a T-shirt. Her dark gaze flicked around the room, skimmed past Lauren and Wrath and fixed on the feline who'd just frozen steps away from the open cage door.

"I'm formerly 52 but I've taken the name Midnight." She stopped a few feet away from him, openly studied his features, and smiled warmly. "You are safe from the technicians who held you and are no longer at their mercy." She paused. "You are free. You are going to go home with us, to our people, and you'll never be locked up again." She bowed her head to him slightly, before meeting his stunned stare once more. "We call ourselves New Species and you have family now." She glanced at all four males before facing the feline male again. "All of you are family."

"I can't believe this is real." The blond feline moved away from his cage and turned to look at Lauren. "You weren't trying to fool us with the stories you shared."

Lauren shook her head. "No. I wasn't."

The dark canine stepped out of his cage and stalked toward Midnight. The tough-looking Species woman tensed slightly, faced him but didn't back away. He moved a little too close to her, his gaze roamed her body and he sniffed. Lauren would have smacked any guy who openly showed his sexual interest but Midnight seemed not to be offended. He hesitated.

"May I?"

Midnight's gaze narrowed. "You wish to get a better sense of me?"

He just stared at her.

"Fine but don't touch. I don't know you."

Her body language remained on alert but she held still as he slowly circled her, sniffed a few times and seemed to take in every inch of her body and clothing.

"What is he doing?" Lauren whispered to Wrath.

"He's not sure what to make of her and all the scents he's picking up have to be new to him. We take pleasure handpicking everything we use for how it smells. Shampoo, body wash and even our laundry soaps. He won't approach a male with his curiosity so we brought in a female, hoping it will speed up the process of them learning to trust us." Wrath kept his voice low, his lips almost against her ear and his hold tightened. "She's less threatening to them."

Lauren watched the canine finally back off a few feet, a frown firmly curving his lips. "You're one of ours but you smell so different."

"This is freedom." Midnight glanced at the other New Species who'd just left the cages then turned her attention on 140. She sniffed the air, slowly stepped closer to where he waited in his cage and paused by the open door. She glanced at Shadow.

"Where's the female Species? Is she his mate? I can pick up her scent coming off him."

"Brass and the team are getting her. She was held in a separate location in the building."

140 growled. "I want her."

"Easy," Midnight crooned, opening her hands on her side. "She'll be safe with them. They will bring her as soon as she's freed." Her gaze darted to Shadow again. "What is the holdup?"

"I don't know."

"What happens to us now?" The canine stepped closer to Midnight. He invaded her personal space again but didn't touch her.

Midnight held her ground once more and just met his intense stare calmly. "You will follow me out of this building.

There are vehicles outside waiting to take us home and you'll meet more of us." She paused. "We have kind, nonthreatening humans who work for us. They will check you over to make sure you don't need medical treatment and you will be nice to them."

His eyebrows rose.

"They are our friends." Midnight hesitated. "I know you can't understand that but these humans never harmed our kind. They didn't work for Mercile and they help us. We aren't doctors but they are. Do you understand?"

He growled and Midnight did something that made Lauren gasp while Wrath tensed. The woman suddenly spun, her foot shot out and she knocked the canine's legs out from under him. He hit the floor hard on his back and Midnight dropped on top of him. She straddled his waist and growled as she leaned over him. Her hands cupped his face and she got so close they could have kissed.

"Don't move," she demanded. "Be calm and listen to me carefully. One of those humans is a female mated to one of our males. I'd hate to take you home only for you to be killed by him when you give him no choice but to protect her. Any of the humans you come into contact with are our friends. Do you understand me?"

He snarled but didn't fight.

Midnight hesitated before she released him and rose to her feet. She offered him a hand. "You're weaker right now. You've been caged and I doubt they fed you well. I could take you in a fight. Behave. You are free but that doesn't mean you can be an asshole."

Lauren closed her mouth and watched the tough female pull the male to his feet. He didn't snarl again but kept away from her. All his anger seemed to have been knocked out of him as effectively as the air in his lungs must have been when he'd been dumped on the floor.

The golden-haired feline made a rumbling noise and Midnight spun toward him. She tensed and her features tightened.

"Do you need to be taken to the floor and talked to?"

He shook his head and slowly grinned. "You're a fierce female. Are there more of you where we are going?"

A chuckle escaped her and her hands dropped to her side. "Yes. You're a lover more than a fighter, aren't you?"

He sniffed. "I smell no male on you. Is there one in your life?"

"There is. I'm not mated to him but there are plenty of females for you to get to know better. We'll discuss that on the drive back to our home. I'll inform you of the right and wrong way to approach them."

"Good."

"Where is my female?" 140 began to pace his cell, agitated. Midnight moved closer to him.

"Easy," she whispered. "They will bring her soon." She shot a worried look Shadow's way.

"Can I go to her? I know where she is. Please? She will be—" 140 stopped talking and snapped his head in the direction of the hallway. He lunged forward, left his cage and rushed in that direction.

Brass appeared suddenly carrying a tall, frail-looking New Species woman in his arms. A blanket was wrapped around her body but it didn't hide how thin she was. Her head rested against his chest and it didn't appear she was conscious. He saw 140 coming and froze, staying that way.

140 reached them and opened his arms. "Give her to me."

Brass hesitated. "She needs a doctor. We need to airlift her to our medical facility." He glanced around the room, searching for someone. "Tim? Get one of our helicopters here right now. She's in critical condition."

"Give her to me," 140 snarled.

"I'm going to," Brass assured him. "You can hold her but we need to get her to our doctors." He inched closer to the upset Species and transferred the woman into his waiting arms. "Do you know what they did to her? The humans we captured won't talk."

140 gently cradled the woman in his arms and rested his cheek against the top of her head. Pain sounded in his voice.

"They have been giving her pills that make her sicker. I don't know what. They refuse to tell us what they do. Please help her."

Brass turned to one of the human task force members. "Call Homeland and tell them to get everyone awake. Have Medical standing by." He looked at one of the New Species. "Slash, call Justice. Let him know what is going on and that we need to find out what they did to her. We're sending the prisoners to Homeland and I want Darkness there to interrogate the bastards. He'll make them talk." He finally looked back at 140. "We are going to do everything we can to save her. You have my word."

Lauren blinked back tears. The woman was so pale, so lifeless, that she already seemed dead. The grim mood in the room assured her that everyone was more than aware of how ill the New Species was.

"Follow me outside," Brass urged 140. "I promise no one will take her from you. You can stay with her but our doctors need to work on her when we reach them. You have to allow them to do that. I swear that they will do everything possible to save her life."

"Please," 140 whispered.

Brass moved and everyone parted for them to make their way outside. A few of the men kicked down the wall under one window so 140 didn't have to step over it to get outside. A helicopter could be heard approaching and Lauren hugged Wrath tighter, grateful they were together and had a happier outlook than 140 and his mate.

"That could have been you needing a doctor."

Lauren stared into Wrath's beautiful, haunted eyes and knew they both pondered the same thing. He continued to hold her until she wiggled.

"You should put me down. I'm not exactly light."

He shook his head. "No. Let's get out of here. I'm taking you back to my home."

She probably should have felt embarrassed from the many eyes that had to be watching them but she wasn't as Wrath walked with her outside. She buried her face in his neck, closed her eyes and just clung to him.

He had to put her down when they climbed into the SUV to open the back door. She scooted inside, he came after her and Shadow opened the other door. The men were on either side of her and she felt safe. Her gaze drifted to the mostly destroyed building, all the windows were gaping holes now and she hoped to never see it again. Jasper's had once held fond memories but not anymore.

Wrath suddenly turned in his seat, his hands dug behind her back and under her thighs, he lifted her and settled her sideways over his lap. She didn't protest, instead just leaned against his chest and curled into his big body.

"Are you really well, Lauren?"

She nodded against him. "I am. I'm just glad it's over."

"You are very brave," Shadow stated. "We found the male you killed inside your home. I was proud."

Her stomach rolled at the reminder and she wasn't sure what to say to that. Her silence stretched until the front doors of the SUV opened. Two human task force members climbed inside and both glanced back. A familiar face grinned at her from the passenger seat.

"Hey, Lauren," Brian greeted. "We're glad to have you back. How are you doing?"

"Much better. How are you? You were bleeding and out cold the last time I saw you."

"I'm fine. What's a little concussion and blood loss? That's why I'm not driving you today. I heard what was going down, who was taken, and I wasn't going to miss this assignment."

"Thank you." Emotion choked her voice. "Please thank everyone for me who was here today."

"Let's go home," Wrath roughly snarled. "Now. Lauren needs a shower. Start the engine and return us to headquarters. I don't know how much longer I can keep in control."

Lauren's gaze flew to Wrath. It surprised her at his blunt intentions to get her naked but she was amused by it too. "You missed me that much, huh?"

He growled instead of answering but he didn't appear turned-on. His angry expression confused her as she watched him in the dim interior of the vehicle, hoping it wasn't because she'd talked to Brian. She remembered that he thought the guy was flirting with her before.

"You reek of another male," Shadow explained. "He's already agitated because he was worried that we wouldn't get you back alive and well. He had all kinds of horrible scenarios running through his mind of what those assholes could do to you. He's highly stressed and the smell of another male on you makes it a lot worse. You'll need a shower before he can calm down. It's a Species trait. We don't enjoy smelling another male on the female we have feelings for." Shadow chuckled. "Sharing sex with him after ridding your body of the other male's scent would probably put him in a much better mood too."

Lauren stared into Wrath's eyes, not sure she really understood the reason for his distress. She could accept that he wasn't like other men. "He just kept me warm and nothing happened between 140 and me. I'm sorry you're upset. I'll let you wash my back, okay? It's only temporary."

"I know. I hate that I wasn't there to protect you."

She wasn't sure how to comfort him. He was really upset and she just curled back into his body. His arms wrapped around her tightly.

Shadow answered a cell phone when it rang and listened for a few minutes. He hung up. "Our new people are on the helicopter safely. The on-flight doctor is looking over the female but it doesn't look good. They are going to do everything they can."

Sadness crept through Lauren. *Poor 140.* She lifted her head and met Wrath's eyes. *If I lost him forever…* She pushed the thought away. She didn't even want to contemplate a life without him.

"I could smell the sickness on her," Wrath admitted. "Will it never end, Shadow? Will those assholes never stop hurting our people?"

"We'll find them all," Shadow swore. "We captured the humans and they'll tell us what they did to the female." Shadow paused. "By the way, you are brilliant, Lauren. I wanted to compliment you on your intelligence. We are all very proud of how you manipulated the human into calling Homeland. Wrath would mention this himself but he's too emotional right now."

"I was scared and Mark was desperate enough to go for any plan to get him out of that mess. He said he used to work for Mercile and ended up working for the woman running that hellhole. I'm sorry about the lies I said about being Wrath's mate and the way I implied I could make deals for the NSO." She met Shadow's eyes. "I had to say a lot of things to survive and try to guide you and get you to come for us."

"You did very well and the lies you told were good ones." Shadow chuckled. "You amused and impressed Justice North. I'm sure he would like to meet you, Lauren. He said you are a very brave female."

"That's good to hear. I've seen him on television a lot. He seems really nice."

Shadow grinned. "He is unless he deals with someone who worked for Mercile or betrayed our kind. Then, not so much."

"We'll speak of all this later." Wrath brushed his fingers through her hair, stroked her cheek and pulled her tightly against him. "I need to hold you to assure myself you are really here."

Lauren settled against him until they arrived back at headquarters. She still had no idea where it was located, had forgotten to pay attention again. Wrath helped her out of the SUV, scooped her into his arms and strode for the elevator with Shadow at their side.

"I can walk."

Wrath ignored that and turned his head to talk to Shadow instead. "Could you please bring her food? Her stomach is growling."

"Of course. I'll send out someone to get her something good to eat. It shouldn't take long and I'll knock to let you know it's outside the door."

"Thank you." Wrath stepped into the elevator when the doors opened. "I'll put her clothes in the hallway. Will you dispose of them for me?"

"My clothes?" Lauren's eyes widened. Why did he want her clothes thrown out? They needed to be washed but they weren't torn or stained that she could see.

"I will," Shadow agreed, pushed a button on the panel and spoke to Lauren. "He never again wants to see what you're wearing. It will only remind him of how close he came to losing you."

Shadow followed them all the way to Wrath's room and opened the door for his friend since Wrath was determined to carry her everywhere. Lauren watched him close the door firmly behind him. She glanced at Wrath. They were finally alone.

He avoided her gaze, carried her into the bathroom and lowered his body enough to set her on her feet. The room wasn't very big, Wrath was, and it was cramped as he bent to turn on the shower.

"Undress," he urged, his voice gruff, as he adjusted the temperature of the water. "Hurry."

"I'm really okay, Wrath. You're being so sweet but you can relax now. We're here, together, and everything is going to be fine."

A snarl tore from his throat. He spun around and his hands gripped her arms. It didn't hurt but he could move fast. His size was intimidating and it shocked her when his fangs were displayed.

"Don't be afraid of me. I'd never hurt you. I'm enraged at myself for allowing you to come to harm. You are trying to make me feel better but nothing will do that. I never should have allowed you out of my sight. I should have made certain everyone at Homeland knew that I didn't want to come back to find you gone and I should have insisted that they bring you to me immediately. I let you down, left you vulnerable to my enemies and you could have died."

Tears filled her eyes. It broke her heart to see him so distraught and to realize how deeply he cared about her. "It's not your fault, Wrath. Please don't blame yourself. Do you know who you should be mad at?"

His hold gentled. "Who?"

"The assholes who took me but I'm glad it happened."

Rage tightened his features.

"We never would have known about those five New Species if I hadn't been kidnapped. I was scared, hungry, and it really sucked, but let's not forget the bottom line. Five of your people are at Homeland now because I was taken. That makes it all worth it to me."

"Your life is more important to me."

Her heart raced and tears filled her eyes. "You mean that." Hope flared that he was in love with her as much as she loved him. The words rose in her throat but she didn't have the chance to tell him how she felt.

He glanced away, let go of her arms and took a step back. His hand shot out and slammed the bathroom door, closing them inside. "We'll talk of this later. I need his scent gone, Lauren."

"Okay."

He stared into her eyes. "Don't fear me."

"I'm not afraid." She wasn't.

His hands tore at the shirt. He jerked it right off her body. She didn't protest when he dropped to his knees, frantically removed the rest of her clothes until she stood totally naked before him. He rose to his feet, gripped her hips and she grabbed his upper arms to keep her balance when he lifted her into the spray of warm water.

He paused while half in, half out of the shower stall. Material tore when he shed his clothing quickly and discarded them to the floor. Lauren appreciated every beautiful inch of perfect skin he bared and her heart raced faster when he finally stepped completely into the small space with her. No guy had ever been in such a rush to get buck naked in a shower with her before and it left her a little breathless.

Wrath was sporting a major erection as her gaze lovingly examined him. His raw masculinity made her feel even more feminine, and even tiny, compared to his size. He pressed closer, peered down at her and growled in that deep, sexy voice of his.

"I need to wash every inch of you."

Lauren pressed her back against the tile and spread her arms and legs apart to give him total access to the front of her body. "I'm all yours, baby."

The hot desire that flared in his dark-brown eyes nearly melted her where she stood. His hand shot out to the built-in shelf, grabbed the bottle of body wash and dumped a bunch of it into his palm. The bottle hit the floor and made her jump from the loud sound but Wrath's hands were suddenly all over her. Big hands gripped her shoulders, slid down to cup her breasts, and kept exploring down her hips.

She had to remember to breathe as she leaned against the tile, his hands leaving soapy trails from her throat to her waist. It became harder to do when he lowered to his knees and those hands trailed down to her feet. The rough texture of his calloused fingertips turned her on.

"You weren't kidding about getting me clean, were you?"

"No," he growled. "Turn around."

Wrath battled the urge to howl. He'd nearly lost Lauren, another male could have claimed her and the knowledge that she'd been touched by one lingered even after he'd washed away 140's stench.

She is mine! That thought drove him to slide his hands up her legs to the vee of her thighs, part them, and explore her sex. Lauren's small gasp urged him on. His knuckle teased the seam of her pussy and his gaze focused there. He needed to remind them both who she belonged to.

He pressed her legs farther apart. The urge arose to bury his face there and lick her until she begged him to take her. He snarled from the overriding desire to taste the arousal that would assure him that she wanted him too.

Mine! A feral emotion gripped him and he pushed her tighter against the wall. He nuzzled her stomach with his face as his fingers explored the tempting seam of her pussy. He knew he was losing control but at that moment it didn't matter. He needed her and he would take her.

His enhanced hearing picked up the sound of the outer door to his room opening and frustration struck fast. A growl rumbled from his throat as he hoped they'd go away. It didn't happen though and it took every ounce of his control to pull away before he forced Lauren to open her thighs wider to allow his tongue to delve inside her warm, enticing pussy.

Chapter Eighteen

ജ

Someone knocked on the bathroom door and it startled Lauren. Wrath stood, grabbed Lauren and spun her around to face the tile before she could do it on her own. His body pressed against hers, pinned her there, and he turned enough to hide her behind his body from anyone who entered the room. She couldn't miss the hard length of his cock trapped between her lower back and his hips.

"Come in."

Lauren jerked her head up and gawked at Wrath over her shoulder. They were naked in the shower and he'd just invited someone to come in.

"Relax," he urged. "It's Shadow. He's taking your clothes away."

She had to wiggle enough to see the door. Shadow didn't even glance toward the shower when he picked up all their clothing off the floor. He turned away, closed them inside once more, and Wrath backed off her. Lauren turned to face him and Wrath shrugged.

"Sorry. I forgot to take them out to the hallway. He knows I'll want that male's scent removed and it lingers on our clothing—yours from being with him and mine from holding you."

Lauren remembered the advice Shadow had given her in the SUV about improving Wrath's mood and inched closer to him. She was all for sex and so was he, judging from the condition of his body. Her hand reached for his cock but his fingers gripped her wrist before she could caress him there. He spun her back around, pinned her facing the wall again and she gasped when his free hand fisted in her hair.

He didn't hurt her but he gently forced her head back. She stared into his eyes but he looked away and released her wrist. He yanked the detachable showerhead from its holder and water soaked her hair as he aimed it there. She closed her eyes to keep out the water.

"I need to wash your hair. I can smell him still," Wrath growled.

"Is it that difficult for you?" It amazed her that he could still detect any traces of 140 on her.

He released her hair and the water stopped pouring down the back of her head. "Yes," he admitted gruffly. "I can't stand smelling another male when I breathe in your scent." The shampoo was cold as he poured a generous amount on her hair and worked it in with both hands, from her scalp to the ends, lathering it well. "My scent and only mine should be on your body."

It felt good as he rinsed out the soap. He worked in conditioner next and massaged her head while doing it. He made sure he rinsed it all out before he suddenly gripped her hips from behind and his body pressed against hers. His head lowered and he growled.

"You keep telling me that you're mine. I told you not to do that but you didn't heed my warning. I believe you."

Lauren opened her eyes and peered up at him over her shoulder. His gaze held hers and the intensity she saw there made her heart race again. So did the feel of his cock pressed against her lower back. Her lips parted and she blurted out the one thing that she wanted to say most.

"I love you, Wrath."

He growled low, inched back and suddenly turned her in his hands. He pushed her against the tile when they were facing each other, pinned her there and stepped into her again. She tilted her chin up and his mouth tried to take possession of hers. She twisted away before he could kiss her.

"I need to brush my teeth first. I ate bloody meat. Kind of gross. Hold that thought and give me a minute." She tried to wiggle away to go do that but he held her against the wall.

"I don't care. I want you."

"I want you too, baby. I just want to brush my teeth first."

Amusement lifted the corners of his mouth. "I'm too big to be a baby."

"It's an endearment, remember?" She smiled.

A serious look suddenly wiped away his good mood. "I could have lost you. I won't allow that to happen. Do you really feel love for me?"

She tensed a little and prayed he wouldn't lecture her about how they hadn't known each other long enough for her to confess those kinds of feelings. Most guys would run, commitment wary, but she didn't regret telling him.

"I do. I know what you're probably thinking but I—"

He pulled away and released her. "Let's get dried off and you can brush your teeth."

Shot down. Damn. She nodded. Wrath faced away, turned off the water and opened the shower door. He handed her a towel, stepped out of the stall to dry off out there and the silence became slightly uncomfortable.

Wrath opened the bedroom door, sniffed and exited, leaving it open. "Shadow has come and gone. There is food here for you on the nightstand."

Wrath tried hard to calm his racing heart and the urge to grab Lauren, take her to his bed and claim her. The wild side of him wanted to do just that. He just figured it might scare her if he threw her over his shoulder, carried her to his bed and showed her why he was the right male for her. He'd fuck her until neither of them could move.

It wouldn't just be sex. With Lauren it was so much more. She claimed to feel love for him and he wanted to throw back his head and howl out his joy. She kept saying she was his. His hands clenched at his sides to keep him grounded in reality. Lauren was human, not Species, and they were different. He needed to remember that. She hadn't offered him forever, probably wasn't even aware that's what he wanted and he wasn't certain what to do about it. He was still a mess, too newly free, and logic stated he wasn't ready to take a mate. He wanted her though.

The desire was so strong his body shook. *She's mine. She said she feels love for me. Take her. Keep her. Mine!* He wanted to roar out his frustration as he battled with his urges. He knew she'd need more time to make that kind of commitment to him. He was ready to make it to her.

He had given his word to work with the task force team. His gaze darted around the drab room—it would be hers too and could he do that to her? Ask her to live in the small space? She deserved better. He wanted to give her a real home but all he could offer would be the equivalent of a cell with an unlocked door. Not that she could leave the building. It was too dangerous and what had happened to her just proved it.

He'd put her in danger by association. His enemies had tried to use her against him and all Species to gain what they wanted. He growled when the water turned off in the next room, trying to come to a decision. He knew what he wanted, what he needed, but love was about putting the needs of someone else above his own.

She needed to eat before he touched her. That would be his first priority. They would talk. It wasn't a choice. She needed to understand that every time she claimed to be his that he took it to heart. Letting her go would be hard but keeping her against her will would be unforgivable. It was Lauren's choice. Pain squeezed his chest. He'd want to lie down and die if she walked away from him. He would never stop thinking about her, longing for her to be near him or wanting to hold her.

He'd never seen this coming. He was antisocial and afraid to trust himself with a human woman, yet Lauren had managed to change him. He'd learned to yearn for things he hadn't even known he wanted.

* * * * *

Good going, Lauren berated herself. *I should have kept my mouth closed and not blabbed about loving him.* She took her time brushing her teeth before she followed him into the other room with just a towel wrapped around her body.

He stopped pacing when she entered the room. The towel hooked around his waist was all he wore, he hadn't gotten dressed while she'd tended to her teeth. His dark gaze fixed on her.

"Come here." He pointed to the spot in front of him. "Please."

Lauren walked to him without hesitation. The serious look in his eyes alarmed her but her spine stiffened. She'd faced a lot of tough things in her life but being rejected by Wrath would probably top her list of "moments that sucked". She stopped where he pointed and refused to look away. She wanted to see his eyes, read his emotions. She wouldn't cry in front of him. She loved him enough to want to avoid making him feel guilty.

"I'm not one of your males."

That wasn't what she had expected him to say. "I know."

"I'm not even fully human. I'm part canine."

"I know that too."

"I snarl and have mood swings because I battle with both sides of myself. I've also suffered abuse."

Ah, the reasons why he's going to dump me. The sensation of tears made her blink rapidly to fight them back. "I know that too, Wrath."

"I don't understand what normal is. I have nothing in common with you and we grew up very differently." He looked away from her to glance around the room before he caught her gaze again. "This room is nice to me. It's far better than anything I could have ever expected. There are no chains here, no locks to keep me inside and no one comes to hurt me. I've seen inside your home and there's a drastic difference."

She couldn't refute anything he said but she could point out what they did have. "None of that matters to me. Do you know what does?"

Something flickered in his gorgeous eyes but she wasn't sure what emotion caused it. She waited to see if he even wanted to hear what she had to say or if he'd already made up his mind.

"What?"

"You make me happy. I hope I make you feel that way too. This..." She waved her hand at the room. "Doesn't matter. It's just being with you that does. I know your past and mine are drastically dissimilar but it's the here and now that I care about."

He took a deep breath.

"Is this goodbye? Don't drag it out." Her voice dropped and her heart broke a little. "Tell me if you want to end this. I love you, I probably shouldn't have blurted it out that way, but there it is. I don't regret letting you know how I feel because life is too short. I'd regret not telling you that. You can make excuses all night for why we have no future but just tell me the truth, okay? You don't feel the same way about me? Just say that. I can take it."

He inched closer. "I feel more for you than I ever thought possible. I don't want to say goodbye to you but I don't want you to hate me either."

"I could never do that." She wanted to touch him and her fingers curled into her palms just to resist.

"You will if I stop fighting what I want from you. I'd keep you with me, Lauren. I'm stuck here in this place until my duty is done and you deserve better. I know this. I would never let you go if you were to stay. I couldn't." His voice deepened. "You keep saying you are mine and it taunts me to claim you." His gaze traveled down her body. "I'd mate you and your life would change forever. Your world is too dangerous if you were with me. You'd have to live in mine, give up everything you have, and..."

"And what?" Her heart raced and hope soared that he loved her too.

"I love you too much to ever make you choose between your world and me."

More tears filled her eyes but she didn't bother to blink them back. *He loves me!* "It's an easy choice to make if you're asking me."

He tried to turn away but she reached out and grabbed his arm. He peered down at her and she saw raw pain staring back at her.

"Ask me, Wrath. Please?"

"I can't. I'm not fit to be a mate and I have nothing to offer you."

That did it. Anger rose. "Nothing? You're wonderful and amazing, Wrath. You've had such a rough life yet you're the kindest man I've ever met. You've given me more in the short time we've had together than anyone else ever has. You risked your life to get me back. You fought for me when Vengeance went a little nuts and I love you. Do you know what it does to me when you hold me? I feel like I'm exactly where I belong. You touch me and I've never been so alive. You have scars inside and out but you faced your fears to make love to me. That's the best gift anyone could give."

He shrugged off her hold. His hands rose to cup her cheeks and leaned down until their faces were just a few mere inches apart and searched her eyes. She wasn't sure what he looked for but she knew he'd find honesty.

"I won't ever let you go if you agree to be my mate. Ever. It won't be easy but I'd do anything for you to make you happy. I would die if you ever left me. I couldn't survive missing you."

"I choose you, Wrath. Always you. You're not going to lose me."

He inhaled and nodded. "I'll put my scent back on you."

She gasped in surprise when he suddenly dropped his hands and hooked her around the waist. Lauren was yanked against his big body and pressed flush against his firm torso. He rubbed up and down along her front and she laughed.

"What are you doing? That tickles."

He stopped and adjusted his hold on her, scooped her into his arms and grinned. "I have a better way to put my scent on you. Don't be afraid."

"You can stop worrying about that, baby. I kind of get hot when you make those noises and I love how aggressive you can get."

His eyes widened when he stared at her as he walked over to his bed. "Honestly?"

"Oh yeah. And the fact that you can pick me up so easily and do it often? You make me feel sexy and feminine. I really appreciate that."

"You are very desirable and all female." He lowered her to his bed until she lay on it, released her and backed up. His hands gripped his towel and he dropped it to the floor. "See what you do to me?"

"Yeah." She licked her lips, staring at his rigid cock, aimed right at her. "I see. Very impressive and I hope I do it for you all the time." She wiggled, tore at her towel and tossed it to the floor. "I love looking at you. I could do it all day. I hate it when you get dressed."

He moved to the night table, tore open the drawer and grabbed the lotion. Lauren smiled when he brought it back to the bed, lowered next to her and shoved the discarded towels under his knees to cushion them from the hard floor.

"You won't need any of that. I'm already turned-on." She knew she was wet and it had nothing to do with the shower. Wrath loved her and he was naked, wanted to mate her and that was all the incentive she needed to be ready for him.

A smile curved his mouth as he opened the lotion and held it out to her. "Touch me."

She sat up and hesitated. "You want me to use that on you?"

"Yes. I'm too excited and I won't last. Make me come first. Sit on the edge of the bed and face me."

Okay. She was eager to put her hands on anything he wanted. She shifted enough to spread her legs open so he was between them. Her gaze locked on his cock and she opened a palm.

Wrath poured a generous amount of lotion into it and capped the bottle, just dropping it to the floor next to him. He hissed when she wrapped her hand around his shaft to spread the lotion and gripped him with her other hand too. The slick one slid to his nuts, cupping him there and she gently scored him with her fingernails while gripping his cock to give the hard length a gentle squeeze.

Wrath threw his head back, his body tensed and he growled. Lauren loved watching him, the way his body tightened to reveal the definition of each muscle, and her gaze fixated on his six-pack abs. Her tongue darted out and wet her lips as she leaned in and inhaled the smell of soap and man.

He jerked when her mouth opened on his ribs, her tongue laved the skin under his nipple and the tip traced the round, flat disk that grew taut at the slightest touch. His hands reached up, gripped her thighs, and his hips started to grind in slow, sensual thrusts to rub his cock in her hand.

"So sexy," she breathed and backed up enough to look down and watch him, imagining him doing that inside her pussy. "I love the way you move."

He growled as she stroked his shaft one-handed, teased the sensitive skin along the underside of his balls and scooted a little closer until her stomach brushed the head of his dick. His hands tightened on her, his breathing grew harsh and his cock began to swell bigger in her hold.

"That's it, baby," she urged. "Mark me."

He jerked his head down to stare at her. She looked up and the raw passion in his eyes made her almost come. He snarled, flashed those sexy fangs of his and hot semen shot across her belly and ribs. His features tensed, his eyes narrowed, and watching him get off was enthralling.

His body stilled, the tremors eased as she stopped stroking him and his hold on her thighs relaxed. Lauren gasped when he suddenly gripped her arms, pushed her flat onto her back and released her. Big hands opened on her abdomen and she could feel him spreading his release over her skin. Her gaze met his as he leaned closer with a nearly feral expression.

"Mine," he rasped. "I need you now. Spread your thighs wider and let me claim you."

She parted her thighs more, a little stunned that he'd just come but wanted to be inside her. He did the unexpected instead of fucking her. He backed up a little and inhaled, growled loudly and glanced up once more.

"You carry my scent now." A wickedly handsome grin curved his mouth, he licked his lips and adjusted his hold on her again, pinning her legs open and slowly lowered his face until hot breath fanned her pussy. "I want yours now."

Her fingers clawed the bedding as a hot, thick tongue teased her clit. Wrath didn't go at her gently or slowly. A hungry, near desperate mouth fastened onto the bundle of nerves, licked rapidly and snarls added a slight vibration to the ecstasy he was dishing out.

"Oh, Wrath," she moaned.

He grew more aggressive, as if he was frantic to make her climax, nuzzled his face in tighter against her pussy and his bottom teeth lightly raked the supersensitive spot he paid special attention to. She moaned and he did it again, then again. Her back arched and she would have slammed her legs closed because it was too intense but Wrath wouldn't allow it with his strong hands pinning her.

She cried out his name and enjoyed every mind-blowing wave of ecstasy that shook her body. His mouth tore away from her pussy, he rose and she opened her eyes just as he collapsed on top of her. Her arms were pulled above her head, he shackled her wrists together with the fingers and thumb of one hand and cupped her face.

"I'll never let you go. I'll die for you. I have to have you right now."

He entered her pussy with his thick, still-rigid cock in one steady, slow thrust. Lauren gasped at being parted, taken. She unquestionably felt claimed when he paused while buried deep inside her and his body surrounded hers as he came down over her even more.

"Look at me," he demanded.

Lauren couldn't have looked away from his piercing gaze if she wanted to, not that she did. She watched his eyes narrow as he slowly withdrew until he almost left her pussy, he paused, but drove back into her deeply. Pleasure and oversensitivity made her gasp, her body still recovering from her climax.

"Take me, Lauren. Let me love you."

She'd have done anything for him, given him anything at that moment. He moved again, slowly pulled back until he almost left her body then surged forward abruptly to make all those nerve endings inside jolt awake from the way he stroked them.

"I want to hold you," she panted and tried to free her wrists but his hold just tightened.

"I'm in control and I need to stay that way. Your hands on me make me lose my mind."

He held her down. Their gazes locked as he kept fucking her and Lauren had to admit it was sexy as hell being pinned, unable to do anything but feel Wrath, his powerful body driving into hers. He shifted his position, adjusted the angle of his cock and did it again. She cried out louder as more pleasure raced to her brain and Wrath grinned.

She wanted to ask him what was so amusing. Her body burned, the need to come again nearly unbearable, but she didn't get the chance. He released her face, reached down to clutch the top of one thigh and began fucking her in earnest. He hammered her with his cock, hit that same spot over and over, rapidly, and she threw her head back. Her eyes closed—she couldn't keep them open—and she forgot how to breathe as rapture rippled through her. A haze of white wiped out her ability to think, she screamed and the body over hers jerked enough to shake the bed.

A howl deafened her. Wrath's hips bucked against her pussy and he came hard inside her. She could feel the swelling as he locked inside her. He released her wrists and thigh, braced his arms to avoid crushing her under his body and his face lowered until hot breath fanned her neck.

"Always, Lauren," he whispered. "I give you my life, my loyalty and my heart forever."

Her arms lifted, wrapped around his neck, and she clamped her legs around his ass to hold on to him as tightly as her exhausted body could.

"I love you, too."

His mouth opened and he gently nipped her throat. "I hope you meant it when you said I have you because I can't let you go. You're my mate, my other half, and my soul."

Tears filled her closed eyes and she smiled. "I'm all yours, baby."

Chapter Nineteen

ꟗ

Lauren opened her mouth and shook her head. "This is ridiculous, Wrath. I can feed myself."

He growled at her, dark eyes narrowed and he waved the fork in front of her mouth. "Open."

Her lips parted and he eased the bite inside. She took it, chewed, and enjoyed the taste of sesame chicken. Wrath turned a little, stabbed the fork into a veggie and watched her eat. She knew he waited for her to finish it so he could make her take another bite.

His cock twitched against her vaginal walls, a reminder that she straddled his lap, and they were still connected. He'd rolled her over, their bodies still locked together after a third round of hot sex and he'd shifted their bodies until he sat on the edge of the bed to be able to reach the nightstand.

She'd forgotten about the food Shadow had said he'd bring until Wrath had torn open the plastic bag, opened the large container and she'd smelled the Chinese food. Someone had run for takeout, gotten a huge amount of it in a big to-go tray and had even remembered to bring a few sodas in cans with two forks. Wrath had insisted on feeding her.

"Eat more. You're little and you need your strength."

Amusement made her chuckle and she allowed him to feed her another forkful of food. "You're going to be bossy, aren't you?"

Uncertainty flashed in his gaze. "I'm sorry but your care and well-being are my first priority. You are hungry, your stomach sounds reminded me that you haven't eaten and I'd be a bad mate if I didn't make sure all your needs were met."

He inhaled, puffed up his chest and a stubborn streak shone in his stare. "I will learn to be the best mate."

He was so damn cute and if he didn't already have her heart, he would have won it over in that moment. She reached up and traced his cheekbone. "You already are the best."

His cock twitched again, was rock hard, and she wiggled a little. He felt so good and she wanted to ride him. His hand released her hip and his open palm tapped her ass. It didn't hurt but it was enough to startle her.

"Stop that and eat. Food first and then I will mount you from behind. You will enjoy it."

Laugher boiled up and she didn't smother it. "I believe that."

He fed her more food. She grabbed the second fork, and offered him a bite. He hesitated and opened his lips, accepting it.

"I want to be the best mate too."

He swallowed. "You already are. You make me happy, Lauren."

A knock sounded at the door and Wrath responded by snarling. "Do not enter!" His voice lowered as he gripped Lauren's hips and lifted her off his lap, abruptly parting their bodies. "Go into the bathroom and close the door." He rose to his feet, got in front her and effectively blocked her body if anyone walked inside the room.

She fled for the bathroom, noticed Wrath stayed at her side the entire time and bit back a laugh. He was making sure no one got a glimpse of her body. He closed the door for her and she wrapped a towel around her. She couldn't hear what was going on in the next room but waited patiently for a few minutes.

The door opened and Wrath had donned on a pair of loose sweatpants but nothing else. His expression was grim as he met her gaze.

"Is everything all right?"

"We've been requested to go to Homeland. Justice wants to meet with us."

"Justice North?" It shocked her. "The leader of the New Species? I see him on television all the time. Why does he want to meet us?"

"I believe he wishes to meet you and discuss your relationship with me." Wrath took a deep breath. "We need to discuss a few things."

"Okay." She tried not to feel apprehensive. Wrath loved her, had claimed her as his mate and he didn't want to lose her. That was the worst thing he could say and he wasn't about to do that. "What do you want to talk about?"

He took her hand and led her back to the bed, sat and pulled her down on his lap. He hesitated, met her gaze and took a deep breath.

"There are things you should know as my mate. I don't want someone else to tell you before I do. They will assume we've discussed everything but we haven't."

"Kind of hard to do when we're having sex. A lot." She grinned. "Not that I'm complaining."

He didn't smile back. A serious look settled over his handsome features. "You and I may be able to have children. No one can know that in your world, even the human males who are on the task force don't know this. It's too dangerous with the hate groups and crazy humans who believe we are animals. They wish for New Species to die out after a generation but a few babies have been born with human and Species mixed mates."

Lauren let that information settle in and understood why they'd want to keep it a secret. "I'm on the shot. I can't get pregnant unless I don't take any more of them. I'm due for another one in two months." Her heart speeded up a little. "Do you want to have a baby?"

"I'm not certain." He glanced away before meeting her gaze again. "I need to learn how to care for a mate first."

"We should have some time together before we think about having a child."

He seemed relieved. "I am not opposed to making a family with you but I am wary due to my past."

Her arm wrapped around his neck and she leaned into his chest to rest there. "I understand. We'll talk about this later when we're both ready but I'm glad that is an option. I always wanted to have a baby or two but only when we're both prepared."

A smile curved his lips. "I am sure once I learn to be a mate that I will want to learn how to be a father." He took another deep breath and his body tensed. "I am afraid Justice will have issues with our mating."

That killed her good mood. "We're already mated, right? You said that. What's involved?"

"I want you for my mate and you agreed. We are mated," he firmly stated, getting a little emotional when his voice deepened. "My worry is that he won't want you to live here with me but you can't return to your home. You were already taken once and you are in danger. I won't allow that. I will not permit him to separate us even while I fulfill my obligation." His gaze left hers to drift around the room. "I will make it more of a home for you here. Brass is in charge and he said I could keep you. Tim has some issues but Brass overruled him."

"Good."

"I will get you a television, a bigger bed and whatever will make you happy. I have to leave sometimes for my duties but I won't be gone long. I will always return to our bed to sleep with you and the time will pass quickly. We'll visit Homeland and Reservation, see which of them you feel would make you happy and live there when I leave here for good."

"My best friend lives near Homeland. I'll be allowed to see Amanda if we live there, won't I?" Worry struck her hard at the thought of something preventing her from doing that.

"Homeland is nice and Amanda will have to visit you there. I am certain it won't be an issue."

"Good." Lauren knew Amanda was going to be thrilled to have a reason to visit and see Flame whenever possible. "That's a relief."

"Do you have family?"

"Yeah but they live back east."

"Will they hate me? Will they be upset that you chose me over a human?"

"No." She shook her head, sure of that. "They are going to love you, Wrath."

Her grandmother was going to be thrilled she'd found a man to settle down with, her grandfather was going to think it was cool he was related to New Species since he found them fascinating, and her sister was going to turn green with jealousy once she got an eyeful of Wrath. She smothered a grin at remembering all the times her thinner sister used to warn her that she'd never find a man until she lost weight. *I not only found one but he's amazing!*

"Do you have family?"

"All Species are considered family to each other. Very few have blood ties to each other but some do. There are two sets of twins and some who were from the same DNA that was donated to Mercile when they created us. No matches were found to mine but I consider Shadow a brother. We were in the cells next to each other in the same testing facility, we were moved to a new location together, and have been inseparable since we were freed. We count on each other."

"I understand that. Amanda and I aren't blood related but she's more of a sister to me than my biological one. We grew up together."

He smiled and lifted a hand, pushing her hair back from her cheek. "You and I are inseparable now, mate. I will deal with Justice if he is concerned about you living here. It is safe. The building is very secure and no harm will come to you."

"He seems really cool on television."

"He is a very wise male and I am sure he will see reason."

"No worries then."

"I have you. That is all that matters and we will face whatever happens together."

Lauren liked that.

"We need to shower and get ready. I'll ask Tim to send some men to your apartment to get clothing and bring your pet here."

"That isn't a good idea. He'd hate it here. He likes going outside. I'll ask Amanda to take him home. She loves Tiger and her condo allows cats. I would like to have him live with us once we get our own place."

"We can do that."

"The helicopter leaves in twenty-five minutes to fly us to Homeland."

Nervousness struck Lauren but she fought it down. It was going to work out. She had faith in that and in Wrath.

"You shower first while I make the arrangements. I'll be right back. Wear my clothing. What is mine now belongs to you."

"I love you, Wrath."

He softly growled, desire darkened his eyes, and his hands tightened into fists at his side. "I want you but we don't have time. Later I am going to mount you from behind. I will show you love."

She couldn't wait.

* * * * *

Wrath worried. The helicopter ride had been too short. He had no idea why Justice wanted to talk to him alone and he hated leaving Lauren in the reception area with one of the Species females. His mate hadn't seemed to mind. She was very friendly and the other female seemed happy to have a human to chat with. He stared at Justice, sitting behind his desk. Wrath closed the door and slowly stalked forward.

"I've taken a mate and she has agreed to live with me at headquarters." His body tightened, poised for a fight, and he was prepared for one if Justice refused to allow Lauren to stay with him. "Brass said we could make it work."

Justice's eyebrows arched, his expression unreadable, and he pointed. "Please sit."

"I'd rather stand."

"You can calm down, Wrath. I'm happy you've taken a mate. I'd never ask you to be parted from her and I'm glad she agreed to stay with you. I know that had to be a difficult decision for a human to make. They are used to having a lot more freedom to roam wherever they wish in the outside world. Please sit."

Wrath folded into the chair, still wary, but relieved Justice hadn't asked him to have Lauren live behind the protection of the NSO walls. "Why are we here?"

"I wanted to meet your mate, mine wanted to meet her as well, and we wished to congratulate you."

"You could have done that over the phone or with her at my side."

A grin curved Justice's mouth. "You want to be alone with your mate. I understand that and I'm sorry I pulled you from your bed." He hesitated. "You haven't been free long. I wanted to share information about having a human mate that will help you. That's why I asked to speak to you alone first."

"Lauren and I are different but we share love. We both are dedicated to making it work."

"I'm really happy to hear that. We mate a female and it means everything to us. Mating is unfamiliar to them. They have marriage in their world."

"I am familiar with what that is."

"Good. Here's my first bit of advice. Ask her to marry you. I saw her file, she has family and they will accept you easier if you're her husband. They won't understand that mating is a deeper commitment but marriage will assure them that you are in her life permanently. My mate, Jessie, has made some calls and we can have a minister here within the hour if you wish to do this."

"I do. I want Lauren to be happy."

"I assumed you would. Tim sent a team to her house to collect her clothing and I had one of them look inside her jewelry box to learn her ring size." Justice got a baffled look. "They need rings for some reason. It is a visible way for them to show they belong to a male and they expect males to wear a matching ring to show females they belong to her." Justice lifted his hand to show the gold band. "See? I don't wear it all the time since Jessie and I have managed to keep our mating from the press but I do while at home and at the office. It feels strange at first but you will adjust to something being on your finger."

"How do I get rings?"

"Jessie is taking care of it."

"We will thank you."

"Lesson number two. Human females love romantic gestures. No need to be confused. It means giving them surprises that show our love while being thoughtful at the same time."

"That's a mate and what we do. We try to make them happy and put them first."

"We are good at this. We just have to learn not to be so blunt. Don't thank Jessie. She wants you to tell your mate that you had the NSO handle the arrangements when you spring marriage and the rings on her. It's not a lie, the NSO did make all the arrangements since Jessie is considered Species and she had our people working on this. I trust my mate on these things and she said your female will be 'blown away' by the romantic gesture." Justice chuckled. "I don't argue with my mate on human matters. That's lesson number three."

"Don't argue with my mate regarding human issues?"

"Exactly. You can't win and I'm always learning new things. Humans are vastly different from us. That's lesson number four."

"Thank you."

"Lesson number five is easy. Just be yourself. They know we're Species, accept us for who we are and they chose to be with us over human males. Don't try to be something you are not, thinking it will make her happier. Just expect to answer a lot of questions when she doesn't understand something about us, be honest and remember that we're aggressive by nature. Try to refrain from going over the top."

Wrath nodded. "Thank you, Justice. I will remember."

The other male stood. "Any questions?"

"She'd like to live here at Homeland once my duties to the task force are fulfilled. She has a friend living in the outside world and she wants access to her. They are very close."

"We'll work it out. Her friend is welcome here."

"I don't want to live with my mate in the dorms."

"You'll be assigned a real house, Wrath. We have the dorms because they were already being built when we were given Homeland. Our males enjoy spending time with each other and it's easier for them to be closer to where they work. Mated males and some of the higher-ranked officers prefer some space and privacy. We'll take care of it."

A weight lifted from Wrath's shoulders. "I am going to be the best mate possible."

Justice stood and smiled. "I know you will. Congratulations."

* * * * *

Lauren laughed. "Really? You refuse to take a mate?"

Breeze nodded. "We enjoy our freedom and our males tend to be overprotective and like to keep us close. Just be firm with yours. Do what I said."

"Don't take any shit." She really liked the New Species woman. "I can handle that but Wrath is a sweetheart."

"Our males never do anything half-ass, I can assure you of that."

Lauren hesitated, unsure if it would be okay to ask. A question bothered her though. "Did 140's mate make it? Wrath and I haven't heard anything."

The female nodded. "She is holding steady. Her mate is at her side and our doctors know what was done to her. I'm not sure of the details but they are hoping for a full recovery. It will just take time for her to regain her strength."

"What about the others?"

She chuckled. "They are adjusting to life very well. One of them keeps asking to share sex with me but he's got an attitude problem. Canines can be a little too aggressive when they are on the hunt. He's been without a female for far too long and is attempting to make up for it now."

"Is he the one who gave Midnight a little trouble and she dropped him on his ass?"

"Yes." Breeze glanced at the door and smiled. "Your mate and Justice are coming. It's just like I said. Justice was giving Wrath helpful hints about having a human mate. We always look out for each other and want everyone to be happy. You are Species now too."

"Thank you. That means a lot to me." She meant it.

The tall Species stood. "Okay, my babysitting duties are over. I have a training session to barge in on. Some of the task force newbies are here and they get to fight some of our males to improve their skills. I enjoy watching that and sometimes I like to step in. Human males think women can't take them down on the mats and it's fun to see their shock when they find me pinning them down." She winked. "Plus, I am considering sharing sex with one at some point. My best friend has told me some things that have piqued my interest."

"What kinds of things?"

Breeze strode for the door. "You would consider it TMI. I know that saying. Happy mating, Lauren. Welcome to the family."

The door to the hallway opened a second after Breeze left and Wrath smiled at her. The man behind him made Lauren nervous and she hoped she wouldn't embarrass herself. Justice North was a celebrity and she'd never met one before.

"Are you well?" Wrath sniffed. "Where is Breeze? I smell her but she's gone. I asked for a female to stay with you while I spoke to Justice."

"She just left a few seconds ago. She is really nice." Lauren glanced at Justice and her cheeks warmed when he smiled at her. He looked much more handsome in person. "Hi."

"Welcome to Homeland, Lauren." Justice nodded. "I would shake your hand but your mate would want to break mine for touching you. You'll learn that he won't respond well when other males get too close to you. It is an instinctual act for us."

The door Breeze had just exited opened and a redhead walked in, wearing a black T-shirt, jeans, and biker boots. Her fiery-colored hair hung past her butt and she walked right up to Justice, put her arm around his waist and leaned against him. Her gaze fixed on Lauren.

"I'm Jessie." She grinned. "Justice is my husband and mate. We heard what you did to get that asshole to turn on the people who held you by tricking him into placing that call to us. I'm damn impressed. Great job."

"Thank you. I was terrified and got lucky."

"Well, it's over and you're safe now. That's the important part."

"We captured all of them."

Jessie glanced up at her mate who had spoken. "And that." Her attention returned to Lauren. "I hope you don't mind but we're throwing a little celebration for you both. It's always a huge event when someone takes a mate and it cheers everyone up."

Lauren was surprised by that news but refrained from asking why.

Jessie seemed to read her mind. "Between the shit we get from the media, the protestors and the occasional kidnapping, good news is something to throw a party over around here. I hope you don't mind."

"We are honored," Wrath admitted and pulled Lauren to his side to put his arm around her. "Would you mind if we spoke alone before we go?"

Justice grinned. "Of course. We'll be outside waiting."

Lauren watched the couple leave and wondered why Wrath needed a private moment with her. He waited until the door closed before he released her, sat in one of the chairs and hauled her onto his lap.

"Will you marriage with me?"

Surprise smacked her and her heart did a flop in her chest. "You're asking me to marry you?"

"Yes. Marriage. It is a ceremony humans have and your family will know I am sincere about my love for you. You're my mate and I want your family to understand that I respect their human world."

"Oh, baby. Yes! I'll marry you!"

He grinned. "Good. I was hoping you would agree. The NSO is putting our wedding together and we will have matching rings."

Tears filled her eyes and she didn't bother to blink them back. "That's so sweet and my grandmother is really going to love you. She'd have been happy that I was with you but she's going to be over-the-top thrilled that she won't have to tell everyone we're just living together. I think it will help me feel mated too, with a ceremony. I don't want anything big, just something fun and casual."

"I will make sure you get what you want."

That made her love him even more.

"We can do it today."

"Today?" *Wow, he never stops stunning me.*

Apprehension tensed his face. "Is this a bad thing?"

"No. Not at all. I'd marry you any day, any place, any time. My family will understand me not waiting but I do have one request."

"Anything."

"I would like Amanda to be here."

"Call her." He nodded toward the desk across the room. "Invite her. Tell her to come and I'll inform the gate she's on her way. They will bring her wherever we are."

Lauren leaned against him and brushed her mouth over his. He growled, fully taking possession of her mouth and she had to admit the guy was a quick learner when passion flared between them. He could kiss like nobody's business. He was the one who broke away, panting, and desire darkened his eyes.

"Call her and let's hurry with this marriage. I want to mount you."

"And I want you to do that."

He lifted her up. "Make the call. I will tell Justice we want a minister and the rings. Just come out when you are done."

Lauren dialed Amanda and blinked back more tears. It amazed her how drastically her life had changed since walking into that warehouse. Her friend answered on the third ring.

"Um, hello?"

"Why do you sound so unsure? Is it hello or not?" Lauren teased.

"Lauren! I saw the caller ID and had no clue why Homeland would be calling me."

"I'm getting married."

"Oh. My. God! No way! You lucky fucking bitch!"

"Can I borrow that blue dress you bought for your Christmas party? I love that."

"You're not wearing white?" Amanda snorted. "Kidding. Wouldn't that be a hoot though, to do that? Not only can you borrow it, you can have it. Do I get to throw you a bachelorette party? We could do strippers."

"Nope. The only hot guy I want to see naked is Wrath."

"Yeah. That's true. He probably looks better than anyone I could hire anyway."

"Did Flame call you?"

"Yes." Some of Amanda's happiness faded. "They had an issue up north at Reservation and he was called up there for a few weeks but he promised to call me when he gets back. I mean, he called so that's got to mean something, right?"

"Yes. He'll call you."

"I'm hoping so because I'm kind of obsessing over him but we'll talk about that later. When is the happy day? I'm totally going to hit up a sex shop and buy you guys a ton of shit you'll have to show him how to use. Well, maybe not. I mean, do they have a sex shop at NSO?"

"I don't know but that's going to have to wait."

"Why?"

"Today is the day. Grab the dress, put something on that you want to wear to my wedding and jump in your car. I'm at Homeland."

"No shit!" Amanda shouted.

"Really. Also, can you keep Tiger for me for a few months?"

"You know it. Where are you going to be?"

"You can't tell anyone about any of this. I'll handle my family later. I'm going to be living with Wrath but we can't keep Tiger there. We'll be getting a bigger place though and then I'll get him back from you as soon as possible."

"Wow. This is so cool. I'll be there. I was your getaway driver so what's having a wedding sprung on me at short notice?"

"You're the best."

"Tell that to Flame when he gets back. You've got pull now with the New Species."

Lauren laughed. "You got it. Bring your camera too. I want wedding pictures."

"Hell, I'll grab that and the video camera. You'll want to tape your honeymoon. That man of yours is scorching hot."

"Leave the video camera at home." Lauren chuckled. "I'm not into sex tapes. That's more your speed."

"I'd upload that baby on the internet and send it to those skinny girls from high school who used to call us names."

"You would not."

"I wouldn't but it would be funny if I did, right? They'd totally understand that bigger is better then."

Lauren laughed again. "Hurry up and get here. Don't forget the blue dress please. They'll be expecting you at the gate."

"Don't start without me."

"I wouldn't dream of it." Lauren hung up and left the office. Wrath waited outside the door.

"Are you ready to go to the party?"

Lauren stared into his eyes. "Yes."

Chapter Twenty

ஐ

Lauren blinked back tears as she stared around the room. Her bed from home sat in the corner of Wrath's room, taking up a good portion of space but she was so touched. Battery-operated candles flickered where they had been randomly placed and a nice meal had been laid out on a table set up by the end of the bed. She turned her head to stare up at Wrath.

"This is so romantic."

He smiled. "I wanted you to know this is your home and thought your bed would help you feel comfortable here. Tim and the task force are responsible for the rest. They know we mated and were married. They said it is a honeymoon gift. Your clothes are here too but I don't have closets. They are assembling something called wardrobes that will be placed against the walls near the bathroom tomorrow, along with a television."

"Wrath, I love you." Tears slid down her face.

He growled, used his foot to kick the door closed behind them and pulled her into his arms. "Did I do something wrong?"

"These are happy tears. This is so sweet."

He lifted her up his body. "I am not sweet."

"Yes, you are."

"I am not having sweet thoughts." He walked her to the bed and halted. "I want to tear off your pretty dress and mount you from behind."

"Put me down."

He eased her to her feet and released her, backing away a few feet. "Sorry."

She reached back. "Don't be. I want to keep the dress but I'm all for sex." She winked. "Strip, baby. The food can wait."

A carnal grin curved his lips and he bent, tearing at his boots. Lauren unzipped the dress Amanda had given her, tossed it over the end of the bed, and shimmied out of her underclothes, kicking her shoes away. She beat Wrath getting naked, climbed on the bed and positioned her body on her hands and knees.

Wrath growled at her while he shoved off his pants and joined her in a heartbeat. He rose to stand on his knees behind her and one hand gripped her hip, while his other one cupped her pussy.

"Spread your thighs wider apart for me. You're already wet." His voice deepened as his fingers stroked her clit. "I need you."

Lauren could relate. Her body was aching for him. The wedding had been everything she could have hoped for. New Species had packed the bar, Shadow and Amanda had stood at their sides and the minister had kept the ceremony short but sweet. They'd posed for pictures and then she'd learned something new about her husband. The man liked to practically fuck her on a dance floor.

It had been torture having him rub up against her, growling as he kissed her neck. The feel of his rigid cock against her belly had made her want to find the nearest private room to consummate their marriage. Instead they'd had to take a helicopter back to headquarters to finally be alone. Now she knew why he'd stalled taking her home. He'd been giving the task force time to set up his room for their honeymoon.

The slow rub of his index finger against her clit made her rock her hips, moan, and she shoved her ass up at him while her chest lowered. Wrath's heavy breathing filled her ears and the bed shifted as he placed his legs on the outside of hers. He stopped playing with her, removed his hand and the thick crown of his cock slid through the slit of her pussy. He teased her at first until she made a protest by groaning.

"Mine," he rasped.

"I'm all yours." She was never going to get tired of telling him that.

His cock pressed against her and she clawed the bed as he slowly filled her, stretched her and staked his claim. He bent, curved his body over hers and braced one hand on the bed near her head. He paused when he was seated fully inside her pussy.

"I love mounting you. Tell me if I'm too rough."

"I will but I don't think that's possible."

He growled, nipped her shoulder with his teeth and the slight bite of pain made her vaginal muscles clench. His other arm wrapped around her waist, his fingers found her clit and he rubbed furiously as he started to fuck her slowly, picked up the pace, until the sounds of their heavy pants and his hips slapping against her ass filled the room.

Lauren understood why Wrath loved doggy style. He was in control with her pinned under him. The way he moved totally turned her on. He didn't just rock his hips in the same repetitive motion most men did. He adjusted the angles of his thrusts and used her vocal pleasure to find out what felt the best to her. When he figured out the one that sent her into near orgasm, he pounded her hard and fast, having no mercy.

Her body tensed and she screamed out as ecstasy erupted. His cock swelled, he threw back his head and howled as he came. His hips jerked in tight movements against her ass to draw out their shared pleasure until he finally stilled.

"Oh yeah," Lauren gasped. "Doggy style is my favorite too."

Wrath lowered his head, kissed her neck and chuckled. "Canines do it best."

She laughed as he eased them to lie on their sides, spooned up behind her and she rested her head on his arm. She turned enough to meet his beautiful gaze.

"Yes, you do."

"We're going to do it again, love. Rest up." Desire thickened his voice and his cock twitched inside her. "I'm going to prove I'm the right male for you."

"You already have but I'm all for you convincing me any time you want."

He grinned. "I can't get enough of you. I have already scent imprinted you. I'm possessive and dominant. We keep being told that our kind has a deep-seated need to control the people around us but you control me. You look at me and I want to do anything to make you happy."

"Mission accomplished. I am."

Also by Laurann Dohner

ఌ

eBooks:

Cyborg Seduction 1: Burning Up Flint

Cyborg Seduction 2: Kissing Steel

Cyborg Seduction 3: Melting Iron

Cyborg Seduction 4: Touching Ice

Cyborg Seduction 5: Stealing Coal

Cyborg Seduction 6: Redeeming Zorus

Cyborg Seduction 7: Taunting Krell

Mating Heat 1: Mate Set

Mating Heat 2: His Purrfect Mate

Mine to Chase

New Species 1: Fury

New Species 2: Slade

New Species 3: Valiant

New Species 4: Justice

New Species 5: Brawn

New Species 6: Wrath

New Species 7: Tiger

New Species 8: Obsidian

New Species 9: Shadow

Riding the Raines 1: Propositioning Mr. Raine

Riding the Raines 2: Raine on Me

Something Wicked This Way Comes Volume 1 *(anthology)*

Something Wicked This Way Comes Volume 2 *(anthology)*

Zorn Warriors 1: Ral's Woman

Zorn Warriors 2: Kidnapping Casey

Zorn Warriors 3: Tempting Rever

Zorn Warriors 4: Berrr's Vow

Print Books:

Cyborg Seduction 1: Burning Up Flint

Cyborg Seduction 2: Kissing Steel

Cyborg Seduction 3: Melting Iron

Cyborg Seduction 4: Touching Ice

Cyborg Seduction 5: Stealing Coal

Cyborg Seduction 6: Redeeming Zorus

Cyborg Seduction 7: Taunting Krell

Mating Heat 1: Mate Set

Mating Heat 2: His Purrfect Mate

New Species 1: Fury

New Species 2: Slade

New Species 3: Valiant

New Species 4: Justice

New Species 5: Brawn

Riding the Raines 1: Propositioning Mr. Raine

Riding the Raines 2: Raine on Me

Something Wicked This Way Comes Volume 1 *(anthology)*

Something Wicked This Way Comes Volume 2 *(anthology)*

Zorn Warriors 1 & 2: Loving Zorn

Zorn Warriors 3: Tempting Rever

Zorn Warriors 4: Berrr's Vow

About Laurann Dohner

ꕤ

I'm a full-time "in-house supervisor" (sounds much better than plain ol' housewife), mother and writer. I'm addicted to caramel iced coffee, the occasional candy bar (or two) and trying to get at least five hours of sleep at night.

I love to write all kinds of stories. I think the best part about writing is the fact that real life is always uncertain, always tossing things at us that we have no control over, but when you write, you can make sure there's always a happy ending. I love that about writing. I love to sit down at my computer desk, put on my headphones and listen to loud music to block out the world around me, so I can create worlds in front of me.

ꕤ

The author welcomes comments from readers. You can find her website and email address on her author bio page at www.ellorascave.com.

Tell Us What You Think

We appreciate hearing reader opinions about our books. You can email us at Service@ellorascave.com (when contacting Customer Service, be sure to state the book title and author).

Why an electronic book?

We live in the Information Age—an exciting time in the history of human civilization, in which technology rules supreme and continues to progress in leaps and bounds every minute of every day. For a multitude of reasons, more and more avid literary fans are opting to purchase e-books instead of paper books. The question from those not yet initiated into the world of electronic reading is simply: *Why?*

1. ***Price.*** An electronic title at Ellora's Cave Publishing runs anywhere from 40% to 75% less than the cover price of the exact same title in paperback format. Why? Basic mathematics and cost. It is less expensive to publish an e-book (no paper and printing, no warehousing and shipping) than it is to publish a paperback, so the savings are passed along to the consumer.
2. ***Space.*** Running out of room in your house for your books? That is one worry you will never have with electronic books. For a low one-time cost, you can purchase a handheld device specifically designed for e-reading. Many e-readers have large, convenient screens for viewing. Better yet, hundreds of titles can be stored within your new library—on a single microchip. There are a variety of e-readers from different manufacturers. You can also read e-books on your PC or laptop computer. (Please note that Ellora's Cave does not endorse any specific brands.

You can check our website at www.ellorascave.com for information we make available to new consumers.)

3. ***Mobility.*** Because your new e-library consists of only a microchip within a small, easily transportable e-reader, your entire cache of books can be taken with you wherever you go.
4. ***Personal Viewing Preferences.*** Are the words you are currently reading too small? Too large? Too... ANNOYING? Paperback books cannot be modified according to personal preferences, but e-books can.
5. ***Instant Gratification.*** Is it the middle of the night and all the bookstores near you are closed? Are you tired of waiting days, sometimes weeks, for bookstores to ship the novels you bought? Ellora's Cave Publishing sells instantaneous downloads twenty-four hours a day, seven days a week, every day of the year. Our webstore is never closed. Our e-book delivery system is 100% automated, meaning your order is filled as soon as you pay for it.

Those are a few of the top reasons why electronic books are replacing paperbacks for many avid readers.

As always, Ellora's Cave welcomes your questions and comments. We invite you to email us at Service@ellorascave.com or write to us directly at Ellora's Cave Publishing Inc., 1056 Home Avenue, Akron, OH 44310-3502.

CPSIA information can be obtained at www.ICGtesting.com
Printed in the USA
BVOW022012190213

313700BV00002B/149/P

9 781419 968082